LIGHT FROM ONE STAR

ENCHANTMENT—that is the word for Virginia Coley. A new and fascinating young television star, she comes into Sir Blaine Belding's life like a creature from another world. And, regretful though they may be, his friends and colleagues can hardly feel surprised when he makes this exquisite young girl his wife. This moving, deeply romantic novel is the story of a distinguished brain surgeon who unwisely marries a woman as empty as she is beautiful, only to meet, too late, as it seems, another girl whose true womanliness, whose gentleness combined with great courage and self-sacrifice, inspire in him a deeper, tenderer love than he has ever before experienced. To Anna Mere, as to Sir Blaine himself, this love brings exquisite happiness, but it brings also great heartache and sorrow, and it is only after many wearying years that they find at last the fulfilment so long denied them. This is an absorbing and warm-hearted story from an author whose wide popularity is well deserved.

NETTA MUSKETT

has also written

LIGHT FROM
ONE STAR

NETTA MUSKETT

THE ROMANCE BOOK CLUB
121 CHARING CROSS ROAD
LONDON, W.C.2

*Set in eleven point Fournier
and printed in Great Britain by
Taylor Garnett Evans & Co. Ltd
Watford, Hertfordshire*

CHAPTER I

"Watch your step with Double B today," said night sister, yawning as she prepared to hand over to day sister.

"Why? Is he likely to be on the rampage?" asked day sister, picking up the book in which the happenings of the night had been logged.

Then she gave a soft whistle.

"Phew! Called him in at eleven, did you?" she asked.

"I didn't. It was Mawby, of course. *I* didn't think it was necessary, but then my opinion doesn't count! And, needless to say, Double B gave me a withering look."

Day sister grinned sympathetically.

"Mawby's always a scarey cat about Double B's ops.," she said. "What was wrong with Number Eight, anyway?"

"Only post-op. exhaustion, but Mawby thought he was going to pass out and wanted Double B to hold his hand."

"I see he didn't pass out—but I bet Mawby nearly did after Double B had left him with a few well-chosen words. He may have been on the point of hopping into bed with some little number."

Night sister laughed derisively.

"Who? Double B? I should say his couch is spotlessly virgin! He's not even married. Well, watch your step today."

Double B, officially Sir Blaine Belding, had certainly been annoyed at being summoned to the hospital just after eleven the previous night, the more so because he was aware that Mawby had only been doing his duty, and part of the duty laid on the house doctors by that eminent surgeon was never to take a chance on their own opinions of his cases being right when they could conceivably be wrong.

Still, there had been nothing particularly wrong with the man on whom he had operated during the day, and the call had

5

caused him to fall down on a much more attractive appointment.

Virginia would be furious.

He had not actually promised to pick her up from the Television Studio, but he had certainly given her the impression that he would do so, and would take her to supper somewhere before leaving her at her home, and since Virginia was twenty and quite marvellously good to look at, she had come quite reasonably to the conclusion that men *could* do what they *would* do when she was the focal point.

It would be too late to go out to Shepherd's Bush by the time he had seen Mawby's man, even if his condition did not warrant his spending much time at the hospital, so he had to telephone to the studio and leave a message for her. That also was annoying, since he had had to give his name to the girl on the switch-board. He could not spare the time to get through to Virginia herself, and in any case she was probably in the studio and not available.

He rang her up the next day at the first suitable moment, which was not before mid-day as far as Virginia was concerned.

"Oh. Oh, it's you," she said ominously when he had announced himself.

"I'm sorry about last night, but it was just one of those things. A late call from the hospital. A man I operated on yesterday."

"Did he die?"

"No."

"Would he have died?"

"No."

"Then why the heck couldn't he have waited till the morning?"

"Actually he could have done, but the house man was not satisfied so quite properly he called me up."

"Was he young and valuable, the man who didn't die?" she demanded.

He gave a little chuckle. He fancied she was coming round.

"No, he was old and probably worthless and I don't suppose

6

anybody but himself would have cared if he had died. A disagreeable old man."

"And you broke an appointment with *me* for him!"

"First things first," said Sir Blaine, "and the first with me is my job. Has to be."

"I rather thought it was me," she said petulantly.

"Where should we be without my job?"

"We? You did say 'we', didn't you, Blaine?"

He gave a relieved smile. She was definitely getting over it. "I did. Yes," he said.

"Oh—well—you can give me some lunch if you like, and if there are no more disagreeable men with a prior claim. I can be ready by half-past one, and I want to go somewhere bright with some music, and I've got to be in the studio by four. A working girl's life. A dog's life!"

He laughed. To a busy and successful surgeon, a day which did not begin till four in the afternoon, even if it did go on intermittently until eleven at night, would be a holiday.

Also he did not merely have to sing for his supper!

"All right," he said, "I'll pick you up at one-thirty, and even if you haven't anything to do until four, I probably have, so don't keep me waiting."

"As if I ever do! Well, not for long, anyway. What shall I wear?"

"I've never seen you look other than ravishing in anything."

She gave a pleased little laugh and he rang off.

He wondered, not for the first time, what it was about Virginia, and about himself, which had made him step so far out of character as he did with her. He made a grimace. What would the hospital people, or any of his private patients, think if they could overhear some of the conversations he had with this gay and glittering star which had suddenly appeared in the television firmament and seemed likely to stay there unless he or some other man did something about it?

What exactly did he intend to do about Virginia?

He had met her for the first time only a month ago.

He had been 'on the air' himself.

'An eminent surgeon performs a delicate and difficult operation on the screen under actual hospital conditions,' the *Radio Times* had informed a public which Belding thought must be ghoulish and sensation-seeking in the extreme if it could be interested in such a performance as laymen in no way connected with the profession.

Virginia had not, of course, been on that particular programme, but he had met her in the corridor when he was leaving the studio which had been given the semblance of a hospital theatre, with all the trappings, the 'patient' being faithfully portrayed by one of his own students.

She stood in his pathway. She obviously knew who he was.

"Well? Did you kill the patient off all right?" she asked saucily.

She was a lovely thing, slim as a reed but with the slenderness of perfect health which owed nothing to dieting. In fact, he was soon to discover that she had a robust appetite for chocolates and cream cakes.

She was like a lily, with pale blonde hair that had a glint almost like silver, and a wild-rose skin, and her eyes were more blue than forget-me-nots. She was not made up for the cameras, and either wore the colouring with which she had been born or had great skill with cosmetics. Another thing which he discovered later was that she used the minimum of artificial aid to make her the astoundingly lovely thing she was.

Involuntarily his thin, firm lips relaxed in a smile.

"He refused to die," he said. "Perhaps a good thing, as he is one of my most promising students."

"You mean you didn't really carve him up? That it was a fake? I'm relieved."

"Why? Did you know him?"

"Oh, no, but I wasn't able to have a look and I wanted to. I thought there might be buckets of blood."

He laughed, knowing she was trying to shock him.

"Aren't you out of your element here?" he asked. "You should have been a theatre nurse."

"Not me! I couldn't be any kind of nurse. I'm much too busy

looking after myself to want to look after anybody else. And I like doing my own job."

"What is the job?"

She lifted her eyebrows and made a wry grimace.

"You mean you don't know me? Virginia Coley? I'm flattened—but *flattened*! Don't you look in?"

"Never. Should I?"

"Definitely. On Wednesday nights anyway, and quite a few other times as well. Why don't you stay and see my act? You can, you know. I can arrange it," with a little arrogant toss of her head which made him think of a child in proud possession of a new toy and wanting to show it off.

"What time are you on?" he asked.

She told him. It was quite impossible for him to spend the best part of an hour here, but he smiled, nodded, said he would try to see the act and went his way.

When he had got back to Harley Street and seen one or two of his patients in the small, expensive nursing home which occupied two of the floors of the house, he was on his way up to the top floor, where he had his own luxurious flat, when he glanced at his watch, paused, smiled, and turned aside to tap at the door of the matron's sitting-room and, always a privileged visitor, walked in.

The middle-aged, grey-haired woman was, as he had expected, watching the television screen. He had given her the set himself, and she was an ardent viewer.

She rose at once.

"Oh, Sir Blaine! I'll switch off," she said, but he stopped her with a gesture.

"No, don't. I'd rather like to watch it. I've never yet really watched a programme at all, though now I've appeared in one!" with an almost boyish look on his lean, good-looking face, a face so perfectly suited to his profession and his position in it near the top. "What's going on at the moment?"

Miss Dove smiled, offered him cigarettes and matches, and sat down again.

"Nothing you would care for," she said. "One of those song

and dance and glamour programmes. This is one of their latest discoveries, Virginia Coley, whom of course they have just introduced with quite fulsome epithets and for whom they have provided a suitable audience to clap in the right places and with the right degree of enthusiasm. I suppose it is the price they are expected to pay for the otherwise free entertainment."

Belding smiled. He knew so well the acid flavour of the caustic comments of this invaluable woman to whom he owed so much. The acidity did not go further than her tongue.

Then he looked at the screen, and there was Virginia before him, losing a little of her radiant beauty from the lack of colour but still a most lovely thing to look upon.

She wore a topless gown, its only-just-adequate bodice glittering with sequins, the full skirts swirling about her so that she seemed to be floating on a cloud, and she was singing a gay little song in a gay little voice that was not really a voice at all, but merely an excuse for her being there. At the end of the song, she danced, tripping and dipping and twisting amongst the swirling draperies, an enchantment of grace and movement.

Yes, that was the word.

Enchantment.

She seemed so full of life and gaiety, and of a delight in herself and her lovely body which surely could not have failed to find some sort of response in any man watching her, even a confirmed old bachelor nearing forty whose life was entirely concerned with the sick and the pseudo-sick.

Perhaps that was the explanation of Virginia's power over him, that her tremendous vitality and sheer joy of living could impart something of itself to him so that in her company, in her mere presence, even the smallest things became worth while.

But just then, watching her act for the first time, all he said was, "She's very pretty."

"Pretty, yes—but quite empty, of course," was Miss Dove's indifferent comment.

"She fulfils a purpose," he said.

"That of making other women envious and giving men thoughts they'd be better without? Oh, yes, I suppose so."

He laughed and took another cigarette.

"Does she make you envious?" he asked mischievously.

"Does she give you thoughts you'd be better without?" she retorted, and then they both laughed, good friends who had had many years together.

"Envious? I hope I've got more sense," said Miss Dove, who was in her fifties, and square, and with a face rather like a nice horse. "I hope I've lived to rather better purpose than that young woman is likely to do."

"How about the thoughts I'd be better without? Don't they serve a useful purpose in the scheme of things?" he asked, smiling still.

"I suppose so," giving him a contemplative look.

"Why that look, Emma?" he asked, stretching out his long legs towards the cheerful fire he was always sure to find in this room whenever the day was a bit chilly. The house was centrally heated, and in his own flat he augmented this with electric fires when necessary, but he enjoyed the matron's old-fashioned hearth.

Now that Virginia had danced herself off the screen, he had no further interest in it and she switched off. Much as she enjoyed looking in, he was better than a television programme any day.

"Why don't you get married, Blaine?" she asked. "You give neurotic women and irritable men that sort of advice, so why not take it yourself?"

"Physician, heal thyself? Am I neurotic and irritable?"

"Often," she told him serenely, the only person in the world who would have dared to tell him so.

"And you think that adding a wife to my other troubles would help?" with a slightly cynical smile.

"The right sort of wife, yes," she said. "Some sensible, intelligent, attractive woman who would understand your needs and be a good background for you."

"But women who are sensible and intelligent and prepared to be backgrounds are so rarely attractive—and if I did marry, I think I'd want her to be in the foreground rather than the background. And haven't I got a background in you? Haven't you been there long enough for me not to have any need for another?"

She snorted, picked up a fresh skein of knitting wool and shook it out vigorously.

"Twelve years," she said, "but it's not a professional background I was talking about but a personal one. You haven't any private life, Blaine. You need one. Every man does. Here. Hold this," giving him the skein of wool. "You might as well make some use of your hands," with a grim smile that hid the deep tenderness of her heart for him.

She was nearly old enough to be his mother. She had been aware of that from the first moment she had come into his life, first as the theatre sister he always insisted on having, then as the matron in charge of the small private nursing home with its six beds kept occupied by wealthy patients at exorbitant prices.

She had admired and loved him in those early days; she had admired and loved him ever since, but if he had ever had any suspicion of it, he had given no hint of such knowledge and her attitude to him was that of employee, friend and mother, whichever need in him was uppermost at the moment. She had accepted spinsterhood as long as she could remember. She knew about the unlovely square body and the horse face and that a man does not look beneath these things to see if there is a heart of gold as well.

Much later, sitting in his own comfortable room with a final cigarette and a mild whisky, he found his attention wandering from the learned treatise on intracranial glioma which he had intended to study.

He was quite absurdly thinking of Virginia Coley, of her vivid face, her laughing eyes, of the tossing pale gold of her hair and the swirling movements which seemed to epitomize the whole radiant joy of just being alive.

What must it feel like to be so glad of life? So carefree, as of course she must be to look like that? Did she ever think of tomorrow, or even of yesterday? Had she perhaps found the secret of life in just living for the day, the hour, the minute?

He wondered what her background was, what sort of home she went back to, what kind of place could possibly house this bright butterfly without bruising her wings? Parents, brothers, sisters? A middle-class home where there were such mundane things as washing up to be done, floors to be cleaned, food to be cooked and clothes to be washed and ironed? Ridiculously, he could imagine her living in the heart of a rose and living off honey-dew.

The everyday home he had pictured had once been his own background. His father, a builder in a small way, had grudgingly given him a slightly better education when he had begun to show his brilliance at a council school and, sent to sudden death by a collapsing scaffold, had left considerably more money than he had ever given evidence of possessing.

Blaine (he had been George Blaine Belding at the time), determined to be a doctor, a surgeon if possible, had been able to prevail upon his mother to let him have such other facilities as he needed beyond his own capabilities, and by the time he reached his early thirties, a lucky break in being able to perform a delicate brain operation on one of the lesser royalties had brought him fame and his title.

But he still remembered all about washing up and even scrubbing floors, for with his education and training to pay for, there had been very little left, and until his mother died and left him entirely alone, he had accepted his share in the toil he had imposed on her.

It was difficult to imagine anyone like Virginia doing that sort of thing, however. What did she do when she was not careering about the television screen in a revealing gown?

But, anyway, what on earth business was it of his what she did?

Yet the next day, when he had taken an opportunity to have a surreptitious glance at Miss Dove's *Radio Times* and saw Virginia's name, he did an incomprehensible thing.

He rang up the studio and asked if he might speak to her!

He was told, very politely, that he could not do so, and that in any case the programme was a pre-recorded one so that Miss Coley herself would not be in the studio. Would he care to leave a message?

He hesitated, and then left it.

Would Miss Coley ring up Gate 2116? No, no name. Just the number.

He realized at once how absurd it had been, and how very unlikely it was that she should respond to such a fatuous invitation. She must have hundreds of young fools (and old ones!) trying to get in touch with her.

But she did ring him up.

She thought a Gate number might be interesting, and she was amused that he had not even left a name.

"Are you Gate 2116?" she asked.

He had given her his private number which led directly to him and not by way of the nursing home, and no one answered calls on that line but himself. It was his one attempt at a private life, though very few people used that number.

"You know, I've not the least idea who you are," said Virginia's gay voice. "Who are you?"

"A congenital idiot. I realize that," he said, and she recognized not the voice but the quality of it, its cultured accents, and that it was not the voice of some callow, adventurous youth.

She laughed.

"That isn't complimentary," she said, "but where do we go from here?"

"Where would you like to go? Out to tea somewhere?"

"That's a nice mild beginning anyway," she said.

"Then will you—Miss Coley? Can I pick you up somewhere?"

"Haven't you picked me up already? I'm so terribly intrigued. Do we know each other? Have we met in the flesh?"

"Once, yes, though I don't flatter myself you would remember. How can I find you? Where? What time?"

"Well, as I have no means of identifying you unless you wear a cauliflower or some other little thing in your lapel, hadn't you better call for me? Say about half-past four? 15 South Mansions, Little George Street. That's Westminster though not recognizably Westminster. A back street behind Victoria Street. Do you think you can find it?"

14

"I'm quite sure I can. Half-past four then, and is it a place where I can park my car?"

She chuckled. It had a young, gay sound.

"Oh, have we got a car? Good. No, you can't park right outside because of the barrows. I told you it wasn't recognizably Westminster! You'd better look for a place near and finish up on your own two feet. I take it you've got two?"

"Oh, yes. I've got my full quota of parts," he said, and heard her chuckle again as he rang off.

What on earth had possessed him to make such a fatuous remark?

He knew very soon that it was Virginia who had possessed him.

CHAPTER II

NUMBER 15 SOUTH MANSIONS was at the top of an old block of flats, built for the wealthy and exclusive but now so far brought down in the social scale that, as Virginia had said, fruit-vendors had their stalls in the street and the steps to the outer door were littered with blown straw and paper.

But the flat itself was a bright enough little place, reached by toiling up several flights of stone stairs and a bright orange door with a card tacked to it which read:

Miss Yvette Gray
Miss Virginia Coley

It was Yvette Gray who came to the door, he surmised; a tall, dark girl in a painting-smock with some wet brushes in her hand.

"Oh," she said when she saw him. "Oh, have you come for Virginia?" and she held the door open for him and called over her shoulder, "Virgie! A gentleman friend!"

"Do you mind if I get on with my work?" she asked Blaine. "The paint dries so quickly," and she showed him into a pleasant, untidy living-room, gay with cushions and flowers and vividly striped curtains. Magazines lay about, and there was a small piano. A large black cat was curled up before the fire, and from an open cage a budgerigar greeted him with "Hullo, ducks, have a whisky."

Blaine did not know what he had expected, but it had been nothing like this. In spite of jarring colours and general untidiness, the place had a homely atmosphere, as if people lived in it and were happy in it.

"Have a gasper," said the budgerigar, hopping down to the table.

"Thanks, I will," he replied gravely and lit a cigarette and removed a pile of magazines and some flimsy under-garment from a chair in order to sit down.

Yvette Gray had disappeared with her paint brushes, and he settled himself down to wait, aware of the unprecedented position he was in but rather enjoying it.

Virginia came to him, buttoning up a fur-collared coat over a warm woollen frock. A gay little hat in matching blue perched precariously on her silver-gold hair.

She stopped in the doorway, astounded.

"Oh—it's *you*!" she said. "It never occurred to me that it could possibly be *you*!"

He gave a rather wry smile.

"I don't know whether I am to take that as complimentary or not," he said.

"Oh, but definitely! I'm flabbergasted, of course, but really honoured! Sir Blaine Belding, isn't it? I simply can't get over *your* wanting to meet me again."

"Well, do get over it," he said, "won't you? Is the arrangement for tea still on?"

"But of course. Do you mind me being all wrapped up in wool like this? I'm such a chilly mortal."

"You didn't appear so the other night."

"Oh, you looked in? It's different, of course, when one is under the blaze of the studio lights. One would be too hot in nothing then! How I'd love to scandalize the B.B.C. and the viewers by appearing in that! Not that one would ever get as far as the cameras, of course, and I saw the producer looking rather anxiously at my top, or lack of it, then! He was terribly afraid it might slip."

"How do you keep those things up?"

"Faith, suction and bones," she said. "Not your sort of bones, of course. Did you like my show?"

"Immensely. You looked as if you liked it yourself."

"I did. I do. I've only got on to the screen lately, you know, not being Lady Anybody, or having friends at court. I've been singing and dancing for ages, but I couldn't get a break until Martin Everton happened to see me in a cabaret show, not much of an affair, and gave me an audition, and even then I was only in one of his beauty shows and almost static."

"I can't picture you static," he said. "Are you ever still?"

"Only when I'm asleep—and Yvette says I plunge about even then. You met Yvette. She's a commercial artist, and we have to share a room here so that she can have one to work in. This isn't quite my idea of the way to live," looking round the crowded little room, "but it has to do—until I get somewhere, of course, and can branch out on my own."

"Have a drink," said the budgerigar, and they both laughed.

"Joey's Yvette's, and so's the cat," said Virginia. "I'm not the domestic sort. Yvette is. She ought to be married with a clutch of kids."

"And you ought not to be?"

She gave a shrug.

"Oh, I suppose I shall marry some day, but just now I have too much fun to be cluttered up with any permanent belongings. Shall we go?"

That had been the beginning of it, and it was very soon obvious to Blaine that it was not to be the end, so far as he was concerned, and by the time he had to break the appointment with her because of the man who had not died, he had to ask himself just what his intentions and his hopes were with regard to Virginia.

She had brought something so new into his life that he knew himself to be dangerously at sea with no harbour in sight. At first, in the atmosphere she created by her frank speech and careless attitude towards life, he had wondered if she wanted an affair with him, the sort of affair he had very seldom allowed himself to have. His profession and high position in it had always kept him aware of the danger of risking his reputation in any way, nor had his devotion to his work left him with any very great desire for the closer society of women. There had been one or two casual and very fleeting contacts, entered into during holidays at sea or abroad for the most part, but none of them had made much impression on him or had any lasting effects. He had never been in love and, now that he was approaching forty, he did not expect or want to be. He knew that Miss Dove was right in her contention that he ought to have a wife. For one thing, it would serve as a protection against the too obvious machinations of some of his women patients, and for another, he had had a feeling lately that he would like to entertain on a larger scale, live a rather fuller life than was possible in his flat over the nursing home. He did not feel the need of companionship, and he certainly did not hanker after a woman to go to bed with— or, at least, he had not so hankered until he had met Virginia Coley and taken her out a good many times.

On one occasion, he had brought her to his flat, impelled to do so by her frank curiosity about the way he lived.

"It's so odd," she said. "I mean, you actually living in Harley Street. I didn't know anybody lived there. I thought it was just a place you went to with your aches and pains, paid a fabulous fee and came away without them."

"Unfortunately people don't always, or even often, come away without them," he said, smiling at her in the indulgent, amused way one smiles at a nice child.

She had been intrigued with everything she saw, though she had not been allowed to look into the rooms where his patients, most of them women, lay under the ministrations of the starched, competent nurses and of Miss Dove, whom she saw fleetingly as they came out of the lift to find her leaving his private door.

"Did you want me, Miss Dove?" he asked.

"It can wait, Sir Blaine," she said in her most correct manner. Her use of his unadorned Christian name, and her attitude of friend and mentor were never allowed to appear save when they were alone. "Lady Mary Grever wants to know if she can get up."

"Tell her she can, for half an hour or so. That all?"

"Yes, Sir Blaine."

"Oh—er—my matron, Miss Dove. This is Miss Virginia Coley, Matron."

The two women eyed each other circumspectly, murmured unintelligibly, and then Miss Dove disappeared into the lift and Blaine opened his door.

Miss Dove sent the message to Lady Mary Grever, and went into her own room and sat down without even picking up her knitting.

She had recognized the girl at once. What in heaven's name was she doing here, with Blaine, being taken up into his holy of holies to which she had never known a woman to be admitted alone before, very rarely any woman at all and even then only in company with a husband who was a particular friend of the surgeon's?

Emma Dove was amazed and not a little worried. She knew that, being a normal man, he must have his little affairs with women at times, but to bring one here!

The visit had been conducted with the utmost propriety, Virginia given a cigarette and a mild drink before, having collected the papers for which he had had to call at his flat, he had conducted her out of the house again and driven her to the studio before going to see an important patient with whom he had an appointment.

But the visit had left its mark, for all its brevity and circumspection and, when he entered the flat again, he seemed still to see her there, something bright and gay that had alighted there for that brief moment and left something of the bright gaiety behind her. The drift of the perfume she used lingered there for several hours and he came across a scrap of a lace handkerchief which she had dropped and, foolishly, put it away instead of returning it to her.

Yes, what did he actually want with Virginia?

He had his answer to that when, watching Miss Dove's television screen, he saw her one evening with a dancing partner, an attractive young man, if one could call anything so obviously emasculate a man at all. He held her supple young form so closely in his arms, her cheek touching his, her eyes dreamy, her lips faintly smiling, that Blaine found his hands gripping the arms of Emma Dove's chair and felt his muscles tighten and the veins stand out on his forehead.

Miss Dove noticed it too, but said nothing. It had become obvious to her that he must know when Virginia Coley was to appear, since these were the times, the only times, when he wandered down to her room and, with his friendly smile, asked if he might share her viewing.

This evening, foolishly, having seen the girl's name in the programme, she had deliberately not switched on, had heard the soft whirr of the lift and had remained stolidly in her chair when he tapped and came in.

His eyes went at once to the screen.

"Not looking in tonight?" he asked.

"I didn't think there was anything on worth looking at," she said without looking up from her sewing.

"Isn't there? Mind if I switch on to see?" he asked, and without waiting for her permission, he turned the knob and sat down to wait for the picture to appear. "I'm turning into quite a television fan," he said with a smile. "I shall have to get a set of my own."

'Or an actress of your own,' she thought bitterly, but without saying so.

Was it possible, she wondered, that there could be anything in this? That he could really have fallen for an empty little nobody like that? It could not be anything but an affair, of course, but why pick on someone like that? There must be plenty of girls, quite nice girls even if their morals were a bit lax, who would have been only too glad to share a little bit of nonsense with a man like Blaine Belding. Why go in for a girl of that sort?

But whilst Blaine watched, growing hot and cold by turns, the new dancing act with a partner, he knew what it was he wanted of Virginia.

He wanted her herself, everything about her, not just as a brief amusement and a satisfaction of the senses which had begun to ache urgently for her, but something complete and permanent.

He wanted her for his wife.

Once he had made up his mind that that was what he wanted and meant to have, he lost no time in reaching out to take it.

He took her out to tea, as he had arranged after breaking that appointment with her and then, finding that she had no more work after eight o'clock, having given up her cabaret job to give more time to her television work, he asked if she would have dinner with him.

"Why, I'd love to," she said. "I'll have to go home to change, of course. I don't go out in the things I wear for the screen."

"Unless you particularly want to go out, why not save yourself the trouble of changing by letting me give you dinner in my flat?"

He saw her face change, and was angry with himself for the blind clumsiness of such an invitation. Of course she thought the worst at once!

They were in his car. He was dropping her outside the studio again.

He laid his hand for one moment on her arm.

"Don't say what you're thinking—or go on thinking it, Virginia," he said. "Don't you know, you *must* know, that there's nothing—nothing unpleasant behind the suggestion?"

"I rather wondered," she said.

"You need not. You should know by now that I don't think of you in *that* way."

She lifted wide blue eyes to his.

"Don't you, Blaine? All right. I'll come," she said, and hopped out of the car before he could open the door for her and disappeared from his sight.

What a clumsy fool a man could be, he thought angrily. Perhaps he had better take her out somewhere after all, but he did not fancy making his first proposal of marriage over a dinner table in a smart restaurant.

So he ordered the meal for them, after all, choosing it with care from the menu sent up to him by the very good chef who was an essential part of his equipment of an expensive nursing home.

"Send up some champagne as well," he said, "and see that it is properly cooled but not iced. Have it ready by about half-past eight and use the food lift. I don't want anybody to wait on the table."

He did not care now what the staff thought. They would

know soon enough what it was all about. It did not occur to him that Virginia might refuse him.

Virginia was appearing twice that evening, once in a popular programme of song and dance, and once as a visiting member of a panel game in which she hoped her youth and beauty would make up for any deficiency she might have in guessing skill. She had been quite excited, if rather frightened, but now all her thoughts about that had been vanquished by Blaine's invitation to dine at his flat.

She was between elation and fear. She felt she could be quite sure that he had meant what he said about that invitation, that it had no intent towards seduction but was a perfectly honourable suggestion. Sir Blaine Belding was not the sort of man who would induce a young girl to go to his flat for such a purpose, though she felt she had been quite right in letting him see that, if he had had any such thoughts, he could forget them.

But if he didn't want to seduce her, why had he asked her there?

The only alternative reason she could imagine sent the blood rushing to her cheeks and brought a new light into eyes that might have the colour of drenched bluebells but which might equally be the blue of sapphire, as bright and as hard.

When the friendship started, and indeed until this afternoon, such a thought had never entered her head. She had been flattered, a little amused by his attraction towards her, and, at twenty, a man of his age could be regarded in almost a fatherly light. How old was he? Forty? Fifty? He had no grey hairs, but there were heavy lines in his face, and there was at times a certain pomposity in his voice, and he was very sure of himself and that he had 'arrived', so he might be any age.

Sir Blaine Belding.

Lady Belding.

She looked at the clock. She'd better be getting ready for her next appearance. She had been told not to wear the topless gown for the panel game, in case close-up pictures of her head and shoulders gave the impression that she was actually wearing nothing at all on her top. Such things had happened, to the scandalization of the viewing public. But now, when the whole of her would be seen, she could reveal rather more of her lovely body, which she proceeded to do with the minutest care and presented herself for the special make-up required.

Whilst she sang and danced, she gave all her attention to her job, until now the only important thing in her life, and after her part in the show was over, hurrying to the dressing-room, she encountered Martin Everton, who stopped her with a pleased smile.

"That new number's good, Virginia," he said. "I've got something else in mind for you. Pop in and see me about it tomorrow. Bray will tell you when I've got a minute. Good child!" and with an encouraging pat on her arm, he hurried away.

She felt her heart lift at his approval. She was determined to get somewhere, to be a big star, perhaps to have her own programme as another stepping-stone towards Hollywood.

Then she remembered Blaine again. Just where would that fit in? Would it fit in at all? Could she hope for the best in two worlds, or would she have to make an irrevocable choice between them?

Virginia Coley in lights—or Lady Blaine.

How maddening to have to make such a choice!

Should she ring him up and put him off, make some excuse of a late rehearsal or something?

She looked at the clock. It was already too late. He would be on his way, for he had told her he would be coming straight to the studio from a patient to whom he had been called as a consultant.

She changed rapidly into her everyday clothes, the trim grey suit and pale blue sweater and the perky little hat which turned her from a glamour girl to a working girl, no different from thousands of other working girls if one discounted the lovely, provocative face and the shining, silver-gold hair with which few girls, possessing, would long remain working girls.

Blaine's car was drawn up outside when she left the building, the first time he had appeared actually there, at the kerb, rather than parked inconspicuously farther down the road. Did that mean anything?

"I warned you I shouldn't be able to change," she told him as she got in beside him.

"You couldn't look more charming," he said with an approving smile.

For once, her ready quip deserted her and she could only return the smile and sit beside him in silence.

It was a big, luxurious car and he liked to drive it himself, though Miss Dove had warned him anxiously more than once that by doing so he was risking possible danger to his hands.

"I should feel I was sixty, with a paunch, if I sat in state behind some other man," he told her and continued to be his own chauffeur, but he always gave his full attention to the job, even when Virginia was sitting beside him.

She stole surreptitious glances at his face, lean and fine-drawn, with sensitive nostrils and thin, firm lips, his eyes of steely grey set deeply so that one seldom saw their real expression. He wore a suit of dark grey, admirably cut in expensive cloth, and a grey homburg was set with no suspicion of jauntiness on his well-shaped head. He looked just what he was, she thought, successful, sure of himself and sure where he was going—and she did not mean merely in the London traffic. He looked a man who would get whatever he meant to have, and she gave a little shiver of mixed anticipation and fear.

He gave her a fleeting glance.

"Cold?" he asked, and touched the switch which turned on the heater. "That suit doesn't look warm enough. You should have some furs."

"Mink for a good girl?" she asked him jestingly.

"Perhaps," was all he said, and she knew that she could have even mink—under certain conditions.

Had she made a mistake, after all? Had he got mink in mind, but not for a good girl?

Well, if he had, that was going to be one thing he didn't get just by wanting it.

There was a table set for two in his big, warm sitting-room, a table beautifully appointed with fine linen and an array of real silver and cut glass, and there were flowers on it, pink carnations in a silver vase, and he mixed a mild cocktail for her when he had told someone, through a speaking tube, that they were ready for dinner.

"Won't you take off your coat?" he asked formally. "There's a bathroom through that door," nodding towards one of the two which opened out of the other end of the room.

It was very much a man's bathroom, workmanlike, nothing fussy, with certainly nothing specially provided for the use of women. She renewed her slight make-up, unnecessarily, ran a comb through the short, natural waves which ended in delicious little curls, and went back to him.

His manner was perfect, rather formal, and as the meal progressed, she became more and more certain that if he had any ulterior motive in bringing her here, it was not to make illicit love to her. Nothing could have been more correct than his manner, and they might have been dining in a public restaurant, except that the few courses, each well chosen and perfectly presented, came up in the food lift and he changed the plates and carried the food to the table himself.

Afterwards, with the table folded away and two chairs drawn nearer to the electric fire, coffee on a small table at her elbow and a huge goblet containing an inch of old brandy, he offered her a cigarette, lit it for her and sat down.

"About the mink," he said with a smile, "and other things."

"What about the mink?" she asked.

"I'd like to give it to you. I'd like to give you so many things —including, for what it is worth, myself, Virginia."

She set down the goblet carefully without looking at him.

"Just—what—do you mean by that?" she asked, her voice not quite as steady as she would have liked.

"Don't you know? I want to marry you, Virginia."

She drew in a deep breath and let it out slowly, still not able to look at him, and he rose from his chair and came to her and laid one hand on her shoulder.

"Well? What about it?" he asked. "I'm not much good at

making a proposal, never having made one before, and I'm not quite sure what will appeal to you about me. I'm a lot older than you, unfortunately. I'm thirty-eight and you're—what?"

"Twenty," she said in a small voice.

"I could be your father then, but I'm glad I'm not. I don't feel in the least fatherly towards you, nor even brotherly. I'm very much in love with you, Virginia, and I want you with me for the rest of our lives. I can give you a good life, with most of the things a girl wants. The one reason I'm glad I'm not as young as you are is that I don't have to ask you to share the struggle with me. I've done the struggling and I think I may say, without puffing myself up, that I've got somewhere and have something to offer you. We could have a lot of pleasant experiences together. We could travel, within reason and having consideration for the needs of my profession. We could go where you like, do what you like and you can have what you like—including the mink," with a smile of extraordinary sweetness as she lifted her eyes at last and looked at him with what was plainly some indecision in her face.

"But what about my profession, Sir Blaine?" she asked.

"Your profession? Oh, you mean this song and dance stuff. Well, that would hardly matter any more, would it?" indulgently.

She stiffened a little.

"I think it would. You see, I like it," she said.

"You like it? You mean, you wouldn't want to give it up?" he asked, plainly amazed. Such a difficulty had never occurred to him. He could not conceive of anybody actually wanting to do what she did without the dire necessity for doing it, careering about a stage, or in front of a battery of cameras, and singing (without even a voice) those ridiculous songs whose meaning, if they had any meaning at all, was quite obscure, the creation of moronic minds for the entertainment of other morons.

He had never willingly listened to such rubbish until he had glued himself to Miss Dove's television set to watch Virginia. Other singers sang the same sort of thing, often in raucous, tuneless voices which in a former age would have had their proper place outside some low-class public house. Virginia's

27

voice was not that sort. It was too small and light, But she sang the same ridiculous songs, giving them a false significance by her assumed earnestness in singing them, though she could not possibly attach any sense to them.

But to want to go on singing them if there were no need!

"No," said Virginia, quite definitely now. "No, I wouldn't want to give it up."

"Why on earth not?" he asked, stupefied. "You wouldn't need the money. You wouldn't need to work at all, at anything."

"You don't understand. It isn't just the money. It's *doing* it, the fun of doing it, being with other people, and people liking it and clapping and wanting more. I don't mean just the television audiences, but real audiences, who've paid to see me. I'm not going to stop where I am. I mean to get somewhere, be a big star, in big shows, or on the films. Don't you understand? You say you've got somewhere, and of course you have, but you must have wanted to."

It was too absurd, he thought, to compare what she did with what he did, but he could not doubt her sincerity.

"So, if you married me, you'd want to go on with all that?" he asked.

She nodded.

"Yes. Yes, I would," she agreed.

He walked away from her, drew aside one of the curtains and stood looking out at the gloomy, starless night without seeing it. All he was seeing was Virginia, her pale hair, her eyes, her soft young lips, her body with its vibrant aliveness, its vigour and its promise.

He wanted her desperately, urgently. He thought he had never wanted anything as desperately before, not even the success for which he had toiled and struggled and denied himself. He wanted her and must have her.

He turned back to her, went to her and lifted her from the chair into his arms. The feel of her body inflamed him with a wild passion.

"I want you, Virginia," he said, and there was no cold calmness in his voice now. "I want you and I must have you—on any terms. On your terms if you must."

She stood within the circle of his arms, her own heart beating fast.

"You mean you'll let me go on with my work if I marry you?" she asked.

"If that's what you really want."

"I do. I do really," she said.

Unable any longer to withstand the allure of her, he bent his head and put his lips to hers, lightly and tentatively at first and then with the burning urgency of his desire for her. She stood there for a moment, unresponsive but not resisting, and then gently drew herself away.

"Is this really happening?" she asked. "Am I awake? Is it really true that you are asking me to marry you, *you*, and that if I do, I can still go on with my work?"

"You can do anything, anything in the world, my darling, if you'll be my wife as well. Will you, Virginia?"

There was a last, momentary hesitation, and then she nodded her head.

"Yes. Yes, I will—Blaine," she said.

He kissed her again, triumphantly and more tenderly. Now that she had said she would marry him, the real ecstasies of marriage could well wait for their complete fulfilment, and she was very young, and perhaps a little afraid. He must go very carefully with her, not frighten her or make her wonder whether she was doing the right thing or not.

He sat in his chair again, and for a while they talked—or rather, he talked and she listened, quieter than he had known her so far and indrawn, but he felt that that was to be expected. She would have considerable adjustment to make in turning from little Virginia Coley, just becoming known, to the wife of Sir Blaine Belding, the eminent surgeon whose name was known all over the medical world and outside it.

It gave him an infantile pleasure to reflect that he could give her his title, that possession so much to be desired by the majority of women. He had liked it himself when it was conferred upon him, and he still liked it.

He outlined for her his plans for their shared life.

"We'll keep on this flat, or one like it," he said, "though I have for some time been thinking of moving from Harley Street as I could take a lot more of my lucrative patients if I had more room. I should have to keep in this district, of course, because one must have the right address as far as the nursing home and my consulting rooms go, but I think we should have our real home a little outside London, say twenty miles or so, and when we need to stay in town, we could stay in the flat. How does that strike you, darling?"

"It would be a long way for *me* to be," she said.

"Ah, your work, yes. Well, need that make so much difference? You could have your own car, and a chauffeur of course, so that you could come and go as you wished—always remembering, of course, that you have a loving and expectant husband in the background!" with one of his most charming smiles.

('Whilst that absurd phase lasts,' his mind added.)

He could not seriously conceive of her wanting for long to continue what she called her 'work', once he had given her a taste of the ease and pleasantness of the life he could provide for her. She would very soon want to give up this silly singing and dancing business, and her romantic dreams of being a Hollywood film star!

"We'll go and look at houses this week-end," he said, continuing his theme. "I try never to have any work on Sundays, at least, so we could make a day of it. I can call for you as early as you like—though I have already discovered how early that is!" with a teasing laugh at her love of lying in bed late. "Perhaps you could make an exception for once?"

She smiled. It really looked as though it might succeed, this amazing thing. She could be Lady Belding and Virginia Coley at one and the same time, both of those two worlds she had believed she would have to choose between.

"Perhaps I might, for once," she agreed.

"Well, now that that's settled, I think perhaps I'd

better take you home," he said, getting up. "How about tomorrow?"

"I've got rather a full day," she said. "In the morning I'm recording. I've never done that yet! And in the afternoon I've got to see Mr. Benner, Jos Benner the theatrical producer, you know, about the part he may be going to offer me in his new show, *Lady of Leisure*, and in the evening I'm doing a number at The Cocktail."

"Rather a lady of no leisure," he said ruefully. "What's The Cocktail? Can I come there?"

"Oh, yes, if you like. It's a sort of club. They don't have a set cabaret show, but just turns. I shall be on at various times until about midnight. We could perhaps snatch dinner somewhere in between?"

He made a grimace.

"I don't approve of snatched dinners," he said, "but if that's the only way I can see you tomorrow, I'll snatch with you. What time? May I call to collect you at your flat and take you there?"

They arranged it, and she went back to tell Yvette her news.

"It won't work, you know," said the practical Yvette.

"Why not? Blaine says he'll give me a car and a chauffeur so that I can get about easily without all this infuriating bus and tube business."

"I didn't mean that. What I mean is that I really can't see anyone like Sir Blaine Belding being content to let his wife work for her living."

"Well, he says he will. He's quite willing. He doesn't seem to mind at all. Why should he? He has his own work and I shall have mine."

"H'm. Well. Virginia, are you in love with him, by any chance? Because if you're not, why the heck do you want to marry him, if you mean to go on working?"

Virginia considered that.

She had undressed by this time and was sitting on the floor in front of the fire, having dislodged Mrs. Robinson, the cat, from the rug but given her a saucer of Ovaltine from her own cup as recompense.

"Am I in love with him?" cogitated Virginia thoughtfully. "I don't know, but I do love him, Yvette. I am quite sure I do. I like being with him. He's interesting and he doesn't put on any side about his work, and he can make me laugh. And when he kissed me, I liked that. He's so very clean and he smells nice——"

Yvette let out a shout of laughter.

"What would you expect him to smell like? Sewers? Or blood? I don't know much about men or being in love and I definitely don't like being kissed, whatever the man smells like, but if you're going to marry him because he's Sir Blaine Belding, well, that's O.K. with me, and quite sufficient reason, but I don't think you should count on not having to give up your work. For one thing, what about a baby?"

"None for me," said Virginia definitely.

"Have you told him so?"

"He hasn't asked me, but if he does, I shall say so. After all, it isn't as if he were a young man any more. He's thirty-eight!"

"Not exactly the sere and yellow," said Yvette drily. She was thirty-five and Virginia knew it. "Men *have* been known to want children at that advanced age!"

Virginia got up from the floor, set her empty cup down and stretched her arms above her head, loving the tensing of her muscles and the feeling of young vigour it gave her. She felt that the world was hers to conquer.

"Oh, well," she said, "I never meet trouble half way. Let that wait till it comes! I'm off to bed. Don't wake me at whatever ungodly hour you get up."

Yvette looked after her thoughtfully.

She was fond of Virginia in a cool, detached fashion, and they had made a comfortable thing of their shared lives in the small, crowded flat and she would miss her badly. On the other hand, she was doing better with her work than she had been when they joined forces a year ago, and she would not be altogether sorry to have the flat to herself, and if Virginia continued to know her when she was Lady Belding, it would provide her with a considerably wider circle of friends and the chance of meeting people who would be useful to her.

But what about Virginia herself?

Yvette felt she knew her fairly well and could assess at its proper value the spur which drove her on, the determination to succeed and the real need she had of popularity and public acclamation. From the little she knew of Sir Blaine Belding, such little confined to the short periods during which he had waited in the flat for Virginia to be ready to go out with him, Yvette had drawn the conclusion that in his domestic life as in his professional life, he would also want to be someone, a more important someone than the other people around him, his wife included.

Supposing Virginia did manage to keep on with her work, supposing she did make a real success of it, how would a man like Sir Blaine take it?

Oh well—it was none of her business.

But she was glad that the chance to marry such a man had not come her way, nor was it likely to come. If she married at all, it would be to some humdrum, everyday person like herself who might even be glad for his own inadequate earnings to be augmented by anything she herself could bring to the communal exchequer.

CHAPTER III

VIRGINIA was married to Sir Blaine Belding in June, barely three months after they had first met.

Because he was proud to show her off, and because none of his friends or acquaintances approved of the match, and because Virginia herself wanted to be 'a real bride', the affair was a public occasion, the wedding at a fashionable church with reporters and cameramen in attendance, and pictures of Virginia, a breathtaking bride, and Sir Blaine, a very personable bridegroom, in all the papers.

She would have liked to make a television appearance with him, apart from a shot of the pair in the news reel, but against this he was adamant.

"I don't mind making a public show of myself if it pleases you so much, my darling," he said, "but an arranged and personal appearance before the television cameras—definitely *no*," and because she seemed to be getting everything else in the world, she laughed and let him have his way.

It was easier in June, he told her, to get away from his work for long enough to have three weeks' honeymoon.

"People don't suffer from so many ills in June," he told her, "and besides, I'm trying to specialize more particularly on work on the brain, and that means I am gradually letting go of other things. I can afford to do that now—and I am determined to have you to myself for a few weeks anyway."

Yvette, tall and dignified, was her maid of honour, and behind her came a train of bridesmaids looking like a bunch of flowers, with Virginia herself looking the personification of her name in gleaming white.

An uncle had been produced from somewhere to 'give her away', and there was a scattering of Coley relations, but for the most part she seemed to be almost as much alone as was Blaine

34

himself, rather to his satisfaction. He knew that in marrying Virginia he might be considered to be going below the social class to which, by reason of his success, he had attained, but he was not anxious to have her family attached to him as well.

He had had to accept a good deal of condemnation from Emma Dove when he announced his engagement.

"I think you must have had a brain-storm, Blaine," she said in her forthright way. "How can you possibly imagine that such a marriage can be successful? You can't have anything at all in common with her, and I should have thought you were the last man in the world to be caught by a pretty face and a pair of legs."

"What makes you think there's nothing more to Virginia than that?" he asked her, angered by her speech but knowing that the familiarity which he had permitted and encouraged throughout the years made her frank criticism to be expected.

"Isn't it obvious?" she asked scathingly. "What could there be in anyone who sings those ridiculous songs, quite apart from anything else? She can't have an idea in her head. Have an affair with her, if you like, but why marry the girl?"

"That's enough," he said brusquely. "I'm quite well aware that I shall come in for a lot of criticism over it, but I don't want any more from you. I'm in love with her, and she with me, and I'm going to marry her. That's all."

And of course it had to be all, as far as the spoken word was concerned. She knew that in spite of their friendly companionship of twelve years, working together in complete amity and singleness of purpose, there was a barrier beyond which she must not go, and she had come up against it and must recognize the futility of battering against it.

He had found the house he wanted for his nursing home, a big old house not too far from Harley Street, its huge rooms easily converted into a large number of suitably-sized ones, and with a wing which could be cut off to provide him with a private flat larger and more convenient than the one which had suite l him admirably whilst he remained a bachelor.

The work of reconstruction was undertaken during the six

weeks prior to his marriage, and Miss Dove was to superintend the removal of the patients and the equipment of the nursing home into their new quarters whilst he was on his honeymoon. Virginia chose the decorations of their own flat, her scheme rather more bizarre and colourful than what he would have chosen, but he let her have her own way, his only proviso being that she should not impose her own ideas of decoration and furnishings on the one small room he had taken as his private study. He had a consulting room within the boundaries of the nursing home itself, so that all he needed in the flat was a room into which he could shut himself if he wanted to work quietly.

They were to look for their more substantial home after they came back, and meantime would live in the flat.

Virginia, delightfully self-important and pleased with herself as the new Lady Belding, felt when she set out with him for their honeymoon on the Continent that life had little left to offer her, and that little lay in her own hands.

Though he had said that it was rather a hackneyed choice for a honeymoon, he had fallen in with her wish to go to Switzerland, and a big hotel on the shores of Lucerne. He would have chosen some smaller, less frequented place off the beaten track, but was in a mood to let her have her way in everything.

"I've never been to Switzerland," she said. "I've never even been out of England, if you don't count Jersey, and Lucerne looks so lovely, all blue and gold and sunshine. I simply *hunger* for the sunshine!" for it had been a cold, wet spring with as yet no promise for the summer.

"You can get sunshine, and more of it, in less crowded places than Lucerne," he said, and suggested Majorca, Sicily, Cyprus, Madeira.

But it had to be Lucerne, and after all, he thought, what did it matter where they went? He would have her, his lovely girl, his wife, and if they had to spend their days being jostled by tourists and sightseers, they would spend their nights alone.

He took a suite in the hotel (Miss Dove had to arrange that), but though she was delighted with everything, thought it "just too dee for words", whatever that meant, and ran out on their own private balcony to look with enraptured delight down over the blue waters of the lake, she vetoed any suggestion that they should have their meals served to them in their own sitting-room.

"I want to show off my clothes," she said, like a child. "How can I, if we stay up here and there's only you to admire me?"

He laughed.

"No one will ever admire you more," he said, "but have it your own way. I shall have something to show off too—my beautiful wife," taking her in his arms and kissing her with something new in his embrace which made her struggle a little, her face flaming.

"Did I frighten you?" he asked very tenderly.

"Well, I—of course we're married, but I—I shall have to get used to it, shan't I?" she asked, turning away.

They had spent the first night in the train, since she had refused to fly, but she had been relieved, and grateful to him, to find that he had arranged separate sleeping compartments for them and, after kissing her good night, he had left her alone until they had had to leave the train very early in the morning for the change at Bâle, where they had had breakfast, great cups of wonderful coffee and hot rolls with cherry jam.

Virginia had loved it all, even being roused at five o'clock in the morning to hustle out of the train and pass through the customs at the frontier. She was like a child in her outspoken delight in everything unfamiliar and suitably impressed by the facility with which Blaine passed from English to French or German as the occasion demanded.

But she could not remain a child. He knew it, and she knew it.

She could not avoid the payment of the one price he would ask for all he was giving her, the fun and new dignity and importance of her title, being here in Switzerland, the gifts he had heaped on her, including the first of his presents, the big, square-cut emerald on her engagement finger and, with loving laughter at her delight, the mink coat.

"It isn't at all the time of year for a fur coat," he had told her when she went with him to choose it, "but I can't wait months before giving it to you, and if we go to Switzerland, as you seem

37

determined to do, you will be able to wear it if we go up the Jungfrau and perhaps spend a night in the hotel up there."

He had given her, too, a substantial cheque to spend on her wedding outfit and her trousseau. She had taken it with pretty thanks and without demur. After all, she couldn't be Lady Belding without looking like it, and her earnings, increasing but still small, would certainly not run to the sort of clothes Lady Belding would be expected to wear.

After that rather startling and revealing kiss, he let her go without touching her again. Rather than hurry her on after the night in the train, he had suggested their staying in Bâle for a few hours, resting for a little while in the lounge of the hotel where they had breakfasted, and driving round the city during the morning, so that by the time they reached Lucerne, it was nearly dinner-time and she was eager to discuss with him the important choice of a dress for her first public appearance in her new dignity.

"I don't mind which of them you wear, my sweet," he told her when she had spread them out for his benefit over both the beds, which had at first made her embarrassed but to which she had now become a little more accustomed, since he seemed quite unaffected by being alone in a bedroom with her.

But then, of course, he was used to being in bedrooms with women, she reflected.

"But I'd like you to choose," she insisted, so he made the casual choice of the one he saw she wanted to wear, a sophisticated gown of pale yellow brocade in which he told her she would look like a primrose.

"A hot-house one, if there is such a thing," he added, laughing.

She carried it off to the bathroom with her, to his tender amusement. How sweet, and how lucky in these days, to have a bride as pure and modest as her name!

He heard the splash of the water, and felt his pulses hammering as he pictured her, naked and rosy, a slender Venus in her bath. Soon, soon now, she would be all his, all her enchantment for his delight.

38

He felt almost a boy again, and if he regretted his greater experience in the arts of love, at least he would not be a clumsy lover to frighten her by her first awakening to it.

He enjoyed her little triumph in the big, noisy dining-room, where a waiter, at first sight of her in her primrose gown and of him, tall and distinguished in his correct black and white, led them at once to the most important table in the room, clearing away without hesitation the little card which had indicated its reservation for some other, less conspicuous, guests who could be accommodated elsewhere.

Virginia was radiant, laughing, ecstatically happy and ready to be pleased with everything. The waiter, speaking excellent English, advised her on the choice of dishes, reduced to slavish adoration by her flawless loveliness and her gaiety so that everything that was particularly choice in the kitchens found its way to their table.

They drank champagne, Virginia taking more of it than she knew to be wise but intentionally producing in herself a state in which she would find it easier to approach the ordeal of her wedding night, though Blaine kept his head clear and cool, knowing that much, perhaps their marriage itself, might depend on his own approach to it with this young, unaware girl who was giving herself to him.

She told herself in the morning, not opening her eyes until he had gone into the bathroom to shave, that it had not been as bad as she had nervously anticipated, that there was, in fact, 'nothing much to it'.

Blaine was vaguely dissatisfied, telling himself that he had been too diffident, too anxious not to alarm her or give her any distaste for the married state. He had induced no response in her, though she had been sweet and yielding, and she had not been able to hide her relief when he let her go to sleep. He could not believe that she was cold. How could she be, with all that abundant vitality? With her enthusiasm for life, and her determination to miss nothing it could offer?

Still, she had come through that initiation, unresponsive though she had been, without any of the fear and dislike which

39

he knew so many women felt after that experience. It had always amazed him how frank and unabashed so many of them were in what they told him, as their physician. He hoped Virginia would never tell any other man that sort of thing! It had always offended his sense of decency that they should be so candid about things which he felt should remain within the close knowledge of just the two concerned, though he had had to listen gravely and without showing any of the disgust he felt at such totally unnecessary revelations.

Well, there would be other nights, plenty of them, and gradually he would be able to teach his little bride that love-making could be fun and intense enjoyment with no fear or restraint. He stretched himself out in the warm bath with joyful anticipation of that happy time of complete fulfilment.

When he returned to the bedroom, she was sitting up in bed, a frothy lace wrapper over the too-exciting, transparent nylon of her night-wear.

He sat on the edge of the bed and took her hand and rubbed it along his smoothly shaven cheek.

"Nice now?" he asked.

"Very," she said shyly, not looking at him.

"I must shave at night as well as in the morning now, I can see," he said. "Last night I was in too much of a hurry—too enchanted."

"Blaine——"

"What, my sweet?"

"You—I can't—I shan't have a baby, shall I?" she asked, unable to look at him.

He laughed and kissed her.

"Not straight away," he said. "Poor child, have you been worrying about that? Don't worry any more. I certainly don't want that to happen yet. I want to enjoy my lovely girl before I turn her into a sober mother. Trust me, darling! I promise you there won't be any complications like that yet," kissing her again, her lips, her soft neck, the little hollow between the small, firm mounds of her young breasts.

'Not yet, nor for a long time, if ever!' thought Virginia, submitting to his caresses and hoping they were not going through 'that' again.

She was rescued by the arrival of the breakfast for which she had rung whilst he was in the bathroom, having received the day before the delightful explanation of the little pictures displayed beside the bell pushes—the waiter with the tray on uplifted palm, the maid with the pressing iron, the bell-boy with the tray under his arm.

It was funny to have a man bringing in her breakfast tray—but then so many things about her wedding trip were funny and new, and at least this one did not produce waves of fear in her, though it was slightly embarrassing to be so very under-dressed with a strange man in her room, and she pulled the lacy wrap more closely about her, aware of the amusement in her husband's eyes.

"Am I too silly?" she asked, when the man had gone.

"No. Very sweet," he told her. "I'm even luckier than I knew."

"Why do you say that?"

"I've been given to understand that it's quite unusual for a girl, at the extreme old age of twenty, to be so modest. It makes me love you even a little more, if possible. Pour me out some coffee, darling. Let's take it out on the balcony, shall we?"

"With me like this?"

"Well, put on a dressing-gown. Here," taking it from the back of a chair and giving it to her whilst he carried the tray out to the balcony which was already bathed in sunshine and the perfume of a thousand lime trees.

"Can one bathe in the lake?" asked Virginia.

"One can, in due season—but this particular one doesn't, not in June!" he laughed.

"Why? Afraid of the cold? I'm not," she said. "I want to swim. It's a lovely exercise, and if I am going to spend three weeks doing nothing but lounge about, with an occasional walk, I must find some way of exercising or I shall get fat."

"Well, what of it?" he asked, stretching his long figure with luxurious idleness in the long chair. "You'd still be lovely even if you did put on a pound or two. There would be more for me to love."

She gave a disparaging sniff.

"I'd be absolutely sunk if I put on even one pound," she said. "How could I dance if I had a tummy?"

"Better than if you hadn't one," he laughed easily not aware how much in earnest she was and watching her with lazy enjoyment as she ran her hands along the lines of her slim figure. "Come and sit on my lap and stop admiring yourself," putting out a hand to grab her and pulled her down to his knees.

She sat there for a moment, taut and unrelaxed. Then she wriggled free and stood up again.

"I mean it, Blaine," she said. "I do want to swim in the lake, but if you don't want to, take me somewhere where I can," and something in her faintly scornful tone reminded him that she, at any rate, had not forgotten the difference in their ages.

"All right, if you insist," he said. "I doubt if the proper swimming place down there is open yet, but in any case, you wouldn't like it. You go down into a sort of dungeon with water for the floor, and if you are very adventurous, you swim out under the bars into an enclosure where the sexes are kept discreetly apart—or that was how it used to be when I was as young as you are. If you really want to swim, though the water is ice-cold from the glaciers, I'll take you along the lake, get a boat with a boatman or something, and you can have your own private beach, but I don't think you'll want to repeat it!"

They did as he proposed, found a boatman who would take them in his small motor-boat round the edge of the lake until Virginia found the right place, where she slipped out of her frock, her swim-suit underneath it, and for half an hour swam and dived and disported herself in the water that could not have been much above freezing point, since the snows were still coming down from the mountain tops into the lake, and she did not appear to mind it at all. Blaine sat in the boat and watched her obvious enjoyment and felt old and rather less alive by the very comparison with her abounding health and vigour.

He got the boatman to land him, with her dress and the dry

underclothes she had brought, mere wisps of things in her hand-bag, and he dried her with the big bath-towel from the hotel and realized that her imperviousness to the cold was no pretence. She was warm to the touch and glowed like a rose.

"I loved it," she said. "What a pity you can't do it with me! Race you to the boat!" and she was off like a puff of wind, leaving him to follow.

It was the same with everything they did, the high spirits, the untiring energy, her enthusiasm for any and every new thing, and in the evenings, when he would have been glad to sit quietly and talk to her, or listen to her or make love to her, she wanted to dance in the ballroom of the hotel, or some other of the many places in Lucerne which she seemed able to discover by instinct.

But, to give her her due, she enjoyed the simpler, easier things as well, such as going by the lake steamers which plied all day between the various little towns or places of interest along its length, or sitting with him in some small, country inn, drinking iced lager, or the hot *gluhwein* which he preferred, listening to him talking in German to the pleased proprietor, insisting on his translating for her what was said, and enchanting the friendly Swiss by her gay attempts to communicate with him herself.

She enchanted everyone, and one evening in their hotel, when she had left him for a few moments and he assumed she had gone to find the place which now she called gaily 'the damen', he was electrified, and horrified, to hear her unmistakable voice from the daïs which held the orchestra, and edged his way through the quickly gathering crowd to see her seated on the grand piano, singing one of her gay little songs to the vamped accompaniment of the delighted members of the orchestra, after which she slipped her feet to the floor and danced, her short curls flying, her dress swirling, her eyes sparkling, her fingers snapping an accompaniment to the music and urging on its speed until it became a delirium of noise and movement and at the end, she sank down amidst a final swirl of her skirts, her glowing face like the heart of an exotic flower, her pale pink skirts its opened petals.

A storm of applause broke out and people, especially the men, were pressing forward as she came down the two steps of the daïs towards them, their cries for 'more' in several languages.

Then she saw Blaine and pushed her way towards him, her hands stretched out in a lovely, appealing gesture, her eyes sparkling with anticipation.

Anticipation of what, he thought angrily? Could she possibly expect him to be admiring and approving of this public display, she, his wife, Lady Belding?

But he was too well-mannered to make an exhibition of his displeasure in public, himself now the cynosure of all eyes, and he forced his lips to smile, though his eyes remained hard and steely.

"Blaine! Were you watching?" she asked gaily, obviously unaware of any cause for disapproval. "It was such fun!" and she tucked her hand under his arm and gave it a little squeeze, though she very seldom touched him voluntarily. It was the first time he had realized it.

"Very charming," he said briefly. "Shall we take a turn outside? Have you got your coat?"

"Oh, I don't want a coat! I never catch cold. You get one, though, for yourself. I'll wait."

It was foolish and small-minded to resent the suggestion that he needed to take more care of his older body than she of hers, but he did resent it.

"Of course you must have a coat, now that you're so hot," he said, and he propelled her by the hand which he held firmly under his arm back to the place where they had been sitting, and to the mink coat hung carelessly over the back of a chair, and wrapped her in it, conscious of all the watchful, curious eyes.

Out in the hotel garden, he spoke to her in a tone she had never heard before, though anyone at any of the hospitals he visited would have recognized it and quailed.

"Really, Virginia! What possessed you to make such an exhibition of yourself?" he asked, releasing her arm.

She stood still and stared at him.

44

"An exhibition of myself? Of *myself*? It was an exhibition of my art! What's wrong with that?"

"Everything's wrong with it, at such a time and place, where you are here as my wife. How on earth did it happen?"

"Quite simply. Somebody recognized me and asked me to," she said. "Blaine, you can't really *mind*?" incredulously.

"Of course I mind. You're not Virginia Coley any longer, especially not here, and whilst you're with me. You're Lady Belding, my wife, not a—a——"

He paused. Even in his present anger, he stopped himself from finishing the sentence with the words that had sprung to his tongue, 'a cheap variety star'.

Her eyes were frosty.

"Yes? Finish it, Blaine. What were you going to call me?" she asked.

"It doesn't matter. What I meant to convey was that I did not expect, and do not expect you to behave as any other than my wife in such circumstances as these."

"I shall never be *only* your wife," she said icily. "Are you going back on your word? You agreed that I should still do my work."

"Yes, but it is not part of your work to give a free performance to complete strangers whilst we are—staying away together."

He could not bring himself to refer to this as their honeymoon, poles apart and even antagonists as they were at this incredible moment.

"Why not? Stage stars live by publicity, or they don't live at all, and this will have done me a lot of good. There are probably lots of people here who have never heard of me before, but they will now, and when they see or hear my name again, they'll remember it."

"Your name? What name?" he asked quickly.

"My own name, Virginia Coley," she retorted, her head high, her blue eyes bright and hard. He had never seen them like that before.

"At least you did not use mine, then," he said shortly.

45

"Why should I? It's not as Virginia Belding that I'm important," she said, and she turned away and walked, head high, back through the front door of the hotel and not, he was glad to see, through the french windows by which they had left the ballroom.

When he went up to their suite later, she was asleep, or pretending to be, and by the morning she was her usual charming self, ready to be amused and entertained, and he was only too thankful that he could be allowed to forget, if he could, their quarrel of the night before, and its cause, and she did not repeat the offence during the rest of their stay.

He knew that it was foolish and undignified, but on the day following what his mind still termed her 'exhibition of herself', he bought her something she had been hankering for, though it cost him most of the joint allowance of money for foreign travel —a jewelled head-band. It was not exorbitantly expensive in itself, and he would not have thought twice about it had she wanted it in England, but, as he pointed out to her rather ruefully when he had bought it, it meant curtailing some of their programme for the rest of their stay.

"Do you mean we've actually got to keep within the absurd limits of the allowance of foreign money?" she asked.

"But, darling, of course we have. I'm not privileged in any way," he said, "and our suite is costing rather a lot, considering that we are the poor British, who are obliged by a near-sighted government to go in for the cheapest available accommodation. We shall have to be very careful, and might even have to cut our stay short after this."

"Couldn't you have fiddled it somehow? Other people do," she said with a pout.

"Perhaps, but I couldn't. I've got my reputation to think of, even if I'd known how to fiddle, as you put it," he said with an indulgent smile. "How about it? Would you like to go home?"

"Not particularly. I like it here. Still, not if it means that we've got to scrape and be poor! I hate being poor!"

"So do I," he agreed. "Well then, let's go home. Not today, but at the end of the week, say, Friday? That gives us three more days, and we've had a good time, and you've got your head-band, though I could have bought you a much nicer one in London."

"Yes, but I wanted this one. It's amusing, and it will look lovely when I'm dancing. All right. Friday then," with a little sigh of regret, regret in which he shared, for when they got back to London she would no longer be all his own, nor would he have unlimited time in which to be with her.

He arranged for their tickets, sent a telegram to Miss Dove, and they made the most of their remaining days. They had to cancel their stay at the Jungfraujoch, to his regret, but he told her they would do that next time they came.

"Next time? Oh, but next time I shall want to go somewhere else! I want to go everywhere, see everything, do everything! I want to pack just *everything* into my life!" and she pirouetted round the bedroom in her short, frilly slip and looked so delicious and so young that he caught her in his arms and kissed her with adoring passion.

"And you've so many years in which to do it all, my lovely girl," he said. "I want to give it to you, everything you could ever want or dream of!"

She let him hold and kiss her without struggling free as she usually did.

"You're terribly sweet to me, Blaine," she said.

"I want to be, if you'll let me. Darling, don't let's go down to dinner tonight. Let's have it up here, just the two of us, and—sweet, I want to make love to you!" pushing off the straps of her flimsy slip and kissing the pearly whiteness of her shoulders hungrily.

She drew herself away.

"But, Blaine, it's only six o'clock!" she said.

"Does love have a clock?" he asked. "Six o'clock or midnight, what difference does it make when one's in love—or when two are in love, better still? Come, my sweet, my little lovely one!"

She let him have his way. After all, she might as well get it over, but she insisted that they should go down to dinner afterwards rather than have it sent up to their suite.

"It's so much more gay," she said. "I love the lights and the people and the music."

"More than you love me?" he asked fatuously.

She pulled a face at him.

"That's different. People and lights and music are my life," she said gaily.

"And I'm not your life?"

"Part of it, but quite a different part," she said. "Darling, go *away*! I've only just made up my lips and now look at them —and your own," dabbing at his mouth with a tissue. "Haven't you had enough *yet*?" for his love-making had been stormy and possessive, seeking urgently to call from her that response he had never been able to rouse in her, feeling that something in himself must be lacking if she could not share his joy in their nearness and the final rapture.

But he laughed and let her alone. Some day she would be wholly his. She must be. He would never be satisfied with less.

CHAPTER IV

BECAUSE of Miss Dove's changed attitude, in which she became formally and only the matron of the nursing home again, and because of the different life he would now be leading, Blaine engaged a secretary when they had returned to England, May Jenner, a bright, capable girl who at once fell under the spell of Virginia so that Blaine told his wife laughingly that he would have to get someone else for himself, if he wanted any of his own work done.

"I know, darling," said Virginia apologetically. "I seem to have a thousand things to think of and arrange, don't I? Once *Lady of Leisure* really goes into production, though, I'll let you have May back, as I don't really need anybody. After all, I do all the deciding for myself, and it's only the small things, stupid letters and things."

"Clever girl, aren't you?" asked Blaine fondly. "Well, have May when you want her, so long as she can occasionally give me a spare half hour!"

"Who did it for you before?" asked Virginia. "You didn't have a personal secretary then."

"Miss Dove used to do all sorts of things for me."

"Why doesn't she do them now? Is it because I'm here? She doesn't like me, you know. It's quite mutual!"

"That's just your imagination. She's much busier since I've had this bigger place, and it wouldn't be fair to ask her to do things outside her own job."

"You know she's in love with you, don't you?" asked Virginia mischievously.

"Emma Dove? What nonsense! Why, she's old enough to be my mother," he said, kissing the top of her bright head.

"So she may be, but she doesn't feel motherly towards you,

49

and when old women like her get the love bug, it bites them badly! Not that I mind who's in love with you. It just makes me laugh."

"It need not make you worry, anyway. Would her ladyship like to have dinner out with me somewhere tonight?"

"Oh, darling, not tonight. I've still got my part to learn, and it's so hard to learn the words that haven't got any music to them. Will you hear me?"

"All right. Give me the book, or whatever you call it. What are you? Sandra?"

"Yes. Just give me the cues—or perhaps you'd better read the lot. I asked for a full script," handing him the bunch of typed papers.

He read the other part with amusement and exaggeration, making a melodrama of it.

"It isn't supposed to be all that funny," said Virginia, irritated by his refusal to take it seriously. It all sounded very futile to him.

"Sorry, darling, but I find it funny," he said. "Who really does say things like this to other people?"

"It's only a play," she said, "and the talking part's only to link up the songs."

"But surely they don't have to be so idiotic about it? 'Whed first you swam into the room, my heart swam with you.' How absurd! Are they in a swimming bath, or what?"

"Of course not. It's just because of the next song," she said crossly. "Who cares about the words, though of course they have to be there. Go on, Blaine."

He tried to be serious, in spite of what seemed to him utter drivel, and when they had gone through her part and got her almost word-perfect, he put down the script and looked at her speculatively.

"How does it really feel, having this Ferdinand person making love to you in public?" he asked.

"It isn't making love," she said scornfully. "Not the way we do, anyway!" with one of her lightning-quick changes of mood and a chuckle.

"I should hope not indeed! But all this kissing. Does he really kiss you?"

"Of course he does, or it would look silly. We're supposed to be terribly in love."

"And do you kiss him?"

"Naturally."

"As if you were terribly in love? How do you kiss when you're terribly in love?"

"You should know!"

"Yes, I should do—but do I? Are you terribly in love with me, Virginia? I sometimes wonder."

Her face hardened. She got up from the arm of his chair on which she had been sitting to learn her lines, but he pulled her back, drew her down until she was on his knees though she stiffened.

"You know I'm in love with you," she said.

"Do I? Are you, Virginia? The way I'm in love with you?"

He knew it was folly to provoke this scene, a scene they had already played several times, at varying tempos but always with the same result, a widening between them of the gulf which he knew, if she did not, kept them apart even in their most intimate moments.

"Why else should I have married you?" she asked. "Just to be Lady Belding?"

"No. No, I'm sure it wasn't that. Why should it be, when you don't even use the name in the most important part of your life?"

"Well, whose doing was that? I was quite willing to call myself Virginia Belding, and you know how fond the B.B.C. are of titles."

"It wasn't—suitable or dignified. Besides, as you told me, it was as Virginia Coley that the public know you."

"Well then, why complain? I find it very difficult to understand you, Blaine. I suppose what you would really like would be for me to stop being Virginia Coley altogether. Give up my work."

"Yes, I should," he said. "I don't find it always convenient to be married to two people, one of them not often available."

She disengaged herself from his arms and stood up. He was beginning to know that expression on her face, the shut-in look which excluded him.

"We agreed about that before I even said I'd marry you," she said.

"I know, but I didn't think it would be quite like this. I didn't think I should be relegated quite so much to the background."

"What you really thought was that I should soon get tired of it and want to give it up, didn't you?" she asked with that shrewdness which now and then turned her from thoughtless child to calculating woman.

"Yes," he agreed with a little shrug. "Yes, I suppose that is what I did think."

"Well, don't go on thinking it because it isn't any use. Anybody could be Lady Belding, but only one person could be Virginia Coley."

"I don't agree," he said steadily. "Just *anybody* could never have been my wife. Only you, Virginia, and it wasn't Virginia Coley whom I married, but the girl I was in love with, *my* Virginia, my wife."

Once, even a few weeks ago, he would have taken her in his arms, overcome her resistance by his kisses and his tenderness, made her yield to him with such response as he could evoke from her until, superficially at least, the breach would be healed.

But now he did not try, and after a few moments she went out of the room and he heard her own door shut.

They had found the house they both liked, a charming old house, long and low and whitewashed, with genuine old beams, and a rambling garden gay with flowers and shaded by trees which had withstood centuries of storm and change. They had had to go further than the twenty miles to find an unspoilt village not threatened by the new dormitory building which was making London into an enormous, continuous stretch of houses and flats where once there had been the open country. It was not very convenient for either of them, particularly for Virginia, and they were spending more and more time in the London flat. There had been too many occasions when Blaine had driven thankfully into the country, looking forward to a long week-end in its quiet peace, only to find, after waiting several hours for Virginia, that she was not coming down, telephoning that she would be too late, even though he had provided her with the promised car and chauffeur.

"Come down tomorrow, then, darling," he might say perhaps. "Come down in the morning and we can have a long day."

"Oh, Blaine, you know how I hate having to get up early when I've had a late night. No, you stay down there, darling, and we'll see each other on Monday. I'll just stop in and have a good rest."

As this did not suit his ideas of married life at all, he soon gave up the habit of driving down to Cotterway by himself, leaving her to follow, though lately he had begun to suspect that she would have preferred him to go and for them to spend their week-ends apart.

She was throwing herself with tremendous energy into what was, to her, of such supreme importance, her first part in a full West End production, and she was looking forward to the time when her B.B.C. contract would come to an end so that she need not let it occupy so much of her time. He had to admire the zest and enthusiasm with which she worked, driven by the spur of her boundless ambition, though he could see plainly that her achievement of that ambition might well be the breaking point of their marriage according to his conception of what marriage should be.

He took to wondering, with increasing bitterness, just why she had married him, and he could not escape the conclusion that in the main it had been for the furthering of her projects, not so much through his social position and the fact that he had made her a titled woman, but rather because of what his financial position could do for her. There was no longer any need for her to do any kind of work which she did not want to do, the cabaret shows, the occasional week's engagement for some variety show in the lesser suburban theatres. She need not even keep up her contact with television or radio now, though this had been not only her stepping-stone, but also her chief means of livelihood.

She undoubtedly appreciated her position as his wife, the luxury of their home, her car, the furs and clothes and jewels which he had been delighted to buy for her. When she entertained their guests, she did it perfectly and charmingly and had worn down any opposition by his friends to their marriage. In her general attitude to him, she was gay, friendly, amenable up to a point, that point being the exigencies of her own work—but that was all.

He had to face the fact and admit it. She was not in love with him and never would be, since she lacked both the understanding of and the ability to encompass the sort of love he had had for her.

Had had?

That was the increasingly frequent and destroying turn of his thoughts.

Did he love Virginia, as he had done? Had he indeed ever loved Virginia herself, or had he merely created out of her enchanting face and desirable body something she was not and never could be? Had he not rather been spellbound by her beauty, by her youth and health and glorious vitality, in comparison as it was with the sort of people amongst whom most of his working hours were spent, people stricken with disease and looking to him, desperately, for healing, people whose bodies held some hidden horror which he must try to remove or alleviate, or the train of neurotic women who, with too much money and time, found their pleasure in fancied ailments and the grave attention and interest of an attractive doctor?

He heaped on Virginia more and more costly gifts, shutting his mind to the knowledge that in doing so, he was trying to preserve his own self-respect and belief in his faithful love. She always received them with joyful delight, thanked him extravagantly, gave him her body for his delight when it was unavoidable—and stretched out her grasping little hands for more.

54

Emma Dove, watching him if she could no longer watch over him, felt her heart contract many times at the signs of strain and worry, even of too quickly increasing age, as the months went by. He worked hard and successfully. People, often very important people, came to him from great distances to be healed, to have operations which few men in the world could perform with so great a chance of success. Whatever his private troubles might be, his brain and his hands lost none of their skill, and Miss Dove wondered wrathfully what more Virginia Coley could want than this man for her husband, and nothing but that. Surely the care of him and of his happiness should be enough, and more than enough, for any woman?

She had never changed her opinion of Virginia, save for the worse, and she saw her now as useless, worthless, self-occupied to the exclusion of everyone else, including Blaine, and greedy, draining him of money as Miss Dove felt she would some day succeed in draining him of everything else he had achieved.

Blaine and Virginia had been married for six months when something happened which was destined to alter the course of several lives, though at first there had been no indication of it.

He was driving home from the theatre where Virginia, released from the cast of *Lady of Leisure*, in which she had made a small, but not outstanding success, was appearing in pantomime.

It was Boxing Day, and they had spent a somewhat unsatisfactory Christmas in the flat, since she had been on call for last-minute rehearsals and was entirely preoccupied with the forthcoming production.

He had wanted them to go to Cotterway, but realized that, for her, it would not be possible and he had accepted the position with at least outward good grace.

He had gone to the theatre for the opening night, and had realized, against his secret hopes, that Virginia, though she might never be a great actress, had certainly 'got something'. His mind had begun to use some of the phrases which were Virginia's rather than his own slightly pedantic respect for the English language.

She was playing 'Beauty', and her association on the stage with the great bear-like creature appearing as the 'Beast' enhanced into a dream of loveliness and grace her dainty person, her provocative beauty and her movements, light as air, as she danced and sang and made delicate love to her unattractive lover.

She was undoubtedly a success in the part. She had answered call after call when the show ended, and flowers had been heaped about her, his own amongst them, and these, he saw, were the ones she chose to hold in her arms at the final call. He had gone round to her dressing-room as she had suggested, but had found it filled to overflowing, so that he could scarcely get near her.

When he did, she told him, flushed, excited, happy, that it might be better if he went on to the flat without waiting for her.

"You've got that big op. in the morning, darling," she said, "and heaven knows what time I shall get away from all these lovely people. You go on, and I'll come as soon as I can."

He had not wanted to leave her, but he knew she was right. He must have enough rest and sleep if he were to be fit to cope with the operation whose magnitude and delicacy only he himself fully appreciated.

Perhaps he was thinking of that, perhaps also of Virginia and their marriage, which was oddly detached and yet which could not be classed with the unsuccessful or unhappy marriages. He was driving with his usual care, though at that time of night, nearly midnight, he had not to contend with the home-going business crowds. But there was a thin fog, and frost had put a layer of ice over the wet roads.

Whatever it was, when a woman stepped off the kerb directly in front of him, he had to brake violently, skidded into a lamp-post, recoiled from the impact, and he had the sickening knowledge that she was no longer walking or standing in the road. If the wheels of the car had not gone over her, at least she had been knocked down and lay out of sight from the driving seat.

He sprang out instantly and was at her side by the time the small crowd, which could always materialize from space at any hour of the day or night, had collected round them.

She was a young woman, slight and not well dressed and she

56

lay, not under the wheels, thank God, but in a crumpled heap half under the bonnet.

"I saw wot 'appened, guvnor," said a rough voice eagerly, as a man of the no-home sort edged his way forward. "Weren't your fault. Stepped right orf in front of you she did, the silly witch. Ain't dead, is she?" with ghoulish interest, though Blaine was thankful that someone, even someone of this sort, had seen the accident.

"No, or even very badly hurt from the way she's lying," he said. "Can you help me to get her out so that I can examine her? I'm a doctor, and my house is quite near. We could perhaps get her into the car when I've had a look at her—that is, if it still goes. Gently. Don't twist her in any way. There may be something broken. She's not conscious."

It was an ankle which he found to be broken, though he did not think there was anything worse, and when he had immobilized it temporarily, one of the bystanders helped him to lift her into the car, which was large enough to accommodate her in reasonable comfort on the back seat.

He handed his card to the man who had been helping him.

"Would you be kind enough to get in touch with the police?" he asked. "This man says he saw the accident so if you would take his name and address for the police, I need not keep this poor woman out in the cold any longer—that is, if my car will start. It got a nasty jar, I'm afraid."

He had no difficulty in starting and moving it, however, and in a very few minutes his new patient was being carried carefully up the steps and into a room which was fortunately vacant.

Miss Dove herself was in attendance. She would not have admitted to it, and nobody was even aware of it, but she rarely went to bed, and never to sleep, until Blaine was in, if he was driving alone, and she had felt pretty sure that tonight Virginia would not be with him. She would be celebrating whatever there was to celebrate! And Blaine himself would not want to do any celebrating, with that operation in the morning.

The injury did not go further than the ankle, which must have been caught by the bumper of the car when she fell, and

when he had set it and left her comfortable, though still unconscious, he went to his own quarters and to bed. There was
nothing now to be done for her which the matron and the night
nurse could not do.

"I'll see her first thing in the morning," he said.

She was conscious, and awake, when he went into the room
again, and he smiled down at her encouragingly.

"Well? Feeling comfortable?" he asked.

"Yes. Rather stiff, and the nurse says I broke my ankle," she
said shyly.

She did not speak in cultured accents, but there was only a
touch of cockney in her voice, and she spoke grammatically.
She had a thin face, pale from the accident, or perhaps she was
always pale, and someone had made her dark hair neat and rolled
it into a bun on the top of her head.

She was not pretty, though not plain either—the sort of face
seen by the hundred any day in a busy city, and the hands that
lay outside the bed-clothes were small and well shaped but not
well cared for.

He looked at the record the nurse had made and had left
fastened to the temperature chart at the foot of the bed.

Anna Mere. Age 32. Nearest relative, married sister. Typist.

An address was given, a street in Chelsea.

"I see that you have a sister in London, Miss Mere," he said.
"Shall we get in touch with her? Unless they've already done
so?"

"No. No, please don't," she said quickly. "She's just had
another baby. That was why I was out so late last night. I stayed
with her until it was born, and I missed the last bus, so I was
walking home."

"All the way to Chelsea? You'd have done better to stop on
the pavement, wouldn't you? Do you remember what happened?"

His tone was kind and friendly, and she managed to smile,
though she had been greatly awed by the discovery of where she
was, and who he was.

"Not very clearly. I was very tired, and the fog must have

58

confused me, but I'm quite sure it was my own fault. I knew at once that I'd stepped off the kerb, but I don't know what happened after that. I was surprised to find myself here," with another of her shy smiles.

"Well, if you had to get yourself knocked down by a car, perhaps it was as well that it was a doctor's," he said cheerfully. "I'll see matron, but I don't expect there is any need for me to look at the ankle yet. It's best left alone now. Are you comfortable? Got everything you want? If there is anybody who ought to be told about you, and where you are, one of the nurses will get my secretary, Miss Jenner, to come and see you."

"But I—shall I have to go into a hospital?" she asked shrinkingly.

"Why? You're all right here, aren't you?" he asked with a smile.

"Yes, but—I can't—I mean, this is a private nursing home, and I can't—I mean——"

He gave her a reassuring nod.

"Don't worry about that. It's lucky we had a room for you. After all, as I knocked you down, it's only fair that I should pick you up, isn't it? We'll look after you here and there won't be anything for you to worry about. Now I must leave you, but if you need anything, just ask for it. You've got some books, I see, but sleep as much as you can," and with another nod and a smile, he left her.

Miss Dove intercepted him in the hall.

"This girl, the one in Number Five. Is she to stay here?" she asked.

"Oh yes, she might as well. There's no one booked in for there, is there?"

"Not until the end of next week, Sir Blaine."

"Oh well, leave her there then. Probably by that time she'll be able to go home. I don't know what her circumstances are. Probably not too good, no mother or anything like that, but you can find out about that before she has to leave. Have they brought the car round from the garage? I told them to send me something to use whilst they fix mine up. I've got that inter-cranial this morning, you know."

"Yes, I know. Not worrying you, is it?"

"Just a little. I'd like to have had my old theatre sister," with one of the smiles which were rare now.

Her grim face relaxed a little. Her heart yearned over him.

"I'm sure you'll have one quite as efficient," she said.

"Maybe, but you were a second pair of my own hands and my own brain to me," he said, and he went out, pulling on his coat as he went.

When he returned, he was glad that Virginia was not in. After the operation, which had been completely successful, he stayed with his patient, or within immediate call, for some hours, and by that time Virginia had had her light lunch and gone to the theatre for the afternoon performance. There were to be two shows a day for some weeks, so he did not expect to see much of her.

Emma Dove brought up his coffee herself. He liked to have it, hot and strong and sweet, before his lunch when he was tired.

"Thank you, Emma. Like old times," he said, taking it from her with a smile. "Don't rush away. Stay and have a cigarette with me until my lunch comes up."

"Is her ladyship not lunching with you?" asked Miss Dove, who always spoke of Virginia with formality.

"No, she's gone off to the theatre—not our kind! Possibly an even more exciting and exacting kind."

"H'm," grunted Miss Dove, and left it at that. She wondered how long things could go on as they were, and when Blaine would put his foot down on all this acting rubbish, and how her ladyship would take it. Time she came home and looked after her husband, and a baby wouldn't be a bad idea—though her heart contracted a little at the thought.

To be able to bear Blaine Belding's child!

You silly old fool, she apostrophized herself. At your age, it would be a darned miracle for you to bear anyone's child!

Later in the afternoon, he went down to see Anna Mere.

He said the name over to himself with a little amusement.

60

Such a plain, unpretentious name! He thought it suited her, though. There were obviously no pretentions about her.

She was comfortable, and inclined to be too grateful, saying that she ought not to be there and would be quite all right, really, in an ordinary hospital, if she couldn't go home.

"Nonsense. You stay where you are," he said with brusque kindness. "Are they looking after you well? What did you have for lunch?"

"Chicken," she said impressively. "Chicken and little roast potatoes and cauliflower, and a pink sweet afterwards."

"Like it?"

"Of course I did. I don't remember when I had chicken last, and the sweet was lovely. Everybody's so nice to me."

"Why shouldn't they be? Is the ankle comfortable, or do you want me to have a look at it? I won't disturb it if it's comfortable, though."

"It aches a bit, but it doesn't hurt."

"We'll leave it then, but tell somebody if it begins to feel any different. Tell me why you're so anxious to go to a hospital, or to your home. Do you live with your family? Friends?"

"No, I just have a room. My mother and I lived there together until—she died. That was three months ago now. I gave up one of the rooms."

"And live in the other? I suppose the people there have been told where you are, so that they won't worry, or go to the police or anything?"

"Yes. Miss Jenner has been to see me, and she said she would ring up my office as well. How long do you think it will be before I can go back?"

She could not bring herself to say his name, never having spoken to anybody but a plain Mister before, and she felt it would not be the thing to address an eminent surgeon as 'Doctor'.

"Oh, a few weeks. It will be quite comfortable and strong in plaster, not going up or down stairs more than you can help, but I like a broken limb, especially an ankle, to be rested first. I don't always conform to the newest line of thought, and anyway, I'm sure it won't hurt you to have a rest."

He was thinking privately that she looked as though she needed rest and a little care. She was too thin, and there were mauve shadows under her eyes and he saw that when she was relaxed, she was glad to lie still.

"Well—I suppose not," she said, "but there's my office. We're short staffed as it is, and Mr. Turner won't be at all pleased about my being away."

"Mr. Turner being the boss? Well, I shouldn't worry about that. There must be plenty of jobs for a girl nowadays."

"I don't know about that. I'm not very good, you see. I can only type. I can't do shorthand and I'm hopeless at figures."

"So am I," he said cheerfully. "Well, don't meet trouble half way. If necessary, I'll see your Mr. Turner and talk to him, and as soon as I think you can go safely, I'll let you go. Meantime make yourself thoroughly comfortable here. I expect they've shown you how the radio works. Can you reach it all right? How about television? Do you like that? There are several sets here, and I'll have one sent in for you if you'd like it—though no getting out of bed to turn it on or off. Ring the bell for someone to do that."

"I couldn't give anyone so much trouble," she said with a return to her shyness.

"It isn't any trouble to people here to do their jobs," he said. "Good-bye. I'll be in to see you tomorrow sometime."

"Good-bye, and—thank you. Thank you very much," she said, and he saw to his embarrassment that her eyes, grey and set wide apart, were wet.

Poor little thing, he thought. Knocked over by a bit of everyday humanity. It takes all sorts to make a world.

After that, he found himself popping frequently into her room. He had to pass the door, anyway, on his way to the lift.

She was so completely different from any other patient he had ever had in his private nursing home, very gentle and grateful and undemanding and, such is human nature, not thought any more of by the staff on that account, used as they were to aristocratic or wealthy patients who rang their bells a dozen times a day on the slightest pretext.

So Miss Dove, who kept her own counsel, was the only one who knew how often the doctor might have been found chatting with the humble patient to whom no bills were rendered and who gave nobody any trouble.

Blaine found Anna Mere intelligent and thoughtful, able and willing to talk with him on almost any subject and showing herself to be widely read, understanding and thinking about what she read, and her tastes were almost as catholic as his own ranging from a book on ancient philosophy, which he found on her bed one day, to the latest whodunit.

"How have you managed to read so much in your short life?" he asked her.

"Short? I'm thirty-two," she said without hesitation.

"Well, I'm thirty-eight, nearly thirty-nine. We're both youngsters," he said, laughing.

He thought she looked younger and a lot brighter for being there and resting and being looked after. He fancied she had not had much looking after.

"My mother was an invalid for a long time," she said, "and before that, my father was bed-ridden with arthritis until he died, and I never went out very much, and as I had to have something to do, apart from sewing and knitting, I read. I got books from the public library, and I took anything that looked to be about something new to me. I couldn't get through some of them, quite a lot of them in fact, but I did manage to read a good many."

He admitted to an affection for the whodunits, and lent her several from his own collection and amused himself and her by sounding her on her theories of the final solution during the progress of the book.

"Don't you ever tell me the end, will you?" she asked on one occasion.

"Never on your life! I should hate that myself, though if my wife ever reads a book, she always looks at the end first."

His wife. It was the first time she knew he had one. She wondered why it gave her an odd little feeling of loss.

When he spoke of Virginia again, it was because he came in to find Anna watching the television programme.

Virginia had installed a set in their flat, but he rarely switched it on for himself and she was not often in in the evenings.

"Will you switch off?" asked Anna when he came into her room.

"Don't you want to look?" he asked.

"It doesn't matter. It was only that—I thought I'd like to," she said with a faint flush and a sudden avoidance of his eyes.

"What's on?" he asked, sitting down in the chair by the bed.

"They're doing an excerpt from a pantomime," she said. "*Beauty and the Beast.*"

"The one my wife's in? Well, leave it on. It might amuse you. It's quite good, though pantomimes are no longer for children, as they used to be. Still, this one isn't vulgar. Sure you won't have a cigarette?"

"No, thank you. I don't want to start, with cigarettes the price they are," she said with a little laugh that was not quite steady. "You have one, though. I know you want one."

"It's against all precedent for your physician to smoke during a visit to you, but it isn't exactly a professional visit, is it?" with a smile, taking out his case. "Let's hope matron won't come in and catch me."

And then Virginia came on to the screen, a very young-looking, very delicious Virginia, floating rather than tripping across the stage on her way to her first meeting with the revolting Beast.

He heard Anna's caught breath.

"Oh—isn't she lovely?" she said in a whisper.

"Yes. Yes, she is, isn't she?" he replied, and something in his tone made her look quickly at him before she looked at the screen again, but his face gave nothing away.

She was in a maze of miserable admiration for Virginia Coley, though she would not admit even to herself the source of the misery. She thought she had never seen anything as lovely as this girl who was his wife—Blaine's wife, to whom he must

64

belong body and soul, this enchantress, and when the short excerpt was finished, he rose and switched off.

"Well, that's that," he said, stubbing out his cigarette. "Now shall we be doctor and patient again? Have you been up at all today?"

"No. I was afraid," she said.

"You?" he asked with an incredulous smile. "Well, let's try it now, shall we? Better put this on," and he helped her get into her dessing-grown, a plain, well-worn garment of beige flannel which had been sent in by her landlady. He thought of Virginia's glamorous satins and velvets and liked the drab flannel.

"Put the good foot to the floor first," he said, "and let me take your weight whilst you try the other out. Don't be afraid. The plaster will hold it safely. That's right. Lean on me until you get your balance," and his arm held her firmly, supporting her whilst she cautiously transferred her weight to the injured foot.

She knew guiltily that she would have been glad if it had not borne her. She was intensely conscious of his arm about her, of the strength and nearness of his body and of the chill of the loss of his support when, after a few moments, he withdrew his arm and then his hand and she was standing alone, trying a few cautious steps.

Nothing in his look and tone suggested that he, too, was a little regretful. He knew that very soon now she would be gone, since she was not one of his wealthy, idle patients who could remain there after the actual need had gone. She had already spoken of going back to work.

"I think that's enough for the first time," he said, when she had taken two or three turns round the room successfully. "No pain?"

"No. It's just awkward."

"It won't be when we've taken off the cast," he said, helping her back into bed. "That won't be for a day or two, and I want another X-ray. How do you feel now? Triumphant?"

She smiled.

"Of course. I've really got to get back to work."

"Any stairs?"

"Yes, a lot. There isn't a lift."

"Well, when you do go back, take it easily. Have your lunch sent in so that you need not do the stairs more than once up and once down," he said with a frown. "Even though the bones have knit, they'll still be a bit weak, you know."

"I have to go down two flights every time Mr. Turner rings his bell," she said.

"Why can't he come to you then?"

She laughed.

"He wouldn't do that," she said. "He's much too important and busy. Besides, quite a big part of my job, since I can't do shorthand, is the filing, and the files are in his office. That's why he rings for me so often. I have to find things."

"Oh, well, see what you can do about it," he told her, and after a few more minutes' chat, he knew he must go. He was making his usual evening visits to his patients, and already they would be wondering what was keeping him.

She was the only one who really wanted to go, he thought, listening to the minutely detailed description of ailments, of aches and pains, many of them quite imaginary.

Did she really want to go, or was it only dire necessity?

It was irritating that she, with far more need of prolonged care and rest than the large majority of them, would be the one he would have to let go, and when, if ever, would he see her again, once she had gone?

He was going to miss her badly. That came home to him with a shock. His daily visits to her had become something to which he looked forward. Her shy smile of greeting told him she had looked forward to the visit, too. She was always ready to talk of anything and everything but herself, though during their talks he had found out quite a lot about her, reading between the lines so much that she did not tell him.

He marvelled at the courage she must have had during so many years of her life.

Several years older than her sister, she had early accepted much of the family burdens. Her father, crippled with arthritis,

66

had given up his work as a city clerk years before he died, and Anna and her mother had had to undertake the care of him and earn the living, Mrs. Mere taking in dressmaking because he could never be left, and Anna having to relieve her in the evenings so that she was not able to go on with the shorthand lessons which would have given her a chance of a better job.

Then the father had died (mercifully, Blaine suspected), and the mother, worn out with years of overwork and undernourishment probably, had developed a disease which before long had prevented her from going on with her dressmaking and she had been in and out of hospitals until at length she had stayed at home to die.

And all that time, Anna had been the mainstay. Beth, the sister, had married young, shifting the full burden on to the older daughter's shoulders before the death of the father, and even, it seemed, adding to it by requiring Anna's care of a succession of ex-babies whenever a new one arrived.

All this he discovered gradually. She made no complaint in the telling, was even quietly humorous about it, so that he was left to fill in the gaps, discovering for himself that the father had been irritable and demanding, thrusting on her services which surely even a badly arthritic man could have done for himself, and making no attempt to do such work as, in the earlier stages at any rate, might have been found for him to do from his bed.

Her deep love had obviously been given to her mother, and that service at least had been a labour of love, tearing at her heart as well as wearing out her body.

And now, for three months, she had been alone, alone with her first youth gone and with few friends or outside interests after the long years which had demanded all her attention.

"What would have happened if you wanted to get married?" he asked her once.

She laughed, a little ruefully he thought.

"Well, I didn't," she said, "but I suppose if I had wanted to —well, I couldn't have done, could I? I could hardly say to a man 'if I marry you, I've got to bring a bed-ridden father and an ailing mother with me', could I? No man would have taken on that packet!" but again there was no sound of complaint, or of being hard done by, in her voice.

"Was there ever anyone?" he asked.

She shook her head.

"No, no one. Beth was the pretty one. She had all the boys. Have I shown you a photograph of her? Give me my bag, will you?" indicating the bedside cupboard.

Yes, he supposed that Beth was pretty, with even features, a round face, curly hair elaborately arranged, but the eyes were a little too close together and the smart frock and high-heeled shoes surely a little too elegant and expensive whilst Anna was spending every penny she could earn on the mother enforcedly at home? He thought of Anna's own clothes, which he had seen only on that first night when he had picked her up from the street and carried her into his car; the shabby, cheap coat, the flat-heeled shoes which had probably been repaired many times, the worn beret which certainly had no smartness and was only a covering against the elements.

"Yes, she is pretty," was all he said, but he preferred the plainness of the older sister's face, the clear, wide-set eyes, the straight dark hair which, when she dressed it herself, she wore parted in the middle and drawn back, madonna-like, from her wide brow and into a knot at the nape of her neck.

He even preferred, he thought with an odd little jerk of his mind, the shabby clothes which were the symbol of her unselfish devotion.

CHAPTER V

IT seemed as if Fate were determined to do something about him—or was it only that he was ready to snatch at opportunity?

A few days before it had been decided that Anna was now ready to leave the nursing home and go back to her home and her work, Blaine came into her room with an odd expression on his face, the look of a schoolboy who has been at the jam.

"Something quite upsetting has happened," he told her, taking a chair opposite the one to which she had now been promoted in preparation for taking up normal life again.

Her foot was out of plaster, and she was walking with the aid of a stick, but would be able to leave that behind her when she left.

"One of your patients?" asked Anna, thinking how desperately she was going to miss these visits and how much readjustment she would have to make to her own way of life after all this luxurious ease.

"No. Worse. My secretary, Miss Jenner. It seems that the man she's engaged to has been offered a post abroad, and he must take it up at once and they want to get married so that she can go with him. It's all most irritating," though his look and tone did not suggest that he was as much annoyed about it as his words implied.

"It shouldn't be difficult for you to get someone else," she said.

She had often thought how lucky Miss Jenner was to have such a nice job and, as she was always well dressed, she probably had a good salary.

"Well, I *hope* it won't be," said Sir Blaine. "I have someone in mind."

"She'll be lucky," said Anna.

"Or I shall be? It's someone you know."

"Someone I know? How could it be?" she asked.

"She is a Miss Anna Mere," he said with a smile.

"Me? Oh—oh, but I couldn't," she cried, her face scarlet.

"Why couldn't you?"

"Well—I don't do shorthand, for one thing. I've told you that already. And I don't know anything about book-keeping."

"Any further objections? You'd have to leave your present job, of course, but in any case I wouldn't want you to do those stairs, and no doubt a personal letter from me would put that right. About the other things. You don't need to know shorthand. The extent and quality of your reading should have made it possible for you to write ordinary everyday letters without dictation, if you are told the gist of them, and I use a dictaphone for anything I want to say in my own words. As to the book-keeping, well you shouldn't find that too difficult, as all the things needed in the nursing home are ordered and paid for by Miss Dove, and an outside firm of accountants deals with income tax and so on. Miss Jenner renders the accounts to the patients, from details supplied by the nurses and by Miss Dove, and she'll show you how to do that. Apart from that, there is only my private account and the actual housekeeping bills, which are supposed to be overlooked by my wife, but her affairs are chaotic and I would not ask you to wrestle with them! *Now* how do you feel about it?"

"Do you really think I could do it?" she asked, longingly.

"Do you think I'd ask you if I didn't think so? As you say, it would not be too difficult for me to get someone, as the work is not arduous and the hours not too long, and I believe that girls should be paid enough to live on. I warn you that I'm not too easy. I'm bad tempered and get irritable over trifles. Can you stand that?"

A tap at the door interrupted them.

It was Miss Dove.

"I'm sorry, Sir Blaine, but Mrs. Murrayne has one of her 'attacks'," and the way she spoke the word put it between inverted commas. "Nurse fetched me, but she simply insists on seeing you."

"A murrain on *her*!" said Sir Blaine testily. "What have you given her? The fifty-seven?"

"Yes, but she insists that it doesn't do her any good."

"Plain water with a touch of soda-bic to make it nasty might be effective," he suggested drily.

"Without doubt, if you gave it to her," said Miss Dove in the same tone.

"Oh well, I'd better go and see her. Meantime, stay and talk to Miss Mere, Matron. You know about Miss Jenner?"

"Yes, she told me."

"I'm trying to persuade Miss Mere to take it on. Add your persuasions, will you? Tell her about the job but don't frighten her. I'll be back."

The last thing he wanted to do at this moment was to see Mrs. Murrayne, the pampered wife of a man who had made too much money not too honestly.

She had been a beauty, but now, in her forties and with the beauty fading and no other interests but herself, she had persuaded herself that she was a martyr to a form of migraine which necessitated frequent periods of residence in Sir Blaine Belding's private nursing home, with Sir Blaine himself in attendance whenever she wanted him. She certainly did have headaches, but she refused to have her eyes tested for glasses, which was the only advice he could give her and since she was a source of considerable profit to him, he accepted her visitations and tried not to see more of her than he could help. She refused the attention of the young house doctor whom he employed, however, and felt that the bills her husband paid entitled her to the services of Sir Blaine himself.

She was lying in the dark with an ice-pack over her brow, though she pushed this off fretfully when he came in, and put up her hand to switch on the light. He was sorry for her as he was sorry for all the women who came there with fancied ailments and not enough to do, but lately her attitude towards him had made him uncomfortable.

Her ravaged face, heavily made up but not in such a way as to give her an illusion of rude health, lighted up at sight of him, though she closed her eyes again and lay back.

"This dreadful pain," she said. "I don't feel that I shall ever be really well again. It's so good of you to come yourself, Sir Blaine, but really, the nurses—and the matron—nobody but you seems to understand and to *feel* for me."

He laid his cool fingers in all the right places, on her wrist, on the forehead now cold from the ice-pack, on her throat where now she said she had pain, and she lay there motionless and he knew, to his intense distaste, that she was drawing a good deal of physical pleasure from his touch. What she really wanted, he thought angrily, was for him to get into bed with her.

"You know, Mrs. Murrayne, the thing that would do you more good than anything is, as I have told you repeatedly, to get some spectacles and wear them. Wear them all the time," he said, taking his hand away and moving some distance from the bed.

"But they're so disfiguring, specially for anyone like me. I'm sure they wouldn't suit me," she said, wishing he would touch her again, would not stand so far away from her, would be a little more *human* with her.

"Would that matter, if you did not have these headaches any more? And if you have to spend so much of your time in here, lying in bed, I should have thought that outweighed what you call the disfigurement of spectacles. Most people have to wear them when they're no longer very young."

She bridled.

"You make it sound as if I were at least fifty," she said, and he forebore to tell her that, though she had given her age as thirty-five, he was quite sure she was a good ten years more.

"Not at all," he said smoothly. "I wear them for close work, and I'm a good long way off fifty."

"But you're a man! That's different. Besides, I should think you look even more handsome and distinguished in them," with a smile which was meant to be provocative.

Once he might have risen to it and pandered to her vanity.

Now he found he could not. It was all he could do to hide his disgust from her. He wondered why he had altered. Was it because he had been spending so much time during the last few weeks with Anna Mere, with her complete honesty and lack of artifice or pretence or coquetry?

"I'll make you out a fresh prescription, Mrs. Murrayne," he said, "and get nurse to give you some of it before you are ready for sleep. But, as I have said, the real remedy lies in your own hands, and you are actually wasting your time and money by being here, where we cannot do anything for you."

"But I feel *better* here, really I do. My husband doesn't understand how much I suffer, and you always understand and do me good when you look after me *yourself*, Sir Blaine. And my husband doesn't have to think too much about the pennies, you know," archly.

"Well, see what the new medicine will do," he said, preparing to go.

Why on earth should he want to quarrel with his bread and butter when it was so plentifully spread with jam?

"And will you ask them to give me something to make me sleep? I am simply a martyr to this wretched insomnia."

Since he knew she spent quite a fair proportion of her day sleeping, it was not surprising if she could not sleep at night as well, but he nodded.

"All right. I'll see to it," he said casually and left her.

Confound the woman, why wouldn't she go, and stay away? She required more attention than any other patient, and when the nurses were hard-driven and ventured to remonstrate at the number of times she rang her bell for small services, she would say tartly, "Well, I can afford to pay for proper attention."

Anna was alone when he went back to her, sitting in her chair with a new, almost excited look in her cool grey eyes.

"Well?" he asked. "Am I addressing my new secretary, or only my departing patient?"

"I'd like to try," she said in her shy fashion, and he smiled contentedly.

73

"That's settled then. Miss Jenner will be here for another week at least, and she will show you what you will have to do—but no using the stairs, mind. The lift's there, and it's for use. Would you like me to write to your Mr. Turner?"

"Oh, would you, Sir Blaine?'" she asked gratefully. "I don't expect he'll mind, but he has kept the job open and perhaps I ought to go back to work out my notice?"

"I don't agree, because of the stairs principally. You leave it to me, and when Miss Jenner goes, you take on from there."

"Can I go home?" she asked.

"If you want to. Any stairs?" with a smile at his insistence.

"Only one flight, and the bathroom's on the same floor," she said, responding to his smile.

"All right. You can go on Friday, but as you'll be under my eye, I shall know if you're doing anything silly."

"I won't. I promise you. If I did, it would be a very poor return for all the care you've taken of me, and now giving me this wonderful job," for she had been staggered at the salary Miss Dove had told her she would be paid.

"Don't be too sure that it's going to be wonderful," he told her. "Remember that I'm a crabby, disgruntled old man, very rarely satisfied," but his smile robbed the speech of any intention it might have had.

Within a fortnight, Miss Jenner had gone and Anna was established in the comfortable little office in his flat which had been found more convenient for his personal secretary than the original one on a lower floor.

She found the work exacting, but largely because of her determination to justify his confidence in her. She did not see a great deal of him, but his voice coming to her from the cylinders of the dictaphone gave her a constant sense of his nearness, and sometimes he would add a few words, a little chuckle, which were for her alone, and she hated to have to clean off those cylinders to be used again.

One of the reasons why she saw little of him was that, now that the pantomime season was over and *Lady of Leisure* had gone on tour, Virginia was temporarily out of the limelight and

74

spent her time between the London flat and Cotterway. When she met Anna, she treated her with casual kindness, got her to do all sorts of jobs for her, including dull errands to the shops which she did not want to do herself, and now and then flinging a handful of bills on her table with a gay "See to these awful things, Miss Mere, will you? And if I've overdrawn my account, tell Sir Blaine, will you?"

That was one thing Anna hated having to do, for Virginia had a very large personal allowance and used it for all sorts of things which Anna, who had never been able to buy anything not strictly necessary, thought wildly extravagant, seeing that Blaine's wife seemed already to have everything in the world any woman could want—including Blaine himself.

When she had to ask him for money to straighten Virginia's bank account, she did it apologetically, red-faced, as if the fault were hers.

"I'm terribly sorry, Sir Blaine, but I'm afraid there's a letter from Lady Belding's bank manager again," she said on one occasion, when he had come into her office with some papers for her to file.

He made a little helpless gesture.

"What on earth does she do with the money?" he asked. "I had to put her straight last month too."

"It's mostly clothes," said Anna in the same apologetic tone. "Two Dior evening gowns on this one. He's started on one of his new alphabetical lines," with a small smile.

"I could become alphabetical about him," said Blaine. "Why on earth women must always be altering their shapes beats me—and I always marvel at the way they manage to do it, since nobody knows better than a doctor what shape they really are. Well, give me the bills and I'll see if I can persuade her to stay this shape for a few months, if these infernal men dressmakers will let her. Wonder if they really are men?" with a grimace as he took the bills, and the bank manager's letter. "By the way, what about you? Are you all right? I don't seem to have seen much of you lately, but I take it the shape of things to come is not being a source of worry to *you*?" with an approving glance at her neat navy blue dress with its crisp white collar and cuffs, freshly washed and ironed every evening. She was modelling herself on what the magazines, which she borrowed from his waiting-room, told her was the perfect outfit for the would-be perfect secretary, and the blue dress, with good shoes and accessories, were some of the first signs of her new prosperity.

She laughed.

"I'm afraid I remain the same shape, whatever Dior says," she told him.

"You couldn't do better," he said. "Look. You need a change of air and surroundings. We're going down to Cotterway, my house in the country—but of course you know about that. Why not come down with us? They can get on without you here for a few days, and if you *must* work, take down any cylinders you haven't had time to finish on the book."

He was writing a treatise, which would probably become a text-book, on his special branch of modern surgery, and though it occasioned her a good deal of anxiety and much recourse to the medical dictionary, she was persevering with it in any spare time she had.

"We can put your half of the machine into the car," he said. "There's plenty of room, and you won't need to take a lot of clothes. We live the simple life down there—at least I do," with a smile at the thought of Virginia leading the simple life anywhere and in any conditions.

"I'd love to go," said Anna gratefully, though she wondered just what clothes she could take with her.

Still, she was not now desperately hard up. She had paid the few outstanding debts left by her mother's last illness and the funeral, and now had a little money in the bank, thanks to her new job.

She decided to consult Lady Belding when Virginia came into her office to see what had been the effect of the straightening of her account. She was in a gracious frame of mind when she had been assured that Sir Blaine was 'taking care of it'.

"It's quite a good idea for you to come down there with us instead of being mewed up here all the time," said Virginia.

"It's frightfully dull down there, of course, and I'm not as hearty about things in the country as Blaine is, but I have a few friends there and generally manage to find something or somebody to amuse myself with. Oh, about clothes for you. Just country things, a tweed suit and a few blouses, and one or two things for the evening."

"But I shan't want anything for the evening," said Anna diffidently.

She always felt tongue-tied and slightly awed by Virginia's radiant beauty and self-assurance, nor could she ever forget that this was Blaine's wife, the woman he had chosen from all other women to share his intimate life.

"Of course you will," said Virginia. "You'll eat with us and everything. You don't imagine we're going to poke you into a corner like a servant? If you haven't got anything suitable, go and see what they've got at Delma's or somewhere. Put it on my account."

"I shouldn't dream of doing that, Lady Belding," said Anna, flushing.

"Just as you like, but you'd better have a couple of things for the evening, one short and one long. Perhaps I've got something. I'm a bit taller than you, but perhaps you can do something about that, or get it done. Come along to my room and let's have a look. I've always got heaps of things I've scarcely ever worn and shan't wear again."

Anna could scarcely bear to look round the big, luxurious bedroom with its two beds and long range of fitted cupboards, their doors, when Virginia threw them open, revealing a breath-taking array of gowns and suits, of shoes and furs and all the panoply of a woman of beauty and fashion.

This, thought Anna with a contraction of her heart, was Blaine's room as well, the place that was at the centre of his private and intimate life, the part of his life shared by no other woman, known to no other woman.

She could not know that he had his own room, across the passage, and that now he seldom if ever entered this room so permeated with Virginia's colourful personality and success.

"Here. What about this? The colour ought to suit you, with your dark hair and grey eyes," said Virginia, throwing across the bed a long evening gown of dull-surfaced amethyst satin. "Goodness knows why I bought it as I simply can't wear that shade. It takes away all my colour, though it will give you some. There's this, too. I'm getting tired of white," throwing a bunch of fluffy, billowing chiffon on top of the amethyst.

"I don't think I could wear anything frilly," said Anna.

Virginia regarded her critically.

"No, perhaps you're right," she agreed. "You're the tailored kind. What else is there?" throwing the white frock over a chair for her maid to put away. "I know. Somewhere here there's a maize-coloured thing, rather nice but I'm tired of it. Oh, here," and she pulled out a soft, sleek dress which Anna saw at once might have been specially designed for her.

In spite of her protests, Virginia threw out half a dozen others and piled them on the bed.

"You can take them home and try them on, anyway," she said, "and if you don't want them, chuck them away. I'll get Roberta to pack them into something and send them to your place in the car. Give her the address."

Anna had an amusing time trying them on that evening, and since at least three of them could easily be altered by her own fingers, and were not too elaborate, she felt, she could concentrate on the tweed suit and the blouses, and some shoes which would go with all the gowns.

When she was settled in Blaine's car, with her suitcase and the transcribing part of the dictaphone, she felt she had never been so well outfitted or so happy. Virginia sat in front with Blaine, and every now and then would turn round to have a friendly word with her, or to point out something of interest.

Cotterway was the dream of all dream houses to Anna, lying back from the quiet country lane in a garden filled with spring flowers, with the mauve and yellow cups of crocus making splashes of colour on smooth green turf, and the trees covered with a fairy lace of green. In a long, rambling pool, goldfish swam amongst water-lily leaves and a little Peter Pan in green bronze sat cross-legged in the middle of it and piped a merry tune which one could almost hear.

Virginia paused beside it for a moment.

"I want to play Peter," she said. "I wonder if I ever shall? Should I make a good one?" turning her laughing invitation to such an assurance to her husband and to Anna.

"I should think so," said Blaine indifferently, and "Of course you would!" more admiringly from Anna.

"My husband is not really sure that I could make a good anything," said Virginia, "not even a good wife!" throwing an enigmatical glance at him over her shoulder as she went on towards the house.

It was the first indication Anna had ever had that there might be a rift within the lute. Blaine did not reply, but turned to give an order about the luggage to the maid who came out to meet them.

They kept a small staff there permanently, a man and his wife, and a house-parlourmaid. A woman came in daily at such times as the Beldings were staying there.

Anna had a charming room, and she realized that Virginia had given her one of the principal guest rooms, since it was beautifully appointed and had its own communicating bathroom. She found herself treated in every way like a guest, and when on the first afternoon she was preparing to betake herself to her own room to do some typing, Virginia indignantly scouted the suggestion.

"Work? Down here? Blaine, don't let her. Take her for one of your exhausting walks if she wants to go, or out for a drive or something. I'm going over to see the Meldrums, and I know you can't bear Beattie."

"What about it, Miss Mere? Not an exhausting walk, as Virginia calls my purposeless ambles, because I still don't feel you should walk far, but a drive somewhere? Down to the coast, if you like, though it may be cold."

"I should like that very much," said Anna. "That is—what about the book?"

"It can wait," he said. "Wear a warm coat in case we get out of the car. Did you bring one?"

"Yes," said Anna and went happily to get it.

It was an experience she thoroughly enjoyed, and it was the first time she had gone out anywhere with him. He was a delightful companion, with no suggestion of her being his employee. They had slipped back into the easy companionship of the days when she had lain in bed waiting for her ankle to heal, and added to that was their new knowledge of a share in his life and familiarity with much that made it up.

They got out of the car and walked along the sandy shore when they reached the sea, but she knew that he was watching her, anxious for her complete safety, and when she stumbled over a half-hidden rock, he said at once that they must go back to the car.

"There's a queer little place somewhere here where we can get some tea, if they're open yet," he said. "I don't like the Oldy Tea Shoppy sort of thing, which is usually spurious, but this one really is old, used to be a smithy and still has the old anvil and the big furnace, though they don't serve up tea on horseshoes!"

They found that it was open, and had an old-fashioned tea of hot scones and home-made jam and cakes, and he enjoyed her hearty appetite.

"Thank heaven you're not one of these women who daren't eat for fear of putting on a few ounces," he said, helping himself to more jam.

She laughed.

"I'm really making a pig of myself," she said. "I don't think I'm the fat kind, and if I don't often eat things like this, it's because I can't be bothered to make them for myself and I don't often eat out now that I get such a good lunch in the home."

"You really do, don't you?" he asked. "You eat it? I'm a great believer in at least one substantial meal a day, though I can't make Virginia agree with me. She's terrified of getting fat."

"Well, of course, it would be serious for her if she did, wouldn't it? Is she going on on the stage?"

"Oh yes. She's wedded to it," he said with an inflection in his voice which oddly hurt her. "She can get any amount of variety and cabaret work, but she wants to do another full musical show, and she is up against the American invasion of the theatres, of course. She thinks she would get a chance over in the States, where they are inclined to go British as a counter-action."

"You wouldn't like her to do that, would you?" asked Anna, who hated hearing him talk about his wife and yet could not prevent herself from encouraging him to do so.

"Not particularly," he said, and talked about something else.

The introduction of Virginia into the conversation seemed to have altered the temperature of their day, and when he suggested making for home, she was ready to agree.

Just as they reached it, he turned to her for a moment.

"Thank you for coming with me," he said. "I've enjoyed it."

"Oh, so have I," she said fervently, and he turned away from her again and said no more.

They had not changed for dinner on their first evening, having arrived too late for it to be worth while, but this evening there were to be guests for dinner, and Anna realized that she would be expected to wear one of the evening dresses which Virginia had given her.

She chose the maize-coloured one, as being the least glamorous though actually it had been the most expensive of them all, cut very plainly in a dull crepe, its severity relieved only by flat flowers of brown velvet set with skill and artistry into the material itself. It had been difficult to alter, since though she was shorter than Virginia her waist was not as small, but she had managed it successfully and, when she was ready, surveyed herself with approval in the long mirror.

'Not mutton dressed lamb, I hope,' she murmured to herself, remembering the ten years, more than ten years, which lay between her and the girl for whom the dress had been designed.

But she felt satisfied that it was not so. The gown was so simple and dignified that it did not need extreme youth to wear it, and its lines showed that she need not fear for her figure.

'You really look quite nice, Anna Mere,' she informed herself—and checked at once the hope that Blaine would think so too.

But his face, at first sight of her in the maize-coloured gown, gave her an unpleasant shock, for it was distinctly disapproving, and he took the first opportunity of explaining his disapproval when for a few moments after dinner, he got her to himself. It was a lovely evening and, huddled in their coats and furs, they and their guests had gone out into the garden.

"Why did you let Virginia give you that dress?" he demanded. "She did, didn't she? I remember her wearing it."

"Yes," said Anna at once. "She was very kind to me. I hadn't anything suitable, and she gave me several. Why? Don't you think it's all right on me?"

"Of course it is. It's very nice on you, but I don't like you wearing Virginia's cast-offs," he said with a distinct edge to his voice. "Don't I pay you sufficient to buy clothes for yourself?"

She was scarlet with mortification.

"Yes. Yes, of course you do," she stammered. "It was only— I mean, coming down here—and I asked Lady Belding what I ought to bring, and—she—she offered me the dresses. I thought it was all right. I thought it was so kind of her. It never occurred to me that you might mind, Sir Blaine."

"Well, I do mind," he said shortly. "Please don't do it again," and he stalked off and left her in a state of the most acute unhappiness.

As he did so, he wished he had not spoken quite so forcefully and in such a tone, remembering the painful flushing of her face and her obvious distress. He might have been kinder about it, might have said it in different words so that she knew what was really in his mind about the dress.

But what was in his mind? He did not know with any certainty himself. He only knew that, at first sight of her dressed in Virginia's clothes, a wild anger had flamed up in him so that he had wanted to tear the dress off, trample on it, do anything so that Anna should be herself again and not that travesty of Virginia. But (the thought seeped slowly and unwillingly through his mind), the resentment had been for Anna and not for Virginia.

Why?

Anna, released from the sight but not the memory of his anger, fled to her room, snatched off the offending dress and huddled down on her bed.

She did not cry. She was not the crying sort. But her heart seemed to be weeping tears of blood.

She ought to have known, ought to have had more sense. Of course he hated the sight of her, the plain little secretary, his paid employee, masquerading in a dress in which he had seen the lovely, peerless Virginia. What man, adoring such a wife, would not have been quick to resent the aping of her by someone like herself, plain, unattractive Anna Mere?

The next day he met her as if nothing had happened between them, was in fact even kinder and more considerate towards her, almost pointed in his endeavours to make her feel at ease in whatever they did, but Anna did not forget, and during the day, when Virginia wanted to be taken to see some friends, she asked to be excused from going with them, the excuse transparently thin, and sat instead in her room with the transcription of his book.

"What have you done to Miss Mere?" asked Virginia lightly as they set off.

"Nothing. What should I have done?" he asked shortly.

"Goodness knows, but she's like a scared cat all of a sudden. Have you been bullying her?"

"I don't bully people," said Blaine.

She laughed.

"What about people at your hospitals? They call you Double B, the Big Bully, only they don't say 'big'. The poor thing looks like a mouse someone's trodden on and is waiting for the descent of the big boot again."

"You're being quite ridiculous, Virginia," he said.

"Oh, well, don't let's squabble about her," she said easily. "In a way, perhaps it's as well she didn't come with us because there's a thing I want to say to you and I might as well say it now. It's about *Lady of Leisure*."

"Oh? I thought she'd gone into retirement," said Blaine, glad that they need no longer discuss Anna.

"Jos Benner's digging her out. He's thinking of taking her to New York."

"Oh? And what does that imply?"

"He wants me to go."

"No," said Blaine, at once and deliberately.

She looked at him sharply.

"Just what do you mean by that, Blaine?" she asked, a dangerous note in her voice. He could feel her body tense beside him.

"What I said. No. Just that."

"You can't stop me if I want to go."

"No, I suppose I can't, but I thought, rather foolishly perhaps, that you were asking my opinion."

"But not your permission!" she said, and though he did not look at her but appeared to be giving all his attention to driving along the quiet country road, he knew how she looked, with two bright flags of colour in her cheeks, her eyes hard, her chin jutting out.

"I gather that you would not feel that necessary," he said.

"I don't, but I should prefer not to have your opposition," she said.

"That's magnanimous of you, but I'm afraid you've got it."

"You can't stop me, but I would remind you that it was a part of our bargain that I was to be allowed to go on with my work," she said coldly.

"Agreed, but there was another part of what you call our bargain, though the word applied to marriage is distasteful. That other part was that I should get a wife, Virginia."

"Well, aren't I your wife?" she demanded, anger coming through the ice.

84

"By the fact that you live in my home and at least partially bear my name, yes," he agreed. "That isn't the whole function of a wife, however."

"I thought you'd got over all that," she said.

"What gave you that idea?"

"Well, you never bother me now about *that*," she said.

"It wouldn't be much pleasure to me to 'bother', as you rather crudely put it, a wife to whom such bothering is plainly distasteful," he said, his eyes fixed steadily ahead.

"I don't know what you mean. I've never locked you out of my room."

"Not with a key, certainly," he said.

"You can come in whenever you like," she said, wondering how the conversation had become so personal and uncomfortable.

"Thank you," was all he said, but she flushed with anger and was silent until they arrived at the house of their friends, where she was her brightest and gayest, deferring every now and then to his opinion in the prettiest fashion, the happy wife of a presumably adoring husband.

She did not return to the subject of going to New York when they left to go home, though they knew that both minds were filled with it, and that night, when they went up to bed, she paused at the door of her room and he saw that her face was set into determined lines.

"You can sleep in here if you like, Blaine," she said.

"Many thanks," he said grimly. "Good night, my dear," and went to his own room and shut the door.

Virginia sat for a long time without undressing, smoking one cigarette after another.

This was not what she had intended, and she was not sure what to do about it. She was well aware, and had been for some time, that she was not in love with her husband. But she was not in love with anybody else, nor likely to be. That was one of the things, she decided, that had been left out of her make-up, and from her observations of other people, she was glad that her life was not complicated by anything as incalculable as love, which seemed able to upset people's plans without rhyme or reason and play havoc with their design for living.

But marriage gave a woman a certain status, and marriage to Blaine a very definite and desirable one. She liked being Lady Belding in private life, and she liked the security it represented and the luxuries it provided. She need not take all sorts of jobs which she did not enjoy doing and she could afford to wait for the coming of such jobs as she did want, this thing in the States, for instance.

Lady of Leisure had not had an outstanding success in London, nor had she set the critics on fire, but London critics are blasé, she reflected, and London audiences phlegmatic about anything but American shows. Jos Benner believed that *Lady of Leisure*, and she herself in it, would be a riot in the States, where there had been a counter-swing towards things typically British and where the people, especially the men, were a lot more beauty-conscious than the British.

From New York, she would undoubtedly have a much better chance of migrating to Hollywood, her eventual objective.

But if Blaine persisted in his attitude of disapproval (it could not be more than that by the very nature of their pre-marriage arrangement), what would her position be? It did not suit her at all to be on bad terms with him. For one thing, he was quite capable of cutting off supplies, and if she did not succeed in New York, she would want to be able to come back to him; and if the unthinkable happened, and she did not succeed at all, she would want to be Lady Belding, with all it included.

It was the first time she had been assailed by any serious doubt of her eventual success, and she could not disguise from herself the fact that in her one play, apart from the pantomime, that success had not been spectacular. The critics had had quite a lot to say about her appearance, but had more than implied that she had nothing beyond that. True, she had been universally acclaimed for her performance as 'Beauty', but the serious career of an actress cannot be made to depend on the appearance for a few weeks in a Christmas pantomime.

No, quite definitely, she wanted to have Blaine with and

behind her, so as to be protected against any eventuality—but how was she to secure that?

She fidgeted uncomfortably at the thought of his refusal just now of her invitation to her room and her bed. If she lost that power over him, what power had she left?

Perhaps she had been neglecting him too much lately, and he had 'taken the huff' and was paying her out, paying himself out too, by denying himself the delights of the marriage bed! Well, she would have to put that right somehow. He had certainly been crazy enough for it once, and not so long ago. It should not be too difficult to get him back into that position.

It was perhaps rather fortunate that at the moment, and until Jos Benner did or said something definite, she had no work and nothing in view. She could devote herself to Blaine.

During the rest of their stay at Cotterway, and after they had returned to town, she proceeded to do so, was her sweetest and most amenable towards him, playing the part of loving little wife prettily but dismayed, and secretly a little frightened, to find that she was getting nowhere at all. Blaine accepted her little attentions, treated her with his usual indulgence and consideration, but seemed almost amused by her change of attitude—nor did he attempt any more love-making than a casual return of the kisses she offered him, though she made it quite plain that she was agreeable to more.

One night she even went to the length of going to his room a long time after he had retired, and sitting on his bed in her flimsy, seductive night-wear within easy reach of his hand, which did not stretch out to touch her.

He was reading, and merely put his finger in the book to keep his place and looked at her inquiringly.

"Hullo, my dear," he said casually, and waited.

She laughed, not quite comfortably.

"Darling, we're not acquaintances meeting on the stairs, or in the street somewhere. I'm your wife. Remember?"

"Yes, I remember," he said quite calmly and still waited.

"Well—how about it? Blaine, don't you *want* me any more?" with a pretty little lift of her head and an inviting look in her eyes.

He laid the book down carefully on the bedside table before he replied, slowly, thoughtfully, not looking at her. He gave no impression of his profound discomfort.

"You don't want me, Virginia," he said at last. "I've realized that for a long time. You never have wanted me. I'm not blaming you, my dear. I ought to have known. As a doctor, I ought to have realized it before it was too late, but I was very much in love with you, and I thought—believed—that you felt the same towards me."

"But I did, Blaine! I do! I *am* in love with you!" she cried.

He shook his head, looking at her now, and smiling in a way which held tenderness but also regret and acceptance.

"No, my dear. No," he said. "Let's face it. I don't know why you married me. I'm not going to insult you by suggesting that it was because I am who I am. You must have been able to marry almost anybody, men much more important than I am. I think you did honestly believe you were in love with me, whereas the truth is that you're not really capable of being in love at all, not as I understand it, or as most men would understand it. Marriage, that part of it, bored you. It did worse. It actually offended and nauseated you, and though some other man might have been able to overcome that, I couldn't. That's why I—refrained. Don't look like that, Virginia. I'm not blaming you. I merely think that it's time we both faced it and met it like civilized people. You want to go to the States. You haven't said any more about it, but I know it's still in your mind. Well, I'm not going to try to stop you, even if I could. That's the way of life you really want, so—have it, Virginia, if it will make you happy. That's what I've always wanted—your happiness."

"But, Blaine, you *have* made me happy!"

"No, Virginia. You've made yourself happy, and now that I realize where your real happiness lies, I want you to have it, take it with both hands and enjoy it. But, my dear, you can't have it both ways. You can't eat your cake and still have it."

Her eyes widened.

"What do you mean by that?" she asked, frightened.

"You know just what I mean. Go to the States. Do your job.

88

Be Virginia Coley to the top of your bent—but you can't be Lady Belding as well."

"Are you telling me that if I do go, you don't want me back?" she asked with a little shiver.

"You're cold. Put my dressing-gown on," indicating it thrown over a chair near her. "Yes, Virginia. I am telling you just that."

"Do you mean that if I went, you'd divorce me?" she asked, making no movement towards the dressing-gown but sitting hunched up on his bed, a delectable and inviting figure for any man's eyes, but not just then for Blaine's.

"I couldn't do that, unless you'd left me voluntarily for three years. And, though I don't know much about the marriage laws of this country, I don't think I could, or you could, until we'd been married much longer than we have been. I wasn't thinking in terms of divorce. That's a thing which does not appeal to me at all. I merely mean that if you choose your career in preference to me, I am willing for you to do so—but not in addition to me."

Her face changed and hardened and there were little fires in her eyes.

"I have no intention of parting from you, Blaine," she said.

"All right, my dear. That suits me," he said. "Now do go back to bed or you'll catch your death of cold. Either that, or wrap yourself in my dressing-gown, though I think we've said all there is to say, haven't we?"

"No. I want to say this," and she leaned forward and put her arms round his neck and drew his face to hers and kissed him, trying to force herself to feel an ardour she did not feel, trying by the last means in her power to draw him back to her.

He felt the warmth of her body through the thin gown, her small, firm breasts and the invitation of all her loveliness.

But it drew no response from him.

He kissed her because her mouth was on his, but his arms did not go around her to hold her, and she withdrew herself again and sat staring at him, humiliated, afraid, one hand going up to the lips he had not desired though his had kissed them.

89

"What's happened to you, Blaine?" she asked in a strained whisper.

"I don't quite know—except that I'm working very hard, using up all my energy," he said, sharing to some extent the humiliation, his surprise at her inability to stir him to any desire for her. "This has been a particularly bad day. I've been at St. Agatha's most of the day."

She caught at the escape he was offering her from the painful moment, reached for his dressing-gown and put it on and took a cigarette from the box on the table beside him.

He picked up the lighter and flicked it open for her.

'She's got courage,' was his thought. 'More courage than I have.'

When she spoke, it was with reference to his remark.

"St. Agatha's? Isn't that the place they call the Nutcrackers' Hospital?" she asked in a determinedly conversational tone, without looking at him.

"I believe they do," he said.

"It's for lunatics, isn't it?"

He gave a half smile.

"I prefer not to call it that. It's the place where they are making a special study of certain mental cases which might possibly be cured by operation. That's why I go there so much. My work is tending more and more towards work on the brain. It's difficult, disappointing and often depressing, but when one has a success, all those things seem to be swallowed up in thankful satisfaction."

"You don't talk to me much about your work now, do you?"

"I didn't think you were interested."

"But of course I am. I'm interested in everything that concerns you, Blaine."

He thought they might be drifting towards a dangerous shore again, and put a stop to it by getting out of bed and wrapping the dressing-gown more closely about her.

"You'd better go back to bed," he said. "It's not warm enough for you in here. I always turn off my radiator before I get into bed, but it's cold for you though it's only September.

Come along," and he opened the door for her and went across to her own room and opened that door as well, leaving her no alternative but to follow him.

He did not go into the room.

"Roberta can bring back the dressing-gown when she brings the tea," he said. "Good night, Virginia."

"Aren't you going to say it with a kiss?" she asked, still not willing to accept defeat.

He kissed her lightly, without holding her, and the next moment the door was shut between them and he had gone back to his own room.

He did not pick up his book again. His mind was occupied with his unexpected reaction, or lack of it, to her invitation to make love to her.

He had known for a long time, since the early days of their marriage in fact, that she did not enjoy his lover-like attentions, and it had given him a good many bad hours before he was able to accept it. What he had not at all realized, however, was that his own desire for her had died, that he now never thought of her in that way, and his rejection of her tonight had shown him just how completely that desire had died.

In its way, it was an intense relief. His urgent, unsatisfied longing for her had threatened to come between him and his work, and his consciousness of that fact had been a considerable source of worry to him, especially now that he was becoming accepted as one of the foremost and most courageous of specialists for the brain. He could not afford to have his attention diverted from absolute concentration by any outside influence, and his physical frustration and denial had diverted it.

Now he was free. He belonged entirely to himself again, and what Virginia did or did not do could no longer affect his work.

But what would happen if she did indeed go to New York? Had he been foolish and precipitate in telling her that if she went, she could not come back to him? Was that what he really wanted? To lose her altogether?

It was a question his mind could not answer. In the fifteen months of their marriage, he had become used to her being in his life, and now that she was not working, a pleasant companion in his free time and a most charming hostess for their frequent guests.

Was that enough? Could he make it enough? Had he, at thirty-nine, really finished with the more intimate side of life for a man with a woman?

It was unsatisfactory, even unethical, if he were to believe what he had frequently told his patients. But if it were true, need he worry? And if he were content to lead such a life, why had he put himself and Virginia into a position where, if she persisted in her resolve to go to the States, they might part?

He shelved further consideration of the problem and turned over and sought sleep.

CHAPTER VI

IT was in October, some weeks later, that Virginia told Blaine that Jos Benner had made her a definite offer to go to New York with *Lady of Leisure*.

She told him with quite unusual diffidence, coming into his private study and making a definite business of the telling.

He looked across his table at her.

"You want to go very much, don't you?" he asked.

"Yes. Very much," she said.

"What's stopping you from accepting the offer?"

"You know, Blaine. I want you to—agree."

"Meaning that you do really mind whether I agree or not?"

"Of course I do. I don't want to break up our marriage," she said frankly.

He was sorry she had added the latter sentence. He would have preferred her to mind for other reasons, having his own views on why she wanted the marriage to continue.

He hesitated, and then gave her a half smile and shrugged his shoulders.

"All right," he said. "Go if you want to—with my blessing."

Her face cleared.

"You mean there won't be any tags to it? About my coming back?"

"No. I give in. How long are you likely to be away?"

"I have no idea. I suppose it will depend on how it goes."

She had reached the conclusion by this time that, no matter what marvellous chances might be offered her out there, she must refuse them to come back to him. She was determined at all costs to remain his wife, and had even resolved to refuse Benner's offer if Blaine had been adamant over the choice she might have to face. She had a gay sense of reprieve in his consent, reluctant though it might be.

"Well, naturally I hope for your sake that you will have a success," he said. "When do you go?"

"In about a week's time."

"So soon? How about money? I presume you're spent out as usual?" with a wry smile.

"Oh, Blaine, I'm terribly afraid I am. You see, not working for so long——"

"All right. Let me know how much you want, and if I can manage it, I'll see to it."

"Blaine, you really are wonderful to me," she said and stood up, wondered if this were an occasion for kisses, but decided not to risk a rebuff. She had never forgotten her humiliation on the night she had gone to his room and practically offered herself to him.

He nodded and, picking up some papers, showed her that, as far as he was concerned, the interview was over.

Later in the day he went into the room where Anna was working.

Though he could not pin-point the time at which it had started, he knew that something had changed, broken down, in his relationship with the girl who had been his patient and was now his secretary, but he knew that the change had taken place. There was more formality between them, and he had lost the habit of calling in to smoke a cigarette in there and chat with her on all sorts of subjects. He had not intentionally broken that pleasant habit, but he had had a feeling that she did not welcome these interruptions to her work, bent as she was on making herself the perfect secretary, as indeed she bid fair to be.

She looked up when he came in, annoyed at feeling her face flush.

"Oh, Miss Mere, can you find a minute to look into Lady Belding's private account and tell me how it stands? Or even if it stands at all," with a smile. "I'm afraid it's usually in too weak a state to do that, quite the most recalcitrant of my patients, in fact."

"I was going into it yesterday, Sir Blaine," said Anna,

getting up and going to a file. "I'm afraid, as you say, that it isn't very healthy."

"Well, let me have a note of the figures when you've got them out. Also of any outstanding bills you know about. I want to get her account squared up. She's going to New York in a week's time, to appear in a play there. I don't know quite how long she'll be away."

Anna felt a leap of her heart. Though it could not possibly make any difference to her, Virginia would not be there, Virginia with her loveliness, her gaiety, her laughter, with her inalienable right to him, Virginia, his wife.

She would have him to herself, and surely they might to some small extent recapture something of the old friendship and comradeship whose loss she, at any rate, could pin-point, for it had dated from that unforgettable occasion when he had been so angry at seeing her tricked out in one of Virginia's dresses.

She had never doubted her complete understanding of his anger. She, his paid employee, had dared to try to make herself look like his adored young wife. It was impertinence, effrontery, lèse-majesté.

But now, for a time at least, Virginia would not be there for his constant delight and for comparison with the mouse of a secretary with no beauty of any sort to commend her to him.

She could have no idea of the essential beauty of her calm face, of the clear candour of her grey eyes, of the peaceful serenity emanating from her presence. She merely saw herself as plain and dull.

Virginia went off in as great a blaze of publicity as those responsible for it could devise, with a suite on the *Queen Elizabeth* and armfuls of flowers, hosts of telegrams, and with the delighted Roberta in attendance.

Blaine went to Southampton to see her off, and returned to town with a holiday feeling which he tried in vain to ignore.

'Now for some work, some real, solid work,' he told himself, for when Virginia was not herself working, she made many demands on him and her mere presence in the flat was a disturbing element.

But the ability to settle to the real, solid work was not to be had for merely the desire to do it, and a few days of close application found him looking for some relief.

He went into Anna's little office.

"You told me once, if you remember, that you were a fan of Beethoven, if one dare use such a word about such an august person as Beethoven," he said. "An orchestra I'm particularly fond of is giving his Fifth tonight, and I wondered if you would care to go."

"Go? With you?" she asked.

She looked so much surprised as to be almost scared.

He smiled down at her. She had jumped up from her chair as she always did when he came in, though he had often told her not to.

"Well, I'm not suggesting your going alone," he said. "Would you like to?"

"I'd love it," she said in her unaffected fashion.

"All right. Then shall we? No need to dress up or anything, but I expect you'd like to go home first, and anyway, it doesn't begin till eight. May I call to collect you?"

"That would be very nice of you, Sir Blaine," she said shyly.

"Good. I think about half-past seven. That will give us time to get into our seats and have a look at the programme, and I know you're a punctual person," with the sort of smile he had not given her for a long time.

But it was only just after seven when her landlady knocked at her door and told her, with a new tinge of respect in her voice, that there was a gentleman to see her.

"With ever such a big car outside, too," she added. "Quite gives the place a tone!"

"Thank you, Mrs. Coleman," said Anna. "I'll come down."

Could she ask him into her room? She looked round hastily, glad that she was ready and that the room was tidy, the remains of her meal put away but the coffee still bubbling in the percolator.

"I'm afraid I'm before my time," said Blaine, when she went down to him in the narrow hall. "I had to run the car into the garage for a small adjustment, and it did not take as long as I expected. Have I made things awkward for you?"

"No. No, not at all. Would you—would you like to come up?"

"May I? Or we could go somewhere and have some coffee, if you like."

"I've just made some," she said, and knew that she wanted him to come into her room so that for ever after she would be aware of his presence there.

"That will be nicer than having it anywhere else," he said, "and I'm sure you make good coffee."

"How can you know that?" she asked with a little laugh that seemed to come bubbling up from somewhere inside her as she led the way up the stairs.

"Because everything you do, you do well," he said.

She turned her head to look at him with a grimace.

"What about the muddle I made over Mrs. Antrim's account?" she said.

"What, charging her at the B rate instead of the A? That was nothing. In fact, it probably saved Mr. Antrim from having a heart attack when he saw the bill," he laughed.

When she had given up the second of their rooms after her mother's death, Anna had spent considerable thought and care on not making her one room too blatantly her bedroom as well as her sitting-room. The divan bed was covered with a gay cretonne, which also turned the pillows into cushions, and the fitted basin which also did duty for a sink was concealed behind a curtain of the same material, and there were no toilet articles in evidence. She had an oak bureau instead of a chest of drawers, and her small wardrobe could be accommodated in a cupboard fitted in one corner. There were yellow chrysanthemums in a blue jar. A gas fire made the room comfortably warm, and on a ring beside it the coffee percolator gave out an appetizing aroma.

He thought it looked bright, homely and Anna-like, with nothing that jarred, nothing which had not its uses.

"This is nice," he said, when she shyly moved the easy chair nearer to the fire and took the percolator off the gas ring to make way for the saucepan containing milk. "Do you have to do all your cooking on that?"

"Oh no. I can use Mrs. Coleman's gas cooker in her kitchen, but I don't if I can help it. I have all sorts of gadgets for this ring, and I do most things in a pressure cooker. I can make toast at the fire."

He thought how natural and unaffected she was as she busied herself with the final preparation of the coffee, setting out two cups and saucers with blue dots on them, and the milk in a blue jug, going in an unconcerned way to and fro behind the screen. She made no apology for her humble way of life, but quite simply gave him of her best with no suggestion that there was any difference between this and his own luxurious setting.

"Is it all right for me to smoke in here?" he asked, when she had given him his coffee, which was as good as he had anticipated.

"Of course. Most of my friends do," she said, and struck a match and held it for him.

"Shall I help you wash these things up?" he asked when they had drunk their coffee.

She laughed.

"What, two cups? But if there had been a dozen, I shouldn't dream of allowing you to help with them."

"Why not? Do you imagine I don't know how to do it?"

"No. I'll repeat what you said to me, that I am quite sure that whatever you did, you would do well. But for Sir Blaine Belding to be washing up! Perish the thought! I'll just cover them with water so that the coffee won't stain them, and then hadn't we better go?"

Neither of them enjoyed the first half of the concert, which consisted of music by modern composers, but when the Fifth Symphony began, they sat relaxed and attentive.

During the slight pause between two movements, Anna's programme slipped from her lap and as she bent down to retrieve it, he did the same and their fingers touched. It was as if an electric shock passed through her, and for a moment she remained as she was, stooping down, and when he had put the programme safely in the rack on the back of the chair in front of her, she straightened herself slowly but the hand which he had touched still hung down limply at her side.

And then something happened which at first she could not believe, but which, as the moments passed, she had to believe.

One of his fingers had found its way into the cupped hollow of her hand and lay against her palm. Almost unconsciously, in that moment of stupefaction and wild joy, her hand closed on it and held it until, with a slow, gentle movement his other fingers joined the first one and lay wholly within her own.

She no longer heard the music for the music in her own heart and in her tumultuous mind which was no longer capable of any feeling, any thought, but that his hand lay in hers, intentionally, secretly, setting the two of them alone in the vast, attentive crowd about them.

When his fingers moved again, it was to release them from hers and to take her hand into his, covering it, holding it, his thumb gently stroking the soft flesh of hers.

She wanted to laugh and to cry, wanted to tell him what that pressure, the gentle caress, was doing to her, sending waves of undreamed-of emotion through her, making her wish that this moment, this contact, could go on and on and never cease whilst she could still live and feel it.

But the moment had to end, and when, as the crash of applause broke out, he withdrew his hand to join in it, her furtive glance at his face told her nothing, nor did he in any way refer to the episode either that evening, when he took her home and left her at her door with a smiling good night and a word of thanks for her company, nor when they met the following day.

It was as if it had never been—and yet for her, it would always be.

She had not blinded herself to the fact of her love for him. She had recognized it for what it was months ago, before she had come to him as his secretary, whilst she still lay waiting for her ankle to heal and he had spent those hours with her, laughing and talking to her.

But clearly it had not meant anything to him, that holding of her hand, and how could she have expected it to? Thrilled and happy though it had made her, it had yet been a subtle disappointment to her—the first sign she had ever had of possible feet of clay. He belonged to Virginia. He loved Virginia. She herself was just a girl whose company he had sought for an idle evening, a girl to whom he might make that small overture and mean nothing by it, but even so small a thing a tiny disloyalty to the woman to whom all his loyalty belonged.

She would have been utterly dumbfounded if she had had any idea of just what that contact with her had meant to him.

It had opened his eyes to something which now he knew he had forced himself not to see, persuaded himself could never happen. He felt again the touch of her fingers, the movement of the small, capable hand within his own, and knew why, long into the night, he could still feel it there.

He loved her, loved Anna Mere, the girl he had knocked down with his car, had taken to his home and guided back to health, the girl who in those weeks had become his friend, the girl who was now his capable, trusted secretary, carrying out his orders and being paid by him for doing so.

He could not doubt it for a moment. He knew it for absolute certainty.

He loved her—but not as he had loved Virginia, not with that idolatrous passion for empty beauty and the satisfaction of his sheer animal passions.

There was nothing like that about this love which he knew he now bore for Anna Mere. He loved her for the lovely thing she herself was, for her calm peace which could give him peace, for her serenity and her utter lack of artifice, for her grave madonna eyes from which looked the sweet and steadfast soul of her.

He loved her and groaned in spirit because it was so.

What had he to offer her even if she loved him, and he could not know that, except that she had left her hand in his and trusted him. He was married, and to Virginia who, he knew, would never let him go. And could he want her to let him go? Go through all the beastly business of a divorce so that he could offer himself, second-hand, besmirched, to this girl who deserved the first and best of any man, and a man much more worth while than he felt himself to be?

If he had any loyalty, any real care for Anna, he knew that he would let her go, send her away from him where her life could not be touched or soiled by him.

He knew he could not do it. The best thing he could do for her, the only thing, was never to let her know, never to let her guess by any word or action or hint of his that she was more to him than just a girl who worked well and loyally for him.

Yet his heart lifted at the thought that, with Virginia at the other side of the world and completely happy to be there, Anna was still here with him, to be seen and talked to every day, perhaps to be taken out again as they had gone tonight, as friends, as companions, nothing more.

He was deluding himself, and he knew it. He could no longer regard her as that and no more, but he could not stay away from her, and he let himself make plans, create situations for being with her, build her into his life as he had never done before.

By the time Christmas came, and Virginia had been away for nearly three months and gave no hint of returning as yet, pleased and happy about her success on Broadway, he had established a habit of taking Anna out two or three times a week, to concerts, to the cinema, to the theatre, or just to dinner in some quiet restaurant where he was not likely to be recognized—that in itself an increasing irritation to him, introducing something furtive into their relationship, something to be kept hidden.

He wanted to give her a Christmas present, not just the money gift which he made to all his staff and in which she would have her share, but something personal.

He wondered how she would take it, or if she would even take it at all, but he would not deny himself the pleasure of choosing a gift, and in the end he bought her a clip for her dress, not very valuable because he could be fairly sure she would refuse that, but a pretty trifle, which surely any girl could accept from any man?

She was surprised when he gave it to her.

It was Christmas Eve, and he had done what was for him a quite extraordinary thing.

He had asked her to have dinner with him, intending to lead up to some shared association for Christmas Day itself.

"I'm so sorry," she said when he asked her. "I'd have loved to, but I've promised to help with the Christmas decorations at the church. We didn't want to put the flowers there until the last minute so that they would be fresh for the services tomorrow."

"How long will it take you?" he asked.

"I don't know. It depends on how many people are there to help. I'm going straight from here."

"What about my coming with you?" he surprised himself by saying.

"You? Come to the church? Why—yes, I suppose so," she said. "I mean—if you really want to help, though it isn't in your line, is it?"

"I've certainly never done it before, but everything has its first time," he said, "and my extra inches might be a help. Perhaps save you having to climb up steps and things."

His presence amongst the helpers caused a mild sensation, for though she had not intended to let them know who he was, she let his name slip out inadvertently. The job was soon done, however, including the placing of the armful of flowers which he had stopped to buy on their way, and they were out on the pavement again in the slightly foggy night, just such a night as the one on which they had first met.

"Now dinner?" he asked, and she nodded.

"I'm hungry after all that," she said. "Do you know it's after nine?"

"The thing will be to find somewhere now," he said, for at any of the places where it was smart to dine so late, he was certain to be recognized. "I suppose you wouldn't consider buying things and taking them home, your home I mean, and having a picnic?"

She coloured with pleasure.

"I'd love to do that," she said, "though unless you are really

102

ravenous, it need not be a picnic because I can cook things, and I've got enough plates and knives for two!"

"Then that's settled. Where can we buy things?"

"There will be shops still open in a little street near where I live," she said, "especially tonight, when they'll be trying to sell out."

They made merry over their purchases, which he bought on a grand scale, a chicken which she said she could fry 'Maryland' for quickness, vegetables and fruit and a bottle of wine, with a huge box of chocolates for her, since she did not smoke, and a big bunch of tawny chrysanthemums for the blue jar.

He insisted on helping with the cooking and was quite ridiculous and like a boy over the carving of the chicken into joints for the frying pan, putting on one of her overalls back to front and tying a handkerchief like a mask over his mouth and nose and conducting the affair with all the gravity of a major operation in the theatre, Anna standing by to hand him the implements for which he asked in the quick, short tones used on such occasions, though she was frequently helpless with laughter.

He prepared the vegetables whilst she cooked the chicken, and she initiated him into the rites of the pressure cooker and did her best to keep the chicken hot rather than have recourse to Mrs. Coleman's kitchen on the floor below.

She was happier than she had ever been in her life. She felt she wanted to take each separate moment and look at it and hold it so that she could store it in her memory for ever. She did not want to think of anything outside this room or beyond this day, not who he was, nor of Virginia, nor even that he was married and probably ought not really to be here at all.

And just before he left, he took the little box out of his pocket and gave it to her.

"Santa Claus," he said.

She opened it wonderingly and took out the clip and held it in her palm, and did not know whether she most wanted to laugh or to cry. It seemed a perfect finish to a perfect evening, this first thing he had ever given her.

"But—Santa Claus has been already," she said a little

unsteadily. "Miss Dove gave me an envelope, you know. Ten pounds! I haven't said thank you for that either, but may I say it now? And now—this lovely thing," holding it so that the facets of the jewels, synthetic but as good as he dared to buy her, caught the light.

"I'm afraid they're not diamonds," he said.

"I should hope not! I should be horrified!" she said. "I'd never dare to wear it if they were—but I will wear it. And—thank you, Sir Blaine. It's so kind of you," with the first return that night to her shyness.

"It's not kind at all, except to myself," he said, and longed to tell her that if he could have had his way, they would have been diamonds.

He thought of all the things he had given Virginia, and of her casual reception of them, with kisses perhaps, but he had often thought that already she had her eye and her mind on something else. Certainly she had never taken a gift with the sincere and lovely thanks that were in Anna's eyes even more than in her voice.

They parted at the door of her room. He would not let her go down to the front door with him.

"You stay in the warm, and hop into bed quickly," he said. "Good night—Anna."

Her hand was warm and soft in his.

"Good night—Blaine," she said shyly.

"I've waited a long time to hear you say my name like that," he said, and let her hand go and went quickly down the stairs before he could say too much, yet knowing how little he had said of all the things he wanted to say. All he had done was to say her name, and she, bless her, had for once spoken his own without the prefix.

She undressed as in a dream and got into bed and snuggled down under the bedclothes and thought of him, of their happy evening, of the way in which he had just called her Anna, of her temerity in saying his name like that, and of what he had said about having waited for her to do so.

Blaine. Blaine. She said it over and over to herself, said it aloud, and then put out the light and lay in the darkness and would not let herself say it again.

They were to meet the next day. He was calling for her in the morning, after she had been to the church he had helped to decorate, and were to have a lovely long day together somewhere. She did not care where they went nor what they did. She would be with him.

It was a lovely day, crisp and cold with fugitive bursts of sunshine, and they drove out into the country, had lunch at a wayside hotel where he told her the excellent food was not as good as what they had cooked the night before, and afterwards they left the car and walked across a wind-swept common and talked or remained silent and were utterly happy.

In the evening he had not been able to avoid accepting an invitation from some friends of his and Virginia's who would have seen no reason why, since she was away and he was ostensibly alone, he should not do so.

"I don't like leaving you to spend Christmas evening alone, Anna," he said when it was time for them to part.

"Why not, after such a lovely day?" she asked. "I don't mind a bit, really I don't. I shall listen to the wireless, and do some sewing, and then I may wash my hair. Besides, I shan't be alone. The Colemans are going out, and they've asked me to have Simon, their darling cocker spaniel, who hates to be left alone. He sits and simply lavishes love on me with his beautiful eyes, and though I'm supposed to put him outside the door to sleep, of course I shan't! He starts on the floor, but somehow by the morning he's always managed to get on the end of my bed."

"Very improper and unhealthy," said Blaine, but he smiled as he said it, for he had met Simon and was glad that she would have at least some living creature with her when he had to leave her, and one that adored her too.

"I've had such a happy day," she said, her eyes so much softer than she knew.

"So have I, Anna," he said, and let her go.

He had not dared even to touch her hand, save once when they had to cross a little stream and she had balanced precariously on the tree trunk set there as a bridge, and then he had let it go again quickly, afraid of even so small a physical contact with her.

Now, leaving her, he ached to hold her in his arms, just to hold her and know her nearness even if he did not kiss her. So small, so gallant, so alone, glad of a dog for company in her solitude.

Anna. His small, brave Anna.

He hated having to leave her.

At length, some few weeks later, it was Simon, the spaniel, who precipitated the crisis that Blaine had known in his heart must come some day. He could not go on indefinitely playing so dangerous a game, since every day drew him closer in thought to Anna.

He had made up his mind that he would not see her one Sunday, after a succession of Sundays spent almost wholly in her company so that he, and he believed she, looked forward all the week to that blessed day.

It had become his custom to find a moment to go in to see her in her office on Saturday mornings before she left. He had told her from the first that he did not expect her to work on Saturday mornings, but he was none the less glad that she always did so, especially since he had arrived at the stage when a day on which he did not see her, if only for a moment and in the presence of others, was a lost day.

On that particular Saturday, though she waited in her office, finding unnecessary jobs to do and hoping against hope that he would come as usual and tell her of some plan he had made for them for the next day, in the end she had to decide that he was not coming and that therefore there would be no plans made for the morrow.

She went home with a dull sense of loss, though she told herself that she could not expect him to want to spend every Sunday, week after week with her and that he had his own friends and interests apart from her.

She did what she always did on Saturday afternoon. She cleaned her room thoroughly, polished the furniture and her little bits of brass and silver and, now that she could afford it, renewed the flowers. After that she cooked for herself a combined tea and supper, a more substantial one than during the week since on Saturdays she did not have lunch with the staff in the home, and then settled down with the wireless, and went to bed as early as the Saturday night play would allow.

Blaine had been restless and irritable because of his decision not to see her the next day. Both patients and staff knew that it was not their happiest day and he practically told Mrs. Murrayne, who had come in as a patient again, that he could do nothing for her and would like her to leave, which was foolish, since apart from being such a frequent and well-paying patient herself, she had introduced the nursing home to a good many of her wealthy friends, to his gain.

The crux came when a letter from Virginia arrived.

After telling him again of the phenomenal success she was having on Broadway, information which he received with mental reservations, knowing Virginia, she told him that 'if he agreed', she was going on a short tour of other American cities with the play.

But darling, she added, *I am in rather a hole. I've been earning lots, of course, and shall earn lots more, but living is frightfully dear here, and of course one has to do a lot of entertaining, keeping on the right side of people who matter and so on, and the awful result is that I'm broke. I haven't a bean. Literally not a bean. In fact, I have simply had to sell things, my diamond watch that I loved so much, and one or two of my rings and things. Of course I just hated to part with anything you've given me, but what was I to do? And, Blaine darling, the worst of it is that I shall have to account for the things when I come home because you're simply not allowed to bring things out here and not go back with them. Isn't it too silly when they're your own things and you ought to be able to do what you like with them? Anyway, I shall have to get them back somehow. I've only pawned them, of course, so I can get them back, but can you get the money out to me somehow? It will be about £500, I am afraid, but I can't work that out in dollars and of course it's dollars I shall have to have. Can you wangle it for me somehow? Get some-*

one to smuggle it out for me or something? I know you have heaps of rich American patients so they ought to be able to do something, perhaps pay for their ops. here to me instead of to you? Anyway, I'm sure you'll think of something. You're so clever, and I really am in a mess about it because of course when I leave New York, goodness knows when I shall be back, and meantime it may be too late to get my things back and I've got to show *them when I get to England again.*

The rest of the letter was filled with her doings, and names of famous people, and he could see quite plainly where the money, *his* money, had gone, on totally unnecessary things and in creating for herself a position amongst these rich people which neither her position nor his justified.

He was bitterly angry. He knew that he had been extremely generous to her, and some of the things she admitted she had sold, the diamond watch amongst them, had represented to him more than the money they had cost him, being tokens of that early, adoring love for her, things with which at the time she had told him she would never, never part.

He was miserable as well as angry. It was for this, for a woman who really cared nothing for him apart from what she could get out of him, that Anna was forever denied him, Anna whom he loved with the whole depths of a being which Virginia had never touched, and who, he was certain, would return his love were he free to offer it.

And it was in order to be loyal to Virginia that he was foregoing the day with Anna.

Of course he could not send dollars to Virginia, and he would not for a moment entertain any thought of getting them to her illegally. It was true that he had one or two wealthy American patients, and at least one of them would be paying him more than the £500 for which she asked, but he would not lower himself by inviting him to connive at defrauding his own government, as of course he would know he was doing.

Somehow Virginia would have to have enough to reclaim the jewellery which she had had to declare, in minute detail, when she went out of England or there would be very unpleasant consequences in which, of course, he himself would be involved.

He had no idea how he was to do it, and in the end, throwing everything aside, he made up his mind to go out to Chelsea and see Anna and make it right with her about tomorrow. There was a telephone in the house to which she would be summoned if he called her on it, but he knew where the instrument was placed, in the general hall, and guessed (rightly) that Anna's doings were already a matter of interest to Mrs. Coleman and the other lodgers in the house. Anything she might say would be overheard, and he did not intend to put her in such a position, so the only thing for him to do was to go himself.

When he neared the house, in the gathering dusk, he saw her come out of it with Simon in tow, and drew up a little way from it.

And then, without warning, the dog dashed into the road, right in the path of an oncoming car, and Anna, with a little cry, rushed after him.

Blaine felt sick, and was out of his own car before the other driver, with screeching brakes, pulled up, saw that he had missed both the girl and the dog, and tore on his way again.

In an instant of time, Blaine was at her side, an arm about her to drag her safely back to the path.

"Are you all right?" he gasped. "Oh, darling, I thought he'd got you! I thought he couldn't help killing you. Anna— Anna——"

Shaken and white-faced, with Simon now scurrying back into the house, aware of his offence, Anna stumbled across to the door with Blaine's arm still about her, and, below the fright she had had, and the bewilderment of the narrowly averted accident, she was aware of what he had said, of the tone in which he had said it, of the only thing it could possibly mean.

He had called her 'darling', and he had been agonized over her, had been terrified at the thought that she might be killed or hurt.

There was no one in the hall, but she would not have known if there had been dozens there. Simon had hastily departed to his own quarters, and, leaving Blaine to shut the door, she stumbled up the stairs and into her own room, where she sank down in a chair and covered her face with her hands, crouching sideways with her elbows on its arm.

She heard him come in, heard the door shut, but she could not look up nor let him see her face.

He went to the window and stood there for a moment, seeing nothing but the sight of her in the path of the car, hearing nothing but the screech of the brakes, and feeling again the agony of that moment.

Then he turned to her, went to where she sat, took her concealing hands and drew her up to him.

"Anna," he said in a low, shaken voice. "Oh, Anna—my dear."

Then, since she could no longer keep her eyes from his, or bear that tender concern, the anguish in his voice, she looked at him, and he knew. There was no concealing curtain between them any more. They looked into the unveiled depths of each other's heart.

"You know, Anna, don't you?" he asked, unsmiling.

"Yes," she said in a whisper. "Yes, I—know, Blaine."

"May I kiss you, Anna?"

For answer she gave him her lips, soft and unaware and trembling, and he took them with a feeling akin to reverence, knowing that no man had ever kissed her mouth before.

When he drew his head away, his arms still held her, and he sat down in the chair and drew her down with him, her dark head against his shoulder, her face hidden.

It was true. The unbelievable thing was happening. Blaine had kissed her, and she was in his arms, and she knew that he loved her as she loved him.

For a long time they sat there in silence, his hand stroking her hair, his lips every now and then touching it gently, without passion but with an utter contentment. It was enough at the moment that she was there, in his arms, close to him, and that he knew of her love.

Presently he spoke.

"Anna darling, what are we going to do about it?" he asked.

She lifted her face. There was a sadness in her eyes which hurt him, but behind the sadness there was glory. Nothing could hide it.

"There isn't anything we can do, is there?" she asked.

"I don't know. I don't know. There must be. We can't just lose—this. It's the biggest thing that has ever happened to me. It is all of me, Anna. Everything."

"Virginia?" she asked, with great courage, he knew.

"Yes. There's Virginia. I loved her when I married her, or I believed I did. She was so lovely, so much alive, so *young*, and I don't mean just young in years, but—in everything. I was enchanted by her, bewitched. She seemed the embodiment of all my dreams, of dreams I scarcely knew I had. I thought it was love for all my life. Now I know it wasn't love at all, but just—well, something there's an ugly name for. I love *you*, Anna, and it's quite a different love. Don't mistake me. I am a man and I want you as a man wants a woman, but that's only part of it, not the whole of it as it was—before. Oh, Anna, Anna my darling, heart of my heart, my little love, my dear little love!" and his lips found hers again and held them, and between their joined lips love flowed and fused their two beings into one until she felt she could never again be just one, never again be Anna Mere, to whom the love of a man and for a man was unknown.

"I do love you, Blaine," she said shakily. "You know that, don't you? I've loved you for a long time, all the time, I think. I didn't want to. I don't think I really wanted you to, but I can't be sorry. I can't be! Not now. Not now."

Presently he talked to her, since there were things that must be said between them.

"You said just now that there's nothing we can do about it, because of Virginia, because I'm married to Virginia, but I can't accept that and I'm not going to. If it is humanly possible for me to have you for my own, my wife, Anna, I'm going to make it possible. Virginia does not love me any more than I love her—less, in fact, because she's never loved me. I'm not quite sure, even now, why she married me, but I suppose it was because of my name, and because I was able to give her the sort of life she wanted; money, clothes, jewels, a good home and influential friends. I think she married me to further what she calls her career rather than for any other reason. Perhaps I ought not to tell you about this, Anna, but there must be complete frankness and understanding between us now, and there can't be unless I tell you about Virginia. She has never wanted a husband, as such, and I doubt if she ever will. She's not made that way, not as a loving, human woman is made, not as you are made, my darling. I know it already, from your kiss, and from the way you trembled in my arms, and because I know you as a *real* woman, with a heart and a body and a most sweet mind. Virginia belongs to herself and always will do. She hasn't a thought in her outside and beyond herself, and her ambition. I don't know if she will ever succeed in gaining her ends. She may do, but whether she does or not, that is what she really wants, all she really loves— success. And it will not materially affect her success if we part. I will look after her, always. I owe her that. Not quite as I have done in the past, because you will be my greatest and first consideration, but you will not grudge what I do for Virginia, bless you. You see how well I know you, dear heart! And if we have happiness, as we shall have, I don't think the things that money can buy will be of such immense importance. Not that I shall not be able to look after you and give you all you can reasonably want. That will be my joy and my pride, and I'm doing well— but I don't need to tell *you* that! I'm glad you know everything there is to know about me, Anna, more than anybody else in the world, my successes and my failures, the things I've tried to do that haven't come off, and the ones that have. I can talk to you, Anna, at last, tell you everything, never being afraid to tell you. Oh Anna, Anna! Some day you will be mine. You must be. I shall find the way. I don't want you in any hole-and-corner way, a little affair to be hidden from the world, but as my own, my wife, my loved and honoured wife, the woman I can show to the world. It must come true. It must. I'll *make* it come true. Say you believe that. You do, don't you?" lifting up her face to look

112

deeply into her eyes and find in them the belief his own heart felt.

How could a woman like Virginia, with her little concerns and her selfish furtherance of her own ends, come between them for long? For even a little longer?

Anna had listened to his words, to his voice that flowed over her like a tide warmed by the sun, lapping at her, enveloping her, but now that she must speak, what could she say? It did not seem nearly as possible to her, not possible at all in fact, that Virginia would give him up, relinquish her claim to him, leave him free for her, for Anna Mere, the little secretary.

Why should she?

That was the focal point. Why should Virginia give him up?

But, with Blaine's eyes on hers, willing her, compelling her to agree with him that it was possible, how could she deny him?

"I want it to come true, Blaine," she said brokenly. "I want it with my whole heart and soul. You know that, don't you?"

He kissed her again, gently, lingeringly, tasting the full savour of her sweet awakening to love, feeling that trembling of her body which told him she was indeed wholly a woman, and ready some day to be wholly his.

"Yes. Yes, I know you do, my darling," he said, and again they were silent, aware of each other and of all that had been said between them and of all the things, sweet things, sad things, things of hope and things of despair, but beyond all, things of love, that were still to be said between them.

When he rose to go, there was no longer any thought that they would spend the next day apart.

"I'd like to be with you early, darling," he said. "Do you go to church every Sunday?"

"I like to," she said. "I always have done, you see, but it's more than just a habit."

"May I come with you tomorrow?"

She gave him a glad smile.

"Oh, Blaine, do you want to? Does it mean anything to you?" she asked.

"I think it might, with you. After all, there must be something pretty wonderful somewhere to have made you."

Her face was very tender, her eyes sweet. She had never thought to have any man say foolish things like that to her, and this man of all men.

"You've got to know a lot about me yet, my darling," she said, and brought out the last words with shy love.

"Well, we've got all the rest of our lives to do that in," he said, "but I know I'll never discover anything worse about you than I know now. Good night, sweetheart, and dream about—well, whatever you want to dream about. Do I know what that is?"

She nodded.

"Yes, I expect you do," she said.

CHAPTER VII

VIRGINIA arrived in England some three weeks later, after a cable announcing her intention, to which she had added *Imperative you do something about my last letter*.

Because he could think of nothing else to do, Blaine had to ask the husband of one of his American patients to help him by paying his bill into Virginia's account in New York, in dollars.

"Of course, of course," he agreed at once, heartily. "You poor British certainly do have to take it, don't you? And we must look after our women, bless 'em. Virginia Coley, eh? Well, well. Saw her picture in the paper somewhere before we left. So she's your wife, Sir Blaine? Never have thought it. Lovely girl," and something in his tone, in the speculative, amused glance he gave him, left Blaine with the uncomfortable certainty that the picture he had seen had been one of those Virginia's husband most disliked, a too revealing, consciously seductive picture which had disgusted him.

That took care of Virginia's immediate problem, but her sudden return meant a great deal more to him even than that enforced subdual of his conscience.

It meant that he would have to do something about himself and Anna sooner than he had expected.

And he wanted to do it.

During those three weeks, they had become very close to each other. Starved of the love he had once hoped he would share with Virginia, he was finding in Anna a happiness of which he had never dreamed, and his urgent desire was to be able to bring about the complete fulfilment of their shared lives. It had not always been easy to keep their love as they meant it to be and were determined it should remain until she could come to him fully as his wife, and there were times when he had had to drag himself away from her and leave her before his physical hunger and need for her committed them to a course which he knew she felt would defile her and spoil their joy in each other.

Anna was innocent but by no means ignorant. She was well aware of the danger they ran, and was both sorry and glad when he told her, gripping his hands so that the knuckles showed white and the nails bit into his palms, that he must not come to her home any longer.

"There's a point beyond which a man can't fight," he said, "and I've reached it. I want you so desperately, Anna, but not this way, not until you can come to me before the world. That's the way you want it too."

"Yes, Blaine," she said, soberly and sadly, for she could not bring herself to share his certainty that that day would come; nor, indeed, had she any real hope of it. This was all of himself and his life which she could ever have, and she must make it enough.

So instead of coming to her home, he had to meet her elsewhere, take her out to a meal, or to some place of entertainment, or, on fine Sundays, into the country or to the coast in his car, but always where there were other people.

Still, they could see each other every day, and her position as his personal secretary had become a thing of bitter sweetness, tantalizing them with its constant reminder that their love was a furtive thing, to be watched and guarded.

He made opportunities for going into her office, if only for a few minutes, ready with an excuse if anyone else were there, Miss Dove, or one of the nurses who had to come to her for an account, or with some of the notes and figures with which she had to be supplied. When he lacked even the time for that, she would hear the light tap of his fingers on the door and know that he was passing, and remembering her.

But he realized that, absorbed in her as he was, this new love of his was not spoiling his work. She was rather, he liked to think, an inspiration to it, her quiet, controlled presence in his life being in no way the disturbing, harassing influence which Virginia had been.

And would be again?

On the evening of the day on which he had received Virginia's cable, they had dinner together in the quiet little Soho restaurant which they had discovered and made their own. Here, if the Italian proprietor knew Blaine, since it was part of his business to know everybody of repute, his manner did not suggest such knowledge, and no one else likely to recognize him came there. In their special corner, screened by a group of dusty, synthetic palms, they could get the illusion of being alone.

He had called in at her office and given her the cable during the day, and when they met, their minds were heavy with foreboding.

"I shall, of course, straighten things out with Virginia at the earliest possible moment," he told Anna when they were seated and had given their order.

There was a tight look about his mouth which betrayed the tension.

"You mean to tell her about us, Blaine?"

"That, if it is unavoidable. But I hope to get at it in another way, without involving you."

"Ask her for a divorce?"

It was the first time, since the evening they had discovered their mutual love, that the hateful word had been spoken between them, but now it had to be spoken. It was the only bridge over which they could pass if they were to be together.

"Yes. I shan't enjoy it. The whole business is nauseating to me. I can say that without being afraid that you will misunderstand. That's one of the blessed things between us, Anna. This perfect understanding. But it's got to be faced."

"Do you think she'll agree, Blaine?" she asked, crumbling her bread and not looking at him.

She could not believe that anyone, even a woman who did not love him, would willingly let him go.

"She must. I must find a way. I'm doing well. You know that. I can ask fees I never dreamed of, even in these days of the National Health Service. I'm getting greedy—for you, my darling. For us. Money is Virginia's god. If I make it enough, she'll agree. It may take a little while, and we don't want to wait the statutory three years. I can't wait for you all that time, Anna. We're neither of us very young any more, and we've already wasted so much of our lives apart."

"But—the scandal, Blaine. You'd hate that, and it might do you a lot of harm professionally," she said in a low voice.

"I know. I'd like to be able to avoid that, naturally, though I don't think it could do me as much harm now as it would at one time. The operations I do now can't be done by more than half a dozen surgeons anywhere in the world, and that counts. When somebody's life, or even more potently their reason, is at stake, the private morality of the man who can save it is light in the balance. There need not to be too much made of it. The usual unsavoury thing. A woman in an hotel—oh Anna, Anna, what a beastly, disgusting mess one can make of one's life! And to have *you* mixed up in this, even though I am determined that no one will know it! Not to be able to come to you clean and decent, but smirched with all this!"

"Blaine—oh my darling, is it worth it to you? Isn't it better to—to——"

He stopped her before she could find the words, stretching his hand across the table to cover hers, to hold it in his firm grasp as if to make her realize how firmly he held her, herself.

"Don't say it, Anna. Don't go on. It *is* worth it. Without you I am only half a man, a brain with no body, with no object or hope in life. Some day, soon I hope, we can be together, belonging to each other, utterly complete. Take that frozen look off your face. Smile, my darling. Haven't I always got the thing I want out of life? And I'm going to get this, the thing I want more than I've ever wanted anything."

But he knew in his heart that this was a thing more difficult of attainment than any of those other things.

He did not go to Southampton to meet Virginia. That, at least, he would not do to Anna. Instead, he asked one of his house doctors to go, young John Murphy. He now had two of these young men, and the senior one could take over his work for the day. Young Murphy, he knew, was delighted with the mission, indulging in a hopeless passion for Virginia, to her satisfaction and amusement.

Virginia arrived at the flat with a large assortment of luggage.

"The big stuff's coming on later," she said gaily, though the place seemed already overflowing. "Oh, how lovely to be home again!" and Blaine was well aware that the way she flung her arms about him, and the fervour of her kisses, were for the benefit of the besotted young man who stood there to witness them, sick with jealousy.

Though Blaine knew (who could know better?) that there was not a spark of real love or feeling in her, she enjoyed rousing in other men the passionate desire for her which she would never have the slightest wish to reciprocate or satisfy.

"Have you missed me, darling?" she asked Blaine gaily.

"Naturally," he said unemotionally, removing her arms from her neck. "Thank you, Murphy. You might tell them downstairs that when the rest of Lady Belding's luggage comes, they had better keep it down there somewhere for the present."

"Yes, Sir Blaine—and it's been a great pleasure to go down to meet Lady Belding," said the young man as he withdrew.

"Isn't he a pet?" asked Virginia. "And so terribly in love with me! Aren't you jealous?"

"No. Should I be?" he asked in the same indifferent tone. "Didn't Roberta come back with you?"

"No. I left her at Southampton. She's lost one of my bits of luggage, the idiot, so I told her she'd better stop there and find it and come on by a later train. What about a drink? I'm dying for one."

"You know I don't drink anything in the daytime," he said, "but you have something, of course. What will you have?" leading the way into their sitting-room, a lapse of his usual good manners which she was quick to note and resent.

"I can see that it's time I came back," she said. "Your manners have slipped a bit, haven't they? Walking into a room in front of me?"

Her tone, now that Murphy was no longer there to hear, had sharpened.

"I beg your pardon," said Blaine formally and opened the cocktail cabinet and repeated his question.

"Oh—a dry Martini if there's any ice," she said. "Not that stupid little glass, Blaine. I want a *drink*."

Anna, in her office, had heard the noise and bustle of Virginia's arrival. How could she not have done? She tried to close her ears to the sound of the light, high-pitched voice, but she could not close her mind. It was going to be worse, much worse than she had even anticipated, having Blaine's wife here under his roof, in his home, again.

Would she be able to bear it? And yet what was the alternative? She shut her eyes for a moment on the intolerable pain which the thought of that alternative gave her. Then she went on with her work steadily, and hoped that Blaine would not come to her, that she would not have to see him, until she had herself completely under control again.

She did not see him again that day. Blaine, no more than Anna, could bear a meeting between them just yet.

Instead, he paid a round of hospital visits and came back after Anna had gone, and took Virginia out to dinner. It was better than having it alone with her in the flat.

Virginia was gay to the point of delirium, professing herself to be delighted to be in England and at home again, enchanted with everything, spreading the cloak of her gaiety all around her to include the manager of the smart restaurant and the man who waited on them assiduously.

But Blaine could see that beneath the gaiety and her constant laughter there was some bitterness, anger. She was a disappointed woman.

After they reached the flat again, she let him see the cause, still talking feverishly, laughing loudly, drinking more than she usually did, for she was abstemious as a rule, caring for her figure and her voice.

"I really hated it in the States," she said, though all the evening she had been telling how wonderful it was and what a good time she had had. "I hate the Americans, too. Thinking such a lot of themselves and being so superior and so sure that everything they do and have is better than anybody else's." Her voice went on and on, her tongue further loosened by her frequently 'topped' glass, and Blaine dug out from all the talking that she had probably been nothing like the success on Broadway that her letters had suggested.

"You decided not to do the tour of the other cities then?" he asked her when she paused to fill her glass again.

"I didn't think it worth while. They wouldn't have appreciated a good British musical, or British stars. They've absolutely no taste at all. No, I decided against it. It wouldn't have done me any good," but he wondered if she had indeed ever had the chance.

"And what plans have you now?" he asked steadily.

She shrugged her shoulders.

"Oh—nothing particular. I'll have a rest. I've earned it, God knows! I want to enjoy being at home again, not being Virginia Coley any longer, but just your wife, Blaine," and she made one of her restless movements and came to sit on the arm of his chair, her hand ruffling his hair, a thing he particularly disliked.

He put up a hand to remove hers, but she stayed where she was, an arm about his neck, her graceful body inclining towards his, though he made no movement to touch her.

"We'll go out a bit, entertain people," she said. "Ugh, it's cold! As soon as it gets a bit warmer, we could go down to Cotterway. We could stay there for the whole summer. You'd like that, wouldn't you, darling?"

His mind rejected, distastefully, the endearment which he knew had no affection behind it. She was merely staging an act. What act? What for?

"I doubt if I could manage it," he said evenly. "I found the double journey last year very trying, with all the building that has been going on between there and London making the road traffic so much heavier. As a matter of fact, I have been considering selling Cotterway."

"Oh, have you, Blaine?" she asked with interest. "Well, I don't think it's a bad idea. It *is* a long way out, and we don't use

121

it all that much, though I shouldn't have thought you wanted to part with it. You've always been so keen about it, with the garden and all that."

"It costs a lot to keep going, with a permanent staff there and the general up-keep."

"That shouldn't worry you," she laughed. "You must be making simply oodles."

"If one makes oodles, as you call it, nobody is allowed to keep oodles," he said. "The taxation on one's earnings is terrific, as you know yourself," for they had had a good many acrimonious arguments about her inability, or refusal, to be responsible for the tax on her own earnings since these, under our unjust system, were Blaine's responsibility.

"Oh well, if I'm not earning, at least that trouble's over," she said lightly. "If you sell Cotterway, we can have a house in town, a proper house, not this crimpy little flat. We can entertain, give parties and so on, have lots of fun."

"The idea in selling Cotterway would be to cut down expense, not incur more," he said.

"I don't know what all this talk about saving expense is in aid of, now that I've come home like a dutiful little wife, prepared to make a proper home for us," she said pettishly, getting off the arm of his chair and going back to her own.

"This flat is quite sufficient for us, and convenient for me," he said.

"Well, what about my convenience? I don't think it's at all convenient, our guests having to come in at the door of your nursing home and seeing nurses and what not in the hall. I want a house, a big house, a real house," setting her lips into a line he knew well, a line which meant that she knew what she wanted and was determined to get it.

Well, in this instance, she was not going to get it.

"How can you lead the sort of life you outline when you are working?" he asked.

"I'm not working. Not at the moment. In fact, I don't think I'm going to work again. That ought to please you. It's what you've been after ever since we married."

He considered this. It gave him a bad jolt. He realized that he had been reckoning on her ambition to succeed in her job as a main factor towards getting his release. He had had a vague plan of offering to set her up in a theatre of her own, paying the cost of a first production there, as the price of his freedom.

"You surprise me," he said at length. "Are you suggesting that you've got where you wanted to get? Done all you wanted to do?"

"Oh—in a way. I've got tired of it, though. All the pushing and the mean tricks to elbow one out of the way, and the petty jealousy. I don't think perhaps it's worth it. After all, everybody knows I'm Virginia Coley and can go back to the stage when I like, but I'm Lady Belding as well, and," with a smile which would once have beguiled him but which now left him cold, "I think it's time I began to enjoy being that."

He was silent for so long that she became more and more restless.

She had known within the first half-hour of her home-coming that something had changed him. He had not even been parti-cularly glad to have her back, though she had shown him that she was prepared to be 'nice' to him. What had happened whilst she was away? Another woman?

Her eyes narrowed into slits. That wouldn't wash. She was never prepared to give up anything once she had got her hands on it, Blaine least of all.

She had been quite right when she said she had come home prepared to be Lady Belding and not Virginia Coley any more, though she would not have given Blaine, or anyone, the real reason for that.

The truth, and a good many people knew it, including Jos Benner, was that she had not had the great success in the States which she had expected to have, and which she had told Blaine she had had. In fact, she had come so near to being a 'flop' that Benner had not even offered to continue her engagement when the company left Broadway.

She had taken, as Benner told her brusquely, the wrong line with the American public. She had let it be widely known that

Virginia Coley was, in fact, Lady Belding, the wife of the surgeon whose name was known and respected in so many quarters, and particularly in New York itself. As a consequence, she appeared to the public as merely a 'pin-money girl', not a serious actress earning her own living by serious application to her job, and Americans have no use, as a rule, for the 'just for fun' worker in any branch of life. That, and her lack of any real talent, reacted against her, as Benner, with his superior knowledge, had warned her that it would.

She knew too, none better, that it had not been easy for her to get the sort of work she aspired to do in London, and she did not intend to go back to the cabaret shows and the odd weeks here and there, or the not-too-rewarding television and radio commissions she could still get.

So, disappointed and frustrated, bitter against everyone but herself, she had come home resolved to make a splash as Blaine's wife, to become one of the most popular and sought-after of London's hostesses, with her picture in all the papers and illustrated magazines, her doings quoted, her dresses described, possibly even get presented at court and move into a circle to which not even Blaine had yet been admitted.

And now he was talking of expense and economy!

He spoke at last, slowly and carefully, not looking at her.

"I'm sorry, Virginia, that you feel like that about giving up your work," he said, "because I have felt for a long time that that is the real answer to the problem of your happiness, perhaps of the happiness of both of us. I have been thinking a lot about this whilst you have been away, and I have been prepared, am prepared, to do something for you in that respect, either to pay the cost of some production which appeals to you, or even to get you a theatre so that you can be independent of all these people whom in the past you have found rather difficult."

She had sat bolt upright in her chair whilst he had been speaking, her eyes fixed on him, her mind trying to probe his.

"That's rather a surprise, Blaine," she said when he stopped. "What's made you change your mind so suddenly about my work? And what do *you* propose to get out of it, if you do this for me?"

He heard the note in her voice and knew that they had reached the crux of the conversation.

He looked across at her.

"Virginia, you know as well as I do that we have not made a success of things, of our marriage. It was ill-advised. We wanted different things out of it. I cannot see the point of continuing as we are."

"You mean you want me to leave you? Break things up?" she asked sharply.

"Yes. I think we have reached that stage," he said.

"Why? Is there another woman?"

He had known he could not avoid that.

"Yes," was all he said.

"And you suggest paying me off so that you can marry her? Is that it? You want a divorce?"

"Since that is the only way, yes," he said and was silent again.

"Who is she?" demanded Virginia in no uncertain tones.

"That I am not prepared to tell you. I am not having what I suppose you would call an affair with her. I love her and want to marry her, and I am prepared to give you sufficient legal evidence, and there would, of course, be no defence."

"Well!" she said. "I shouldn't have thought that you of all people would have wanted to go in for divorce. It wouldn't do you much good, would it?" with a curling lip that was almost a snarl.

"I don't think it would do me irreparable harm," he said steadily. "Since it would be an undefended case, it need not cause much comment in the newspapers. There would be no unsavoury details. These things can be arranged, I understand."

"You've learnt quite a lot during the last few months, haven't you?" she asked unpleasantly. "Well, Blaine, there's nothing doing."

"You mean you would not be willing to divorce me, Virginia?"

"No. Why should I?"

125

"The only reason I can think of is that you are my wife only in name, and have been for a long time, that you don't enjoy being a wife at all, and that you would be happier free, especially if your career were furthered and assured."

"Are you trying to bribe me, Blaine?" she asked with a sneer of scorn.

"In a way, I suppose I am. I want something which I know would not be distasteful to you, and as I am in a superior position to do so, I am prepared to make it worth your while to give us *both* our freedom."

"Well, I am not prepared to accept it. I have told you that I am giving up my work, a thing you've always been at me to do. I have come home to be your wife, your wife in every way if that is what you want, and that's how it's going to be. You can forget this other woman, whoever she is. *I* am your wife, and that is how things are going to remain."

"I suppose what you mean is that you are Lady Belding, and you are not prepared to surrender that doubtful honour to another woman?" he asked bitterly.

He had not prepared himself for this, so sure that she would never be able to resist the chance to make a bigger name for herself at his expense. He had never reckoned on her wanting to abandon her career. That had been his only weapon, and it had broken off short in, his hand before it had even touched her.

"If you like to put it that way, yes," she said stonily.

"You would hold me, a man who openly admits that he loves another woman, just for that?" he asked.

"Just for that," she agreed. "Now let's drop the subject, Blaine. There's no more to say about it. I have come home prepared for it to be a home for both of us, and that's the way I intend it to be. You can leave me, of course. You can go to this other woman with whom you say your relations are so pure, though, knowing the sort of thing you like, I doubt it. But whatever terms you're on with her, and even if you leave me for her, I shall not divorce you. And if you do leave me, I shall go on living here, in this flat, with your staff knowing all about it, and the patients too—though I doubt if there would be many patients when they knew that, and you'd have to go on coming here, wouldn't you? You see, Blaine, I hold the best cards and I shall know how to play them. Good night. I'm going to bed, and you can come too if you like," throwing him a look as she said the words which infuriated him, a look which he could only have described as of evil triumph.

He sat there for a long time and then, though it was already late and he knew she might have gone to bed, he wanted Anna so desperately that he flung himself out of the house and took a taxi out to Chelsea.

Anna had not gone to bed, but she was preparing to do so when the taxi drew up outside and, acting on a premonition, she went to the window and saw him getting out.

She ran downstairs swiftly to open the door to him.

"Blaine! Is there anything wrong?" she asked, frightened by the look on his face, its greyness and strain. He did not even smile.

"Let me come up for a few minutes, Anna. I know it's late, but I must see you, talk to you, be with you for a little while."

She led the way upstairs, closed the door behind them and went to the cupboard where lately she kept whisky and a syphon for him, knowing that he liked an occasional drink.

She put the bottle and the syphon down on the table beside the chair into which he had flung himself, brought him a glass and watched him pour out a much more generous portion of the spirit than usual and drink it down at a gulp, neat.

Then he rose and took her into his arms and held her closely.

"Oh Anna—Anna—to be with you, to hold you like this, to be with your heavenly peace, with your love. Anna—dearest, dearest."

She let him hold her, her own arms about him, offering him that peace and love in her quietness, her heart aching for him, her mind able to guess a little of what had brought him to her because she felt she had known from the first that there was no future for them but this.

"Is it Virginia?" she asked him very quietly when his arms

127

relaxed a little and he sat in the chair and drew her down with him.

"Yes. I hadn't meant to come to the point so soon. I wanted to wait a few days, but—it just happened. She won't divorce me, Anna. I can't get her to do it. She doesn't want to go back to the stage. That makes all the difference."

"Yes. Yes, I see that it could," she said, and pressed his head against her and held him closely and tried to pour into him her protecting love.

"You sound as if you knew she might refuse, Anna."

"I thought she might," she said very gently. "You see, Blaine, my poor Blaine, from her point of view, why should she, just for our happiness? She wants you herself. Naturally she does."

"My name and what I can earn, yes," he said bitterly. "There's nothing else. There never has been. What I want, what we want, Anna, doesn't matter to her."

"Did you tell her about—me?"

"Not by name, no. I'm not going to bring you into this. I didn't tell her. Only that there is someone else and that I want to marry her. Oh Anna, she's so *hard*, so determined. And now that she wants to give up the stage, what can I do? It isn't only the money. If it were, she could have the lot and I'd start again. I'd make a living for you somehow. But it's the name she wants, and me with it. She wants to go in for entertaining on a big scale, make the name of Lady Belding what she couldn't make of Virginia Coley's. Virginia Coley! Oh Anna, how could I ever have been such a fool, such an idiotic, besotted fool, as to think that I loved her or could ever find happiness with her? And I've brought you to this with me, my darling. I've spoilt your life, taken what some other man should have, your love, you for his wife——"

She closed his lips against the softness of her own.

"No, darling, no," she said. "You haven't spoilt anything for me. You've given me everything, something I should never have known, could never know with any other man. Even if there can never be anything for us but this, perhaps not even this, we've had it, Blaine, our love, the joy of being together, of knowing each other."

"But it isn't enough. You know that as well as I do. We want all of each other, for all our lives. Anna, I can't lose you. I can't! You won't leave me, will you? Promise me you won't leave me."

"No, I won't leave you, Blaine," she said, since she must comfort him, but how was she to bear it? How was either of them to bear it? Seeing each other every day, she under the same roof that covered Virginia so much more closely, so much more intimately?

"I think you ought to go now, Blaine," she said presently, still with that gentle, protective, mother-note in her voice. She seemed so much older than he just now, so much wiser, even so much stronger and more able to face the future.

But then she had not lived, as he had done these past few weeks, with the dream of their belonging for ever.

"Yes," he said, putting her from him reluctantly and getting to his feet. "Yes, I must. I've kept you up too late already. Don't come in in the morning if you don't feel like it. I'll make some excuse. Say you've telephoned."

She managed to laugh a little at that.

"Of course I shall come in," she said. "For one thing, it's the day for the patients' bills."

"Oh, damn the patients, and everything else in this utterly damnable world! Kiss me again, Anna. Tell me you love me and will never give up hope."

"Of course I love you, my darling, and of course I'll never give up hope. How could we go on living without hope?"

But when he had gone, she faced the certainty that there was no hope.

For what reason at all, as she had said, would Virginia give him up?

And things could not go on between herself and Blaine like this, nor for much longer. It was so short a time since he had first told her he loved her, had taken her in his arms and kissed her, and yet already she knew that there was much more to it than that, that neither of them could remain satisfied with this half life, this shadow of the loving they both wanted and needed desperately.

She had no delusions about herself. Loving a man for the first time had revealed her to herself, and she knew that she had all a woman's heritage and capacity for fulfilled love. She wanted Blaine just as he wanted her, and she trembled at the thought of what that satisfaction could be.

She had said she would not leave him, but what else would there be for her to do, if Virginia could not be moved? And in her heart there had been all the time the feeling that such a solution would not be right for Blaine, even if it gave him personal happiness. He was a great man. His skill and courage had made him great. Was it right for such a man to be mixed up in a thing like divorce? His private life the subject of newspaper paragraphs? His photograph there, probably, for all the world to gaze at and speculate unpleasantly about?

No, that sort of thing might not matter with a lesser man, but it was not for Blaine. She knew it in her heart, though she would have married him with utter thankfulness if he had been free.

CHAPTER VIII

It soon became as clear to Blaine as to Anna that things could not continue as they were. Her association with him as his secretary had become a danger to them both. At any moment Virginia might find out, and then in any case Anna would have to go. Blaine knew that she was watching him, waiting to get some clue to the woman who had supplanted her and who was waiting somewhere for Blaine to be free.

Apart from the danger, Virginia's return and her presence in the flat had made what was between Blaine and Anna a furtive thing, a thing of subterfuge and pretence and of constant wariness.

He could not even see her in the evenings often, for Virginia was doing as she had intended, enlarging their circle of acquaintances, adding to its importance, entertaining and being entertained on a scale which kept Blaine constantly at hand, since he would not allow any hint of trouble between him and Virginia to appear openly, a subject for discussion and surmise behind their backs.

He had said no more to Virginia about a divorce, and she behaved as if that conversation had never taken place. His one hope was that she would tire of the social round and feel the urge to return to the stage, but the weeks went by without her showing any sign of it, and during the summer they went down to Cotterway, which he had not after all put up for sale.

"If you want to do some work down there, you could take Miss Mere," suggested Virginia. "It will be a sort of holiday for her as well, and she could be quite useful to me."

"She needs a holiday of her own," said Blaine, thankful that his profession had long ago schooled his face not to betray his thoughts. "I'll speak to her about it. I'm keeping the home as empty as possible whilst we are away, so she can be spared just now."

"I think you ought to go away somewhere, Anna," he said when he talked to her about it. "You need a breath of sea air. Will you let me arrange something for you?"

They were having one of their stolen meetings, stolen with difficulty now, and he had met her on a Saturday afternoon and driven out into the country with her. They were sitting in his car, which he had drawn up where they could look out over a great stretch of open land, with no danger from the quiet lane behind them.

"I should like that," she said, knowing that she must not always frustrate him in his desire to do something for her, anything possible. Also it was very comforting occasionally to be looked after and planned for when all her life she had had to do the planning and the looking after.

"Unless you want to go a long way away, Devonshire or somewhere, may I find somewhere for you too not far from Cotterway?" he asked. "On the coast, but not so far that I cannot come to you sometimes? I shan't be quite so much beset down there as I am in town, and Virginia may let me off the leash now and then," with a bitter edge in his voice.

"Please do what you like about that, Blaine," she said gratefully, and a few days later he told her he had booked a room for her at a small hotel on as quiet and unfrequented part of the coast as he could find.

"The only thing that worries me is whether you'll find it lonely," he said. "I shan't always be able to be with you. I wish I could. I'd love to be able to stay with you there. You know that, don't you?"

She flushed a little but did not avoid his eyes.

"Yes, I know," she said. "That isn't what you mean by this though, is it, Blaine?"

"No. I can't put you into such a position, and that isn't the way I want you. Sometimes I think it might have to come to that, or—parting, Anna, but don't let's think about that yet. You have nothing to fear from me. Don't ever be afraid of me, will you?"

"I don't think I could be," she said simply. "As for my being lonely, I shan't be. I have always had a lot of my own company, and when you can't be with me, I shall be quite happy roaming about on my own."

He took as many opportunities as possible for being with her, and though it meant lies and subterfuges which were nauseating to him, he had no other means of spending the long hours with Anna, sometimes in the car, but walking when they could, swimming together or stretched out in the contentment of each other's companionship on the beach, taking advantage of the grudging hours of sunshine whenever they could.

"I do love the sun," said Anna, stretched on her back in the full glare of it, her eyes closed, her face red with the coming tan.

"Some day I'll take you into it and give you your fill of it, real sunshine for hours on end, and a warm sea in which we can stay all day, evenings when one never even thinks of a coat or wrap, and nights—oh Anna, if we can make it come true!"

If only they could! Every hour they spent together, gathering new experiences for shared memories, made them long for the more complete and perfect companionship denied to them, and when it was nearing the time when she must return, they both knew that their idyll could not last, that they would not remain proof against their passionate need of each other.

Sometimes Anna thought wildly that she would be glad if he left her with no more choice, no chance to resist him, if he took her and made her forever and utterly his own. That would be the end of all this yearning and frustration and the constant fight against themselves.

But she knew he would not. He still hoped that some miracle would set him free to take her openly, before the world, not in the furtive, secret way which was the only one now possible for them.

On the last afternoon of her holiday, which he had contrived to spend with her even though he knew Virginia was becoming suspicious of his frequent absences, Anna voiced her thoughts bravely.

"Blaine, you asked me once not to leave you. I want you to absolve me from the promise I gave you. You must see as I do, my dearest, that we can't go on as we are. We've got to make our lives without each other. I *must* leave you. You know that, don't you?"

It was a wet day, the weather in tune with her sad heart, and he had driven out to a deserted spot along the coast and drawn up the car so that they could watch the stormy sea from its warm shelter.

He covered her hand with his own and was silent for a moment. Then he answered her sadly.

"Yes, I do know it, Anna. I thought we could go on as we were. I've always been hoping things would happen, expecting a miracle, I suppose. There still may be one. I'm not giving up hope. But I realize that in keeping you with me, I'm being unfair to you, putting you in an impossible position. Have you thought about what you want to do, Anna?" his voice despairing but accepting what he knew she must do.

"Not in detail, but I think I want to go into the country, away from London."

"Away from me, you mean?"

"Yes. That would be the wisest thing."

"You don't mean we're never to meet again, Anna?"

"I couldn't bear that," she said in a low voice, "but not often, nor for too long at a time, though I know quite well that I ought to have the courage to say 'never'. I can't, Blaine. Not now. Not yet. I couldn't bear it."

"Nor could I, darling. There would be nothing left to live for. Where would you go?"

"It would depend on what work I could get."

"Work for some other man?"

She had to laugh a little at that, but tenderly and with love. "You're jealous, Blaine!"

"Of course I am. I shall hate this other man, whoever he is." She laughed again.

"There's still so much of the little boy in you, Sir Blaine Belding," she said. "It's one of the things I love in you," on a softer note.

"And the other things, Anna?"

She gazed out at the sea.

"Oh—so many. Your brain, of course, and your clever hands, your courage, your kindness, the way you speak to children and to animals, all you are, yourself, Blaine, all the things that make you *you*."

He lifted her hand to his lips.

"You think too well of me, Anna, but I want you to. I don't want you to know my littleness, my bad temper over trifles, my impatience when I don't get my own way, my—my overbearing attitude!" breaking off with a smile because he knew he had the reputation for that attitude, Double B. "Oh Anna, how am I going to get on without you? Live without you?"

They turned to each blindly and were gripped in a close embrace, love and grief, renunciation, acceptance in their kiss.

After she had gone back to London, he was restless and cut his own stay at Cotterway short, with the always easy excuse of a consultation, and in a few days Virginia followed him.

She was sweetness itself to him at this time, consulting him prettily even when he knew she would take her own course whatever he said, asking his opinion on this and that, and spending—always spending.

He knew she was willing to resume normal married life with him, making it quite plain, leaving her door open when she went to bed before him, wandering in and out of his room whilst he was dressing, playing the loving wife in so far as his cold withdrawal from her least touch would allow her to do. He had no desire for her at all and showed it, but she let even the most obvious slights pass off her as if she had never even noticed them. She was a determined woman. He wondered how he could ever have thought of her as sweet and amenable and yielding.

Anna soon found herself a new job and told him about it.

"In Dorset?" he asked with a frown. "Why must you go so far away?"

"It isn't all that far, but isn't it better, Blaine?"

"I suppose so."

It was with an estate agent in a small country town ten miles from the coast, and she felt that, though she knew nothing of that kind of work, it was work that would appeal to her.

"I've always been interested in houses," she said, "and quite a good part of Mr. Trimwell's job is with big houses which have to be cut up, or modernized and he is willing to teach me. I'm going to learn to drive a car as well, so that I can take clients to see houses if necessary."

"I shan't like the thought of you driving about in a car," he said with a frown, but she smiled away his objections and did everything in her power to see that her successor, a middle-aged woman, understood the many small points of her job.

Virginia was surprised though only mildly interested at Anna's departure.

"Why does she want to leave you?" she asked when Blaine told her. "Don't you pay her enough, or what?"

She had the power, and knew she had it, to prick him into unreasonable irritation in a moment. Her question did so now, and she saw his eyes narrow and his lips compress into a frown of anger.

"Of course I do. She's invaluable," he said.

"Then why is she leaving? I thought she was devoted to you. I've seen her looking at you as if she'd like to hop into bed with you."

"Don't be ridiculous, Virginia," he said, too hotly. "Miss Mere is not that type of girl at all."

"No? Well, you should know, I suppose," said Virginia meaningly, though actually she had no such thoughts about Anna and was merely trying to provoke him. "These old maids, though, do get ideas, especially about men like you. Is that why she's leaving? To take her pure soul out of your reach? Have you been making a pass at her, by any chance?"

He was insanely angry and showed it, to her delight.

"Really, Virginia, your mind is like a sewer," he said. "Please don't try to bespatter anyone like Miss Mere with its filth, whatever you may think of me," and he left her before he could be goaded into saying anything more.

Virginia looked after him reflectively.

She had spoken idly and without any real thought, and now pondered his unexpected reaction to her words. It would be funny, she thought, if there were anything in it, if mouse-like little Miss Mere really did cherish a hopeless passion for Blaine so that he, discovering it, had decided that she must go in order to save him embarrassment! That was the sort of thing he would do, of course. He would not risk any entanglement with anyone like that.

She wondered again about that other woman in his life, who she was, what she was like. A beautiful woman, of course, for had not she herself caught Blaine by her beauty? And young, since that was the way he liked them, again thinking of herself.

But who? A patient? That might be quite amusing, but dangerous, of course, for Blaine. A doctor might conduct his little affairs without the too great interest of the British Medical Association, but only if the partner in the affair were not a patient. Then it might step in with all its majesty and power and —phut! Exit the doctor!

No, it was almost certainly not a patient. But who?

Virginia did not for a moment believe that the affair was as pure as Blaine had made out. She felt she knew him, and that the man who had tried so desperately to make her a partner in that beastly business of married life would not have lived all this this time as a celibate.

Still, what did she care what he did, so long as he kept it out of the public eye? She herself possessed him in the only way she wanted him, and no other woman was going to get that!

She dismissed from her mind all thought of the departing Miss Mere.

Anna settled down more quickly than she had anticipated at Kenborne.

Mr. Trimwell was quite a character, well known for his interest in and exhaustive knowledge of the neighbourhood and its considerable history.

He knew every house for miles around, knew who had built it and when and for whom, knew the various people who had lived in it and what each had done to the structure, the plumbing and even the decoration. He could have drawn an accurate plan of any of them, and he entertained Anna with his dry humour about many past and present situations, a thin little man with a drooping moustache, a grey, dusty little man who lived in his books and was only too glad to relegate to his new assistant anything she would take on, his business as a house and estate agent only the rather resented and necessary means of livelihood.

To Anna, therefore, came all sorts of people, young people looking desperately for somewhere to live, older people trying to make their too-large houses fit themselves into the new way of life, over-taxed and servantless and, in many cases, needing to make their houses earn money for them instead of swallowing up what they had.

She developed a flair for the conversion of such houses into smaller and more convenient units and Mr. Trimwell, who, she discovered had in his earlier days passed his examinations as an architect, could help her with his knowledge of what could and what could not be done in the way of removing or building walls, and replacing plumbing.

She missed Blaine badly, but her new job was interesting and demanding, and she threw all her energies into it and tried ruthlessly to make it fill her life.

She had found comfortable lodgings with the village school-mistress, a capable middle-aged woman who was glad to let two of the rooms in her cottage to someone who did not mind being left alone, with a dog, a cat and the chickens to look after, at such times in the school holidays as Miss Balchin went away. In the little sitting-room given over to her exclusive use, Anna worked at her plans and read exhaustively, chiefly books on architecture and house design lent her by Mr. Trimwell, and she became knowledgeable not only about the houses, many of them historic in their associations, but also of the people who lived in them.

She entered into the village life and found it both absorbing and entertaining, joining the Women's Institute and the dramatic and musical and debating societies which flourish so successfully in places where people still have to find or make their own amusements. It was pleasant to find herself regarded as an asset to the village, and she realized with thankfulness that, though she would never forget or cease to miss Blaine, she was re-making her life and finding a quiet happiness in doing so.

She wrote to him as she had promised to do, though they were not the love-letters she received in reply, but a record of her doings, of the small happenings which made up her life, of the people she met, though she knew from his replies that he found them unsatisfactory and unsatisfying. But it was the only way. She would not let his life be spoilt by the continued belief that she could have a place in it, and he must by now realize what she had realized in the first place, that Virginia would not let him go and that unless he were free to marry her, Anna, he must let her go out of his life.

It was their destiny. They must both accept it.

But there were times when her longing for him seemed unbearable, and she would write to him desperately, unreservedly, tell him of her hunger for the sound of his voice, the touch of his hand, for the kisses which had awakened her to the knowledge of herself as a loving, responsive woman. In the morning she tore the letter into pieces. Again, it was the only way.

Meantime Blaine was becoming more irritable and hard to please, as his patients, and even more his long-suffering staff and associates, discovered.

Miss Dove watched him with an anxious solicitude she did not venture to express. With his marriage, their former companionable relationship had ended, and she could not renew it. He was Sir Blaine and she Matron even when they were alone, nor did he ever go into her private sitting-room for one of the old friendly gossips. She had her own ideas about Anna Mere. What she suspected, but Virginia did not, was that any feeling Anna might have had for him was reciprocated, and her heart was both sore and angry that anything there might have been between them had had to end in their parting.

Anna was, she felt, the perfect partner for him. Miss Dove

had no thought of the secretary's social inferiority to him, for she knew he was not made that way. Anna was the woman he needed, gentle, kind, unselfish and, she felt, loving and capable of loving much. With a woman such as Anna for his wife, his private and personal life might have been completely satisfied.

And he had had to tie himself up to Virginia Coley!

Miss Dove's mind was robust about that marriage. Why did he not face whatever unpleasantness, even scandal, it might entail, and get rid of Virginia so that he could marry Anna Mere? It ought to be possible. Surely Virginia was the sort to be committing all sorts of indiscretions, and it was obvious to Miss Dove's mind, which knew Blaine so well, that there was nothing substantial between him and his wife, however the ill-starred marriage might have started.

She longed to say to him the time-honoured 'I told you so', but knew she could not, nor ever would. Blaine must know for himself the mistake he had made in believing that there was anything in Virginia beyond her glamorous loveliness, which she decked out in all the glory of Solomon—at his expense, of course!

And then there began a train of circumstances so cunningly dove-tailed into one another, so utterly circumstantial, that it seemed as if some malevolent spirit had taken Blaine Belding's life into its power and was determined to leave nothing of it untwisted and intact.

It began with the epidemic of influenza which was sweeping the country with the November fogs, and which found its way into the home itself.

Several of the nurses went down with it, and then Miss Dove herself, Miss Dove who had never before, in Blaine's knowledge of her, had a day's illness.

"You've got to stay there, Emma," Blaine told her when he learned that she was struggling against the high temperature which was an early symptom of the complaint. He had ordered her to bed, and the fact that she had gone there showed him, quite apart from the thermometer, that she was really ill. He had come to her room in the staff quarters, and was standing by her bed, something of the old affection in his eyes and his use of her name.

"How can I?" she asked wearily. "With three of the nurses down, and now Dr. Murphy? And before I came to bed, Sister Grant was looking like death but would not give in. I must get up."

"And spread the thing still further? Well, you can't, and that's the voice of your boss as well as your doctor. What makes you think that you are indispensable?" with a smile. "Nobody is, not even the great Double B himself. Though with half the nursing staffs of the hospitals down with it, or crawling about with it, I can't afford to get it myself and I seem to be turning back into a G.P. just now. You stay there, Emma, and that's an order. Understand?"

She nodded and closed her eyes, knowing that she was too ill to do anything else.

He went on to Dr. Murphy, who had now moved into the house to be conveniently on call, the other doctor having his own home elsewhere.

"I'm frightfully sorry, sir," said Murphy. "It's going to be deucedly inconvenient, I know, but perhaps a couple of days will be enough."

"Well, we'll see. No sense in being about for the moment," said Blaine. "Luckily we're not full up, and I shall try to send as many as possible out."

He had recently decided to give up his nursing home. It was no longer necessary for him to augment his income in this way, and it was an inconvenience, especially just now. Also he wanted to get away from the flat and take the house for which Virginia was always clamouring. He had no thought of obliging her in this matter, but felt that in a house he could get farther away from her and her constant stream of noisy guests. Also he was in a mood to welcome any change in his way of life, having the obscure feeling that some change, whatever it might be, might conceivably point the way to his eventual freedom to marry Anna.

Though he managed to persuade several of his patients to

return to their homes, there were one or two he could not dislodge.

One of them, of course, had to be the immoveable Mrs. Murrayne, who said blithely that she was not in the least afraid of infection, and, anyway, were there any better hands than Sir Blaine's in which she could be if she did catch the thing?

"I'm not a medical practitioner, Mrs. Murrayne," he told her acidly, "but a surgeon and consultant."

"I know, but you wouldn't let me lie here and *die,* would you, Sir Blaine?" she asked him with hideous archness, and there she stayed.

Another patient who would not move was a Mrs. Frey, the young and attractive wife of an elderly man, who adored her jealously but did not know at all how to cope with her vagaries and discontentment and was mortally afraid for her even to speak to another man.

She had come into the nursing home, on Blaine's advice, for a minor operation, from which she had now completely recovered, and there was no reason at all why she should not go back to her home and to normal life.

No reason except that she was hopelessly in love with Blaine.

He was not a vain man, and he had not realized it even when it had become apparent to the nurses and was the subject of sardonic amusement to them, but lately Blaine himself had become uncomfortably aware of it and was the more anxious that she should go. He blamed himself because at first, liking her gaiety and her witty, if not always kind, tongue, he had stayed in her room to chat with her after his professional visit was over.

Some of the other patients were aware of young Mrs. Frey's attachment to him, notably Mrs. Murrayne, whose room was opposite Mrs. Frey's, and who took a note of the time when she heard the door open and close, and had even popped out of bed and crossed the passage to listen at the door, annoyed to hear the talk and laughter which she would have liked to have going on in her own room. She herself was never able to detain him for even a minute after she had detailed her symptoms and her sufferings *ad nauseam.*

Her jealousy was fed by gossips she had with a new young nurse who had been taken on when the regular staff started to go down with influenza, a girl whom in the normal way, Miss Dove would never have engaged, considering her flighty and indiscreet. Nurse Holm liked to stay and chatter with the patients, and Mrs. Murrayne was always ready for a gossip, especially if Blaine were one of the subjects.

"He's in with *her* again," Holm said on the evening on which Miss Dove and Dr. Murphy had both taken to their beds. "I can't think what he sees in her."

Mrs. Murrayne gave a snort.

"My dear, what does a man usually see in a pretty girl?" she asked. "I suppose she is pretty?"

"Oh yes, very. Not like Lady Belding, of course, but then she's his wife! Have you had your temperature taken lately, by the way?"

"No, but it doesn't matter. Just put it down at normal. It always is," and Nurse Holm made the requisite marks on the chart and replaced it. "I'd like to know just what does go on in there, all that talking and laughing. Not quite decent, to my mind. After all, he is her doctor and she a patient. I shouldn't like him to treat *me* like that," though she longed for him to do so.

When he left Louise Frey's room, unavoidably he tapped at Mrs. Murrayne's door and came in. Now that Dr. Murphy was not able to do the usual round, Blaine had undertaken it. Dr. Brown could not do day and night as well, and he had gone home.

"Well?" he asked cheerfully. "How's the head?"

She regaled him with the usual list of her sufferings, to which he gave little attention, knowing them so well, and, inflamed by her visions of what might have been going on in the room across the passage, she lost her head.

"Do you think I don't know what's going on over there?" she almost shrieked. "You and that girl? Everybody in the place must know, with the hours you spend with her, talking and laughing. Doctor's visits indeed! I wonder you're not ashamed."

She had abandoned all the superficial refinement which she had worked to acquire with her husband's money and was showing herself for what she was, a common and uninhibited woman, beside herself with rage and jealousy.

"Mrs. Murrayne, calm yourself," said Blaine, his cold voice cutting across hers like tempered steel. "I will send you a sedative, and then you had better make your arrangements to leave at once."

"I can't. I'm ill. You know I'm ill," she babbled.

"If you are so ill that you no longer know what you are saying, which I think must be the case, then this is not the right place for you, Mrs. Murrayne," he said firmly. "I will send a nurse to you," and he turned his back on her and left her, feeling revolted and sick.

As a brain specialist, he had seen distraught women before and knew how to deal with them, but there was nothing the matter with Mrs. Murrayne, and it was quite certain that she must leave at once. It had been a disgusting performance, but he had at the time no inkling of just what the episode might mean for him.

He went to the door and opened it.

"Nurse!" he called. "Oh, Nurse Holm, Mrs. Murrayne's head seems to be troubling her. Give her a sedative, at once please. The usual bromide mixture we use here."

"Yes, Sir Blaine," said the girl, looking slightly scared and aware of a crisis of some sort.

He went up to his flat, in no mood at the moment for other patients, whom he would see later. That demented woman! Well, that was the end of *her*. He would insist on her husband taking her away the next day, and as he now fully intended to give up the nursing home, he need not see her again.

But as he went, he thought of Louise Frey. Perhaps he had been rather indiscreet in the amount of time he had been spending with her, finding her a relief from his other women patients, and now that he had very strong suspicions that she was entertaining unwholesome thoughts about him he would do his best to get rid of her as well. Heavens, what a mess women could make of a man's life! And he certainly wanted nothing of any of them—except Anna, his beloved, lost Anna.

He sat in his room with his head in his hands, her last letter on the table beside him. He had gone to it for comfort, but found none. Just a friendly, amusing letter which anyone might have written to him. No word of love, nor even of missing him. Was she forgetting him? Managing to do without him as he felt he could never do without her? If only he could go to her, be with her for even an hour, listen to her quiet voice, look into the sweet serenity of her eyes, know that here lay the one thing he wanted and had—her love.

But she had asked him not to come, and he had respected that urgent request, for her sake, not for his own. As far as he was concerned, he would not have let her go.

Presently he finished his late visits, but without going into either Mrs. Murrayne's or Louise Frey's room, and nodded good night to Nurse Holm, who felt a little nervous, if elated, at being on duty without a sister.

"There are only a few patients now, Nurse," said Blaine, "and none of them likely to need much attention—except possibly Mr. Ewing, who seems restless and still suffering from post-operative shock. Keep a close eye on him, and if you are at all worried about him, ring my bell and I'll come down. No need to use the telephone. If I hear the bell, I'll come down."

"Yes, Sir Blaine," she said. "Good night."

He sat up reading for a long time, and went to bed to fall at once into a sleep from which the violent ringing of his bell awakened him.

'That'll be Ewing,' he thought with a frown, getting out of bed and pulling on his dressing-gown. 'Don't suppose there's anything seriously wrong, but that little nurse is rather a scatter-brain. Good job when Emma's about again,' because, of course, under normal conditions, the call would have gone first for Miss Dove, who would never call him except in a case of dire necessity and if the house doctor could not deal with it.

But when he reached the lower floor, he found that it was not Mr. Ewing who needed him.

"I'm terribly sorry, Sir Blaine, but it's Mrs. Frey," said Nurse Holm. "She simply insisted on my ringing for you. I couldn't quiet her, and she won't tell me what's wrong except that she says she is in pain."

"Really, Nurse!" said Blaine, thoroughly annoyed. "You know there's nothing wrong with Mrs. Frey and no real reason why she should be here at all," but since he had been called up, he went to the door of Mrs. Frey's room, tapped at it and went in.

"All right, Nurse," he said as he did so. "I'll call you if I want you," which he realized at once had been a mistake, for when he got near the bed, Mrs. Frey launched herself upon him bodily, flinging herself from the bed on which she had been lying in a trembling heap, and into his arms.

"You've come! I said you'd come," she said, and now the trembling ceased and he knew it had been merely pretence. "Oh, Blaine, I've wanted you so. I couldn't sleep for thinking about you and wanting you. Hold me tighter. Kiss me. Kiss me, Blaine, darling Blaine!"

He was completely nonplussed. Nothing like this had come into his experience before, and he had already had one small dose of it from Mrs. Murrayne. These neurotic women!

"Come now, Mrs. Frey," he said, trying to force apart the hands locked about his neck and to avoid by twisting his head the frantic pressure of her lips. "What is all this nonsense? We can't have this sort of thing going on."

"Don't talk to me as if I were a child!" she cried, still holding him in a close grip, try as he might to escape from it. "I'm not a child, and I love you—love you—love you. Love me a little, Blaine! Only love me!"

He managed at last to drag her clinging hands from him, held them firmly in his own and pushed her towards the bed.

"This simply cannot go on, Mrs. Frey," he said sternly. "Get back into bed and behave yourself, or I shall have to send for your husband."

"That old man! What good do you think he is? What do you think he can do? It's you I want, Blaine. Only you!" and she would have got him into her arms again if he had released her hands.

He wished with all his might that he had not sent the nurse away, though he would not have relished her as a witness to this disgraceful scene, with her perky little face and lively, curious eyes.

Somehow he had to control this hysterical woman himself.

He managed to get her into bed, pushed her arms firmly under the bedclothes and tucked them in tightly. He would have liked to give her a good slap, which was what she needed.

"Now," he said, "are you going to behave yourself? Such a disgraceful scene!"

She was somewhat subdued now and lay there looking up at him with big, soulful eyes.

"All right. I will, if you'll stay here a little while," she said, and rather than risk a repeat performance, he pulled up a chair and sat down by the bed, and began to talk to her in a quiet, natural voice about other things, anything that came into his head which was not concerned with themselves.

He knew, of course, what was the matter with her, a young, exuberant woman married to an old man, who could not interest or satisfy her. He had seen it too many times not to know the signs, nor was there any answer to the problem of Louise Frey— unless, of course, she took a lover, which undoubtedly she would do eventually, but it would not be Blaine Belding.

He sat with her for about half an hour, wanting to make sure that she would not try a repeat performance after he had gone. Then, as she seemed calm and quiet, he rose to go.

"Now get some sleep," he told her with a professional smile. "Nurse will give you something to help you if you want it, but I think you could sleep without it, don't you?"

"I'll try," she said in a small, dull voice.

"That's right. And in the morning we'll see about your going home," he said cheerfully. "I shouldn't have the light on, if I were you," and he bent over her to press the light-switch above her head.

He had never been more mistaken in his life than when he

147

believed she was now calm and quiet, for in an instant her arms had shot up and fastened about him, dragging him down to her, and forcing his lips against hers in mad, wild kisses, and for all his superior strength, he could not get away from her, caught in that position, and as he struggled to stand upright, the mat beneath his feet shot across the polished floor and sent him sprawling fully across the bed.

"Oh, I love you. I love you so! Blaine—darling Blaine!" she cried wildly.

And it was at that precise moment that the door was flung wide, and Mrs. Murrayne appeared, an unlovely sight with a skittish cap askew on her curling-pinned head, her face shining with grease, a dressing-gown clutched about her, her eyes ablaze with angry satisfaction.

"I thought so!" she cried loudly, and at the sound of her voice, Louise Frey let her arms drop from their hold, and Blaine struggled to his feet, angrily aware of the utter humiliation of his position.

"I knew what was going on between you two," said Mrs. Murrayne, "and now I've seen it with my own eyes. Disgusting! But don't let *me* spoil your fun!" and she turned and marched out of the room again and banged noisily into her own.

Nurse Holm, who had heard the sound of the furiously opened doors, had come hurrying along the passage just in time to see Blaine struggling to his feet from his prone position on the bed, and she stood with her eyes wide and her mouth open, a foolish and utterly dumbfounded expression on her face whilst Mrs. Murrayne pushed past her.

A moment later Mrs. Murrayne's door came open again.

"Nurse!" she cried. "Nurse Holm! Come here. You saw what was happening? That disgusting exhibition? I told you. I told you what was going on. Now you know!" and she banged the door shut again, leaving the nurse in the passage not knowing what to do.

Blaine spoke curtly to Louise Frey, who was now sitting up in bed, a frightened look on her face, but beneath the fear, excitement and even pleasure.

"You must leave in the morning," he said. "Let your husband know. Nurse Holm, go back to your duties. There is nothing to do for Mrs. Frey," and he stalked away, going first to Mr. Ewing's room to make sure that all the noise had not disturbed him, as it must have disturbed other patients.

He was furiously angry. How could he have permitted himself to be drawn into such a disgusting situation? He knew what sort of woman Mrs. Frey was, and should have had more sense than to go to her on the mere word of an inexperienced nurse. The administration by her of a sedative would have put matters right without his going to the woman at all.

And Mrs. Murrayne!

He felt humiliated and unclean, glad that he had decided to get rid of the lot of them.

Well, both these women with their unhealthy minds and unsatisfied bodies would be going out of the house first thing in the morning, and that would be the end of it.

But it most definitely was not the end of it.

CHAPTER IX

ANNA was sitting at her table with books and papers spread in front of her, busy with a plan for splitting into two separate dwellings one of the large, unsaleable houses in the district, when she heard the knock at the front door of the cottage.

George, the red setter, gathered together all his sprawling limbs from before the fire and stalked towards the door, whilst Bing, the black and white cat (so called because of his melodious voice in the night hours), dislodged from his position between George's front paws, seized the opportunity to get pride of place on the hearth-rug, and Anna, with a little sigh at the interruption, went to open the door.

"Blaine!" she cried, with a rush of pleased surprise.

But there was no smile on his face. He looked grey and tired, and there was an expression in his eyes which she had never seen before, nor ever imagined she would see, a defeated, exhausted look.

'Something's gone badly wrong,' was her first thought. 'One of those terrible operations?'

"May I come in, Anna?" he asked dully. "I had to see you. I had to come to you."

"Of course," she said quietly. "Come in, my dear. In here," eading the way back to her comfortable little sitting-room.

She was glad that this was one of the occasions when Miss Balchin was away. It was very late, nearly midnight, and it might have been difficult to explain such a late call from someone strange to the village.

He walked, almost stumbled, into the room and dropped into a chair by the side of the fire and sat there, his hands gripping its arms, his eyes staring in front of him with that disturbing expression in them.

"Blaine, what is it, dear?" she asked, wishing she had something to give him to drink, for he looked badly in need of it. "What can I get you?"

"Nothing. I didn't want anything but you. Come here, Anna. Come to me. Let me feel that there's at least one sane person in the world!" and he lifted one hand from the chair and caught her own in it and held on to it as a drowning man clings to a spar.

She gave the friendly, investigating George a little push out of the way, and dropped on her knees beside the chair and put her arms about the man who sat there.

"Tell me if you can bear to, my darling," she said. "Or just sit there and we'll be quiet together."

"Thank you. Thank you for your blessed comfort, Anna," he said, and after a time began to speak, haltingly and almost unintelligibly at first but presently with more coherence so that, horrified, she could piece together what he was saying.

It appeared that following the scene with Louise Frey, Mrs. Murrayne, jealous and vindictive, had taken upon herself the quite gratuitous task of waylaying and informing Archie Frey, when he came to fetch his wife, just what had taken place the night before, according to her own interpretation of it, and had insisted on having Nurse Holm, who had gone off duty by then, recalled as a certifying witness.

Mr. Frey, bewildered and angry but inclined at first to disbelieve the jargoned statements of Mrs. Murrayne, herself dressed and ready to leave, had turned to his wife for a refutation of them when, to his dismay, Louise began to simper and look coy, and did not deny the accusations being made against her and against Sir Blaine Belding.

Louise had had time to reflect on the scene of the midnight hours, and to wonder what there was, if anything, that she could get out of it.

Accustomed during most of her twenty-four years to the flattery and admiration of men, and believing that she could turn any of them round her little finger, she did not accept Blaine's refusal of her advances as necessarily final. She had timed them badly, that was all. She ought to have waited until she was back in her own home, and she could get him to herself there, ostensibly for a professional visit and making sure that her husband was not around, nor likely to be.

All she had really meant to do by that half-admission that what Mrs. Murrayne was saying was true, was to establish between herself and Sir Blaine something which might compel him to see her again, to have a shared spot of trouble in which both were on the same side.

Now, however, she saw to her consternation that things would not go quite that way, for Archie was not only jealous and angry, but was preparing to do something about it. His questions, to herself, to Nurse Holm, to that dreadful Mrs. Murrayne, were pointed and aggressive, and he insisted on remaining in the house until Sir Blaine himself had returned to it and become available.

The sister, appalled by the situation, of which she had been apprised when Nurse Holm had come off duty, could do nothing about it but put the Freys into his consulting room, since she could not risk their going on with their acrimonious discussion in the presence of any patient who might come by appointment to wait for the doctor.

Louise was frightened at the turn events were taking, for Archie was adopting an attitude which she had not for a moment imagined he would adopt, and was talking furiously about divorce.

Since she had allowed him to assume that there *had* been something not innocent in the scene of the night before, and that Sir Blaine had been a party to a guilty association between them, she did not see how she could at once retract what she had said or allowed him to think, if she wanted to preserve any self-respect, and when she made a tentative attempt to do so, he did not believe her.

"I always thought you were a hussy at heart," he told her, "and now I know, and it's no good you trying to say now that nothing happened, because I know it did. That woman, whatever her silly name is, *saw* you at it, and when I first asked you about it, you didn't deny it, so it's no use you doing it now.

Well, I've finished with you, Louise, and the sooner you know it, and he knows it, the better. I'm going to divorce you, and I've got enough evidence, so he can put that in his pipe and smoke it, and you can shut up. The wider you open your mouth, the more you put your foot into it."

Louise sat in silent thought, thought that was at first alarmed, but gradually excited. If Archie could, and did, bring a divorce case against her, citing Sir Blaine Belding, and if he won it, there would be nothing for Lady Belding to do but bring a like case against her husband, and then Blaine would have to marry her, Louise.

She would be Sir Blaine Belding's wife—Lady Belding!

It was a deliriously exciting thought, something which she had never imagined could happen to her. She had married Archie for his money, but when she married Blaine, it would be for himself and his title as well!

If Archie won his case.

Then he must win it. She must see to that, and she could see to it by the simple method of not denying Archie's accusation, backed up as it would be by Mrs. Murrayne, and the nurse.

That barmy old woman! Louise was ready to bet she had not thought of *that* when for some unknown reason she had made her attack on Blaine! Probably tried it on herself, she thought shrewdly, and hadn't had any luck!

So by the time Blaine arrived back to keep his appointments, it was to find an apologetic, evasive sister explaining inadequately why the Freys were in his consulting room, that holy of holies, and why Mrs. Murrayne, her husband in attendance, was still there when she should have departed before his return.

Most of this, though not the motive which was actuating Louise Frey in her extraordinary explanation of what had happened in the night, Blaine was able, gradually and painfully, to tell Anna, and when he had finished, she held him closely, his head pressed against her breast, her eyes looking out despairingly over his head.

She knew, none better, what this would mean to him, if

indeed this Mr. Frey brought the threatened divorce action against his wife.

"You see," he said jerkily after a long silence between them, "it isn't only the divorce, which will be so utterly beastly, and with this woman insisting that I—I—took advantage of her like that. She was a patient, under my own roof, and—there's the B.M.A. You know what line they'll take. There could be only one."

"But, Blaine darling, no one—*no one*—could believe that you would do such a thing," said Anna, deeply distressed for him.

"With Mrs. Frey insisting that I did, and with Mrs. Murrayne describing in detail what she saw, and adding to it whatever she surmised? Saying that I had been in the room half an hour or more at that time of night, and in my pyjamas—and Nurse Holm verifying what they both saw? That woman in my arms, kissing and screaming out all sorts of rubbish about loving me? And, believe it or not, Mrs. Murrayne says I tried it on with her!"

Anna had to laugh softly at that.

"Well, if she persists in that, it might do you a lot of good," she said, "for who in their right senses would believe that? Blaine—Virginia knows, of course?" she added diffidently.

"Oh yes. She had to know."

"And what does she think about it? She must know it isn't true."

"How can one be sure what Virginia thinks about anything?" he asked bitterly. "Says she doesn't believe it, and will stand by me—for what that is worth. But I'm not at all sure that she doesn't believe it, Anna. The look on her face, the way she spoke—oh hell, what an utterly impossible and degrading *mess*! I had to come to you, Anna. I had to see you. I just got into the car and drove down here like a madman."

"You drove down, Blaine?" she asked, shocked. She had not heard the car drive up. He had, in fact, left it further down the lane and come on foot to find the house. "All that way, and in that state? You might have had an accident."

"That would probably have been the best way out, if the

154

accident were bad enough," he said shortly. "No such luck! The devil looks after his own, they say."

"Don't talk like that, Blaine. You're of far too much value to the world."

"And what value shall I be if the B.M.A. has me struck off?"

"Don't think of that too much, darling. I can't believe that this dreadful thing will ever happen, that Mr. Frey really will bring this action. He's just saying it to frighten his wife. She's probably made him jealous before."

"Yes, no doubt, but don't forget that in this case she's not denying it! She's prepared to state in court, and under oath, that I made her my mistress," he said in grim despair. "What on earth for? Does she *want* to be divorced?"

"I should say she has in her mind the prospect of marrying you, Blaine," said Anna slowly and quietly. "Might she not conclude that Virginia would divorce you, and that you would be bound to marry her? Would you, Blaine?" painfully.

"Good heavens, are *you* asking me that? If I were free (and it's the only saving thing that might come out of all this mess), there's only one woman in the world I'd marry. You know that!"

"Even if you were the co-respondent in the case of this Mrs. Frey, and her husband did win his case?"

"Nothing in this world would ever make me marry Louise Frey, nor any other woman on earth but you, Anna. You must know that. Oh, my little heart, I could almost welcome this business if it meant that I should be free to do that."

She shook her head, but her eyes were sweet with gratitude for his love.

"No, dear. No, Blaine," she said. "You wouldn't welcome it, even for that, if it meant giving up your profession, not being yourself any more. You couldn't be happy, even with me. I know it. It's why I left you, so that you could go on being yourself and in no danger from what we mean to each other."

He did not at once reply, and she knew he was aware of the truth of what she had said, and when she spoke again, it was with a change of subject and tone.

"I'm going to get you something to eat," she said, getting up from the floor, where all the time she had been sitting, close to him. "You must need it after that journey, and you probably didn't have any dinner, going through all this. Can you do with something eggy? It'll be quicker. Then you ought to have a rest before you go back. You can lie down on my bed, or I can make you comfortable on the couch here, if you can cope with George and Bing, who make this room their headquarters, I'm afraid."

She busied herself with housewifely care of him, glad of even so little to do for him, and had the satisfaction of seeing him make a reasonably good meal of an omelet and some stewed fruit and cream, with coffee made in her own percolator to follow.

"Are you in the house alone, Anna?" he asked, realizing that he had neither seen nor heard anybody else about.

"For tonight I am," she said. "Miss Balchin has gone to see some friends and is staying the night. Perhaps a good thing! She'd probably be horrified at my entertaining a stranger, a *man*, at such an hour!" with a laugh. "I wish you could see her, Blaine. She's quite a character, all square and presenting a challenging front to the four winds of heaven. You know the sort? Miss Balchin against the world, and doesn't care who knows it! And her name always gives me private amusement, for if there's anything she hasn't got, it's a bald chin! I long to tell her about depilatory wax, but I'd never dare. She doesn't even use powder, but she's salt of the earth, the sort the world can't do without."

"I hardly think it right of her to leave you alone here at night though," he demurred.

She laughed and kissed the top of his head as she passed his chair to get him some more coffee.

"I'm so very safe," she said, "but I like you to think I'm not. Will you have another cup, darling, or have your rest now? Here or upstairs? It's warmer in here."

"Will you go to bed yourself if I do?"

"Yes," she promised, and when they had taken George out for his last short run, and left the window open so that Bing could go on his nightly prowl in search of love if he felt like it, she gave him some cushions and a rug, kissed him and went up to her room, promising that she would call him so that he could leave before the village was properly awake and able to take notice.

She could not sleep, tingling with the awareness of his near presence, there in the room below her which was, in effect, her own, impressing the memory of himself on things that would surely always retain it so that after he had gone, she might still see him there.

She was acutely distressed on his behalf, able to realize fully the probable result if he were to be cited in such a divorce case, with that unspeakable Louise Frey not attempting to help him, making it, in fact, fairly certain that her husband's petition would be granted. It was an unspeakable, utterly unjust position for Blaine to be placed in, and she was anguished for him by her well-founded imagination of what it would mean to him if he defended the case, as he said he would, when Louise Frey refused to do so.

She heard him moving about in the room below and knew that he. like herself, was unable to sleep, and after a time she put on a dressing-gown and went down.

He was sitting in front of the fire, with George's head and front paws sprawling across his knees. Bing had departed on his own affairs.

"Blaine, isn't there anything at all I can get you?" she asked anxiously. "I'm afraid I've only got aspirin."

"The woman's panacea for all ills," he said with a tired smile. "No, darling, thank you. I don't think aspirin would do much for me. Don't go though, Anna. Come and talk to me, or listen to me if you can bear any more. Stay with me, anyway, will you?" and he removed George from his knees and Anna came to sit there instead, her head on his shoulder, her whole mind willing itself to give him whatever comfort was possible, little enough, as she knew.

But gradually, in the silence and the warmth of the fire, which gave them their only light, in the awareness of each other's bodies, their minds ceased for a little while to try to bear their

157

burden and he held her closely and presently she lifted her face and their lips met.

"Blaine, I love you so much," she said.

"Thank God, my darling, I know you do. As I love you. As I love you and—most desperately want you, Anna."

She heard the tremor in his voice, felt the quickening of his heartbeats, knew that it was as a man who needed the woman he loved that he held her now, and resolution came to her. It was all she could do for him, and perhaps it would give him, if not peace, at least a respite from all that lay so heavily and inexorably on his mind.

She turned a little in his arms.

"Blaine, why not?" she whispered. "I'm just as much a woman as you are a man, and I—love you with all my heart."

His arms tightened about her in a convulsive gesture. He could not mistake her meaning or intention. Then they relaxed a little and he held his head back so that he could look into her eyes. They were clear and steadfast, all her sweet and loving soul in them.

"You won't ever regret it, Anna?" he asked.

She shook her head.

"I shall never regret it," she said. "We have so little, Blaine. Just now only each other, and there could never be anyone else for me."

"I know I ought to deny myself," he said unsteadily. "I may be doing you a terrible wrong, Anna—but I can't deny myself. I can't just leave you—refuse what you so—so wonderfully offer me. Oh Anna—Anna, my dearest, my darling heart!"

CHAPTER X

BLAINE had one interview with Louise Frey after the divorce papers had been served on him, an interview at which he insisted that her husband and their respective solicitors should be present, but he did not need Jeffrey Templar, his solicitor and friend, to tell him that it had been a mistake.

Louise's attitude was of pathos and injured innocence, of helpless dependence on Blaine and of simulated fear of her husband, under which she had sought and was seeking Blaine's protection. She did, in fact, rather overdo the pathos to the extent of slightly throwing Archie off his balance, a balance which she quickly helped him to maintain by some quite cruel remark at his expense, so that he was purple with anger and the desire for vengeance again.

Had he been able to be an onlooker, with this scene one enacted in a play, Blaine might have admired her performance, and even in such circumstances he found himself thinking that she was a far better actress than Virginia Coley would ever be and might have missed her vocation.

She persisted in her original story, that she had felt 'terribly ill', had asked the nurse to fetch the doctor, never thinking that it would be Blaine, that he came at once, with a dressing-gown over his pyjamas, sent the nurse away, closed her door and proceeded at once to make love to her.

At first, according to Louise, she had resisted, as any virtuous wife would do. Then she realized that Blaine's 'love' for her was returned, and finally she yielded to his importunities.

Blaine, angrier than he had ever been in his life, indignantly repudiated her statement, told the brutal truth without mincing matters, but when Louise wept and tried to throw herself into his arms, asking him over and over again what had happened to him, after all he had said and done, he realized from the expression on the faces of Archie Frey and his solicitor, that he had done himself no good. All he had done was to show himself, in their eyes, as a man who had persuaded a hitherto faithful wife to betray her husband, and who was now cravenly trying to escape the consequences by repudiating her.

He made a final desperate appeal to her to defend the case "even if you really believe this fantastic thing", he added grimly.

He eyes opened widely in shocked amazement.

"But, Blaine darling, how could I?" she asked. "That would be *blasphemy*, wouldn't it? Isn't that what it's called when you don't tell the truth in a case?" appealing in innocent helplessness to the two solicitors.

"Perjury," murmured Templar.

"Is that what they call it?" she asked, baby-eyed. "I couldn't do that, could I? I know I've done wrong, and I'm prepared to take my punishment," casting her eyes down again and twisting her hands in her lap in silent, brave suffering. "I must tell the truth, mustn't I?"

"That's all I'm asking you to do," said Blaine angrily, but she threw him a look of hurt, bewildered surprise.

"Well," said Jeffrey Templar when he and Blaine had left the hotel where, in a private room, the meeting had taken place, "you're in a jam, Belding."

"You don't believe her, do you, Templar?"

"No, I don't—but that's only because I know you and prefer to believe you."

"You mean other people will believe her?"

"We might as well face it. I think it's highly probable. Think of the effect she'll have on the jury! That baby innocence of hers! She's a superb actress. Pity she didn't go in for it professionally. You think the only way for you is to defend, even if she refuses to do so? It's a tricky position for you and the public won't like it, the respondent admitting guilt and the co-respondent denying it and defending."

"I've got to defend it," said Blaine, gritting his teeth. "Don't you see what it means for me if she gets away with it?"

"Yes, of course. I do see. It's criminally hard luck for you,

Belding, but if Frey brings his case, and you defend, isn't it a good deal worse for you? The eventual result, to you, will be the same and in addition you will have all the publicity of a defended action. It'll be a stinking case. The newspapers are going to love it, even with the restrictions on the most lurid details."

"I've got to defend it," said Blaine doggedly. "I can't believe that she'll get away with it in a court of law. What about our vaunted British justice?"

"I'm very sorry for you, Belding, but I'm bound to tell you that I think Frey will get his case. They can call her as a witness, and look at the effect she'll produce in the box! Still, if you're determined, we must get the best divorce man we can and hope he'll be able to get her down. By the way, what about Virginia's attitude? How is she taking it?"

"Does one ever know what's in Virginia's mind?" asked Blaine bitterly.

Jeffrey Templar was one of his closest friends, one of the very few who knew that all was not well between him and Virginia, though it was by observation and deduction rather than by anything which Blaine had said specifically.

"I suppose she'll petition herself if Frey wins his case?"

"I don't know. It's usual, isn't it?" asked Blaine with a sneer.

He was hating so bitterly the whole sordid business that not even the possibility that as an outcome he might be free to marry Anna could have much weight with him just then.

"Yes, but this isn't a very usual case, and if Virginia stood beside you, showed her own belief in you, it might have its effect. And, of course, if Mrs. Frey knew that Virginia was not going to divorce you afterwards, it might alter her attitude."

"I see your point," said Blaine grimly, "but whatever Virginia does or doesn't do, I'd certainly never marry Louise Frey!"

"It might be as well to let her know that," said Templar.

But when he took the first opportunity of getting that idea into Louise's head, he saw that she was refusing to harbour it there.

"He would have to marry me," she said, head in air.

"If you think anybody can make Sir Blaine Belding do what he doesn't want or intend to do, Mrs. Frey, you don't know him very well," he warned her, but she merely brushed it aside with a smile and a shrug.

She was, of course, acutely concerned within herself about what Virginia Belding intended to do, but as she had no means of finding out, she could only leave events to take their course. Of one thing she felt quite sure, and that was that if Lady Belding did divorce Blaine, he would marry her. He could do nothing else. Men in his position, according to Louise's estimate of them, always did. And she could not seriously contemplate Virginia's doing anything but sue for divorce, after all that would be in the papers about it. He would have to marry her then, for very shame, and once she was his wife, Lady Belding, she was quite confident of being able to handle him.

Blaine could not bring himself to open the subject with Virginia, and from her complete ignoring of it, he could almost have believed that she knew nothing about it. That, however, he could not believe, especially after he had seen her reading an evening paper on the front page of which was a short paragraph, headlined, giving the news that the case was set down for hearing.

Nor could he ask her, as both Templar and his counsel suggested, to stand by him openly. He would ask nothing of Virginia, feeling quite sure in his own mind that the very fact of such asking would be enough to turn her from it. She held the cards, and it remained to be seen whether she would consider her ace of trumps to be divorcing him, with the substantial alimony she would be able to extort, or keeping her position as nominally his wife, condoning his offence in magnanimous forgiveness.

Templar had briefed the best divorce lawyer he knew to defend Blaine. He accepted the brief because he knew the case would be notorious, but he warned them that there was little chance of success, once he had seen Louise Frey, and he was right.

Frey got his petition, but not until Blaine's name had been

dragged through the mire, and he left the law courts with the bitter knowledge that he would have been wiser not to defend at all.

On his way out, he found Louise waiting for him, pale and pretty in the special make-up she had chosen with care for her performance. She came towards him, a smile of affectionate pity and apology on her face. She had practised that before the mirror.

"Blaine——"

He pushed her aside roughly.

"I hope I shall never see or hear of you again," he said.

"But—Blaine darling——"

"Oh, get out of my sight!" he told her angrily, and made more headlines for himself by so doing.

SIR BLAINE BELDING TELLS MRS. FREY
TO GET OUT OF HIS SIGHT

In spite of all his anger and disgust at the trial, he was determined to go down fighting, if go down he must, and when, in a very short time, he was arraigned before the tribunal of the British Medical Association, he made a good impression, but not good enough to prevent his being struck off the rolls for 'unprofessional conduct', a rider being added that the Council deeply regretted its inability to come to any other decision, in view of Sir Blaine's distinguished career and his value to the profession.

During the period of waiting for the case to be heard, he had made the arrangements for disposing of his interest in the nursing home, but had remained, under those arrangements, in temporary possession of his flat.

Virginia had busied herself house-hunting, calmly ignoring the Frey divorce case. Blaine took no interest in the house-agents' lists which she showed him.

"I can't think about that just now," was all he said, and he did not know whether she had actually settled on a house at all, nor did he care.

He waited until the decision of the B.M.A. had been made, and then asked her the question she had been anticipating ever since the divorce case had ended.

"What are you going to do, Virginia?" he asked her bluntly.

"About what, Blaine?"

Her voice and face were perfectly calm.

"Are you going to petition for divorce? There's no difficulty about it, of course."

"I have no intention of divorcing you, Blaine," she said coolly.

"What have you got to gain by staying with me now?" he flung at her savagely. "I've just been struck off the rolls. I can't practise any longer. I've no job. I don't see how I can earn a living even for myself. I can't even give you a home."

He saw that she had already weighed all the facts and been prepared for them.

"I still don't intend to divorce you," she said calmly. "I have no wish to be in the position of a divorced woman, even as the innocent party."

He stared at her. Incalculable as she always was, he had not believed that she would keep up this attitude when he no longer had anything to offer her, not even a home or a living once his savings had gone, and Frey had applied for, and obtained, heavy damages against him.

"How do you propose to live then?" he asked her.

"I can work. As a matter of fact, I have been offered a part in a new musical which I should probably have accepted in any case. Now I shall write and do so."

"I'm not going to live with you," he said angrily.

"You must, of course, do as you like about that," she said. "Have you seen this cartoon on the new Russian situation? Rather clever," offering him the newspaper which she had been reading when he came into the room.

He brushed it aside, stood for a moment staring down at her with hatred in his eyes, and then went to his room and began to throw things into a suitcase.

It was Anna he wanted, needed with desperate longing, her

love and understanding, the comfort of her arms, of her quiet voice, of her sane mind.

He sent her a telegram, and she was waiting for him.

She had told Miss Balchin that she was expecting a visitor, but not his name. That was something about which Blaine himself must decide, though, with his picture splashed all over the newspapers at the time of the Frey divorce case, she had little hope of his not being recognized.

Her heart contracted at sight of his grey, exhausted face, the new lines etched there, the grey that faintly streaked his thick dark hair.

He had told her what time to expect him, and she had a meal ready for him in her sitting-room, though to get there she had to take him through the living-room of the cottage and present him to Miss Balchin, slurring over his name in such a way that the schoolmistress was unable to catch it.

She felt she had seen him somewhere, but the memory eluded her. She thought, however, that he looked a very nice friend for her Miss Mere, if a bit old for her, and she let her mind dwell on the pleasant contemplation of a romance.

"Well, Anna, it's all over," said Blaine, when she had closed the door and pulled the chair a little nearer to the fire and set beside it the cigarettes, his special brand, and the whisky and syphon of soda which she had bought after receiving his telegram.

It was four months since he had seen her, wanting her badly but feeling unable to go to her whilst the divorce case hung in the balance and until he knew what Virginia was going to do about it.

"The B.M.A.?" she asked quietly, for of course she knew the result of the Frey divorce case.

"Yes. They've kicked me out," he said bitterly.

They had not kissed. Mere physical contact was the least thing that held them and they had no need of it to make them utterly one.

Now, however, she came to him and put an arm about his

165

shoulders and drew him against her as he sat slumped in the chair.

"I'm so sorry, Blaine," was all she said, but he put up a hand to cover and hold the one which lay on his breast, and there was a long silence between them.

When he moved, he did so with a smile that tore at her heart.

"What about this food?" he asked. "We might as well eat."

"I'll get it," she said. "It's as ready as I could make it. I shan't be many minutes. May I pour you a drink? I got this in for you."

"Bless you. No, I'll do it," and she left him to do so.

She was thankful to see that he made at least an effort to eat the good, simple meal she had provided, that he was doing his best to give a normal appearance to a situation which she knew was fraught with much difficulty and uncertainty. She asked no questions, made no comments on what he had so briefly told her, but waited for him to speak, knowing that he would tell her everything when he was ready to do so.

He told her when she had cleared away the meal, washed the dishes and returned to the quiet peace of the firelit room, taking the chair on the other side of the fireplace.

He told her quite simply, with no unnecessary detail but with nothing important omitted.

"Virginia refuses to divorce me," he said. "I've no job or any prospect of one, very little money when I have paid the costs of the divorce case and satisfied Frey's demands, no home, not even a name I shall care to use. I've nothing at all, Anna. You see what a very bad penny has turned up."

"Have you made any plans at all, Blaine?" she asked him in her tranquil fashion, her hands busy with some knitting though her mind was not on it and she would probably have to undo it.

"Only one. To stay with you, Anna, if you'll have me," he said.

She lifted her eyes to meet his.

"You mean for good, Blaine?" she asked, and wondered if he could hear the pounding of her heart.

"If you can call it good—for you, I mean. For me it can't be anything but good. Will you take me, Anna, with the nothing I have to offer you, not even my name?"

"You know I will, Blaine."

She had given it long hours of thought, known that it might happen, and she was ready to meet it, her mind irrevocably made up.

"You understand what it means?"

"I understand fully."

"Oh Anna—my darling," and now he could take her in his arms and hold her and feel that there was to be no more parting for them, whatever the cost.

"I've no plans," he said presently, taking her with him into the big chair as he loved to do, their faces close together, her soft hair brushing his lips like a caress. "I've no ideas at all. I don't know how we're going to live, or where. We couldn't stay here in Kenborne. In fact, is there anywhere we could live where the thing wouldn't follow us?" with a touch of bitter resentment against fate.

"I think there might be," she said. "Blaine"—hesitating a moment—"I've made a sort of plan, just a sketchy one. May I tell you?"

"You know you may tell me anything, always," he said. "Heaven knows I don't know what to do myself!"

"I hope you don't mind, but I spoke to Mr. Trimwell, about us. He's very understanding, quite uninhibited, and completely to be trusted. He's been a very good friend to me. He doesn't want me to go, naturally, but he sees that I shall have to if—well, if what might happen has happened. And it has, hasn't it? That's a bit involved, but I daresay you can pick your way through it," with a smile. "He has a friend, a Mr. Gracing, who is an architect and who has been employed by a large land-owner in Scotland, on the Isle of Skye, in an attempt to develop his land, build on it, and try to re-establish sufficient industry there to encourage people to stay, or to come back to, a place which is falling into disuse, almost into decay, because of the lack of amenities on the island and the way it seems to have been left behind by modern growth. Mr. Gracing wrote to Mr. Trimwell some time ago to ask him if he could recommend a good assistant to him. I have seen the letter, and we think he means another architect, but Mr. Trimwell suggests recommending me, if I have to leave him, and he also suggests that I go in for it properly, read for exams and things, but I don't know about that. Shall I try for this job, Blaine? Would you come?"

"What to do, my sweet? Live on you?" he asked scornfully.

"Quite honestly, I don't know what you can do, Blaine," she said, "but we've got to make a start somewhere, and together, and you've got to be big enough to take whatever it means at the start. My own idea is for you to write, finish your book as a beginning."

"With my name attached to it? I hardly think so," he said with a wry grimace.

"Nothing can alter the fact that you *are* one of the greatest authorities on your subject, Blaine, and every surgeon knows it and knows that whatever has happened has made no difference to what you can teach them."

"Well, I may do that later. We'll see. When I say I've got nothing, I don't mean literally nothing, of course. A few hundreds. A thousand or two possibly, enough anyway not to have to ask you actually to feed and house and clothe me for the time being, but I shall have to find some sort of job. I don't propose to maintain Virginia, in the circumstances. She's going back to the stage, her own choice of course, and she won't need support from me whilst she's working, but I suppose she can claim it, and if she does, I shall have to find it, though they can't mulct me of what I haven't got! Tell me about this job, this place, Anna. Isn't Skye a bit dreary for you?"

She smiled.

"No place could be dreary for me if you were with me," she said, "and Skye has its own kind of beauty, even if it's a rather bleak and grim kind—and, darling, I think we could be safe there, so far away."

"Safe from discovery of the disreputable character I am?" he asked in his grim fashion. "What I've come to! Have you found a name for me as well, my wise Anna—Mere Anna!" with a little smile at an old name he had sometimes called her.

"No, I've left that to you," she said happily.

"We'll think that out. A rose, or a pole-cat, smells the same under any name!"

She kissed him with lingering tenderness, longing to throw around him the protective mantle of her love, to shield him and cover him until he had found himself again, struggled out of this nightmare, this abyss, in which he was living. She knew that the best she could do was to make him sure of her love and of its endurance to the end. His return to faith in himself must be his own doing. She could only stand by him, her hand in his, her eyes looking forward.

Since for her sake he could not remain in Kenborne, he went to a nearby town and took a room in a small hotel. They had decided that they would not renew their association on any terms but those of friendship until they could be together entirely, and when they met, it was at a spot outside the village where they could walk and talk without attracting the attention and gossip of the village. Miss Balchin had had regretfully to conclude that the little romance she had been prepared to enjoy was not coming to fruition.

Mr. Trimwell wrote glowingly of her to his friend in Skye, giving the name which Anna suggested, Mrs. Banford, her mother's maiden name, to which Blaine had agreed rather sardonically.

"You've got to give me even a name," he said, but she refused to let him go on being sorry for himself, and gradually, under the influence of her optimism and calm assurance of happiness, the bitterness and the resentment began to leave him so that, when she received the offer of a trial month from Mr. Gracing, he was even mildly enthusiastic about it.

At least they would be together, and Anna would not let him look too far ahead.

They left on their long journey to Skye in the middle of April, going in his car, not the big one in which he had come to Kenborne, but a smaller one bought to replace it. Anna thought, and Mr. Trimwell agreed with her, that a car might be of very great benefit to her in her new job, and if it were not, they could always sell it again. The big Daimler was, they agreed, much too opulent-looking in the circumstances, though Blaine laughed at the difficulty he had at first in accommodating his long legs and luxurious tastes to the modest little saloon.

She was happy and excited when she joined him, hiring a car to take her and her few belongings to Salisbury and spending the first night there in order to make an early start in the morning.

They signed the hotel register as Mr. and Mrs. Banford.

Their new life had begun.

It was all new and interesting to Anna, who had done so little travelling that even the north of England was unfamiliar to her, and he chose a route which took them through the Lake District, spending the night in Keswick by the side of Derwentwater rather than try to make too long a journey in the little car.

They walked by the side of the lake in the sweet spring evening, with everything coming to new life again after the winter, matching the new hope with which they themselves were meeting the passing of their winter.

He had told her, that first night in Salisbury, how deeply he felt his inability to marry her.

"I feel married to you, Blaine my darling," she said, lying in his arms. "I couldn't feel more your wife, even with bell, book and candle. And in a way, I think I'm glad I can't be Lady Belding, though I should have been proud to be known by your name. It wouldn't suit me. I wasn't brought up to that, or that way of living. I'm terribly happy, and proud, to be Mrs. Banford."

"I wonder what your mother would have thought about our annexing her name?" he asked, holding her closely.

"I think she might have been glad—glad to help in our happiness. She was a very sweet person. You would have loved each other, Blaine."

"Even though I have taken her daughter to live in sin with me?"

She laughed and kissed him.

"I can never think of it like that. We love each other too much," she said.

"I know, but——"

"Don't let's have any buts, or think about them," she said, but they knew that, deep in their hearts, they both wished it could have been different, not for his name, the wearing of which would have been an embarrassment and encumbrance to her, but because they were neither of them in essence the sort of people who could accept without a feeling of wrong-doing their relationship as unmarried lovers.

She would not let it interfere with their happy joy in each other, however, and he had to believe that she was as completely happy and untroubled as she seemed.

She brought a child's enjoyment to everything they shared, and astonished him by her knowledge of the poets who had lived in and written about the beauty through which their journey took him, speaking poetry in her clear voice as she sat beside him, giving him a hitherto unknown pleasure in words which had been no more to him than the meaningless tasks of school days.

And at last they came to Skye, the Kyle of Lochalsh with the dim, misty greyness of the island itself at the other side of the narrow strip of water between it and the mainland, over which they and their car were taken by ferry, and then the long drive along the coastline to Portree, where Mr. Gracing had arranged accommodation for them for the night.

They walked arm in arm in the little town, looking at the two rows of small shops, their windows crowded with souvenirs of all kinds to attract the tourists who were now almost the only source of income to the shopkeepers. They went into a shop where an old man was weaving, the heavy hand-loom, solid and substantial the same, he told them, as had been in use by Skye weavers for a hundred years and more.

Anna watched him, fascinated, as his gnarled hands threw the shuttle deftly to and fro, and was delighted when she was allowed to try it for herself, though he had to adjust the selvedge, which he told her was always one of the most difficult parts of weaving for the novice.

Blaine bought her a length of Scottish plaid in gay tartan weave.

"Let me," he said when she was about to protest. "I've never bought you anything."

"What about my clip?" she said, showing it to him fastened securely under her coat.

"You weren't my wife then," he told her, his eyes lovingly on hers, and he bought her the plaid and she said she would make a skirt of it.

The girl in the shop showed them a whole range of hand-woven materials, from heavy tweeds to scarves and shawls like cobwebs, and they talked to her about Skye, and about the way in which for many years all the young people had been leaving the island to find a means of livelihood on the mainland or in England, so that the crofts were deserted and the farm lands going to waste, even the sheep and the great horned cattle now in small, scattered herds, for whom the grazing was not now sufficient nor the labour obtainable.

"Perhaps we shall be seeing you again," said Anna. "We are going to live not very far away from Portree," and, encouraged by her interest and obvious intelligence and concern about the island she loved, they told her something of their plans, and of the old Earl of Cothern with his hopes of contributing something towards a return to prosperity and re-establishment for the crofters and in new industries.

The girl knew something about it, and knew and liked Mr. Gracing, and they left Portree with the feeling that already they had made a contact for themselves in their new home.

They found John Gracing a taciturn, uncommunicative man, but one who undoubtedly knew his job and was wholly concerned with its success. They had a small, inconvenient cottage on the estate, one which had been deserted long ago by the crofters and had fallen into a bad state of repair, though, before their arrival, something had been done to make the roof sound and the thick walls of local stone less grim with plaster.

There was no bathroom, and only the most primitive means of cooking and of heating water, but Mr. Gracing told them that as soon as something better was available, they were to have it.

Left alone in the cottage, Anna and Blaine looked at each other in some dismay. Then they went into each other's arms and hugged each other and laughed. It was the only way to take it.

"At least it's a home," said Anna, "and I'm just the right person to see and exploit its possibilities if I can persuade Mr. Gracing to lend me some of the workmen for a little while. That out-house will make us a bathroom, with a door in this wall, and if we have to go into the living-room to get to it, who cares? And there's a kind of heater on the market which will burn wood and peat and give us hot water. Can we afford that? I'll look up the things I've got about it, and see what it would cost."

"You must have it whatever it costs," he told her. "You've got to have some sort of comfort, though it's a ghastly place for you," but he could not wear down by his contempt for it her cheerful acceptance and even delight of having her first home with him.

On their first evening, they were bidden to dinner with the old Earl of Cothern in his half-ruined castle and Anna was delighted to be piped into the great dining-hall, which even in April was icy-cold, by a piper in full dress. They found the old man a mixture of Scottish caution and idealistic dreams, at once a business man and a visionary, and both qualities appeared in his schemes and plans and were often at war with each other. He belonged to an age that had gone by, and, living in almost feudal style, was trying to adjust himself to life in two different centuries, with what success remained to be seen. What was quite clear was that the whole of his personal fortune was being expended on his schemes for, as he told them sadly, since his two sons had been killed in the war and he had no daughters, who was left to him but those he called 'his own people'?

"He's a dear old man," said Anna, as they walked back to their cottage, having decided that it might not be quite the thing to arrive at the castle in their own car the first time they were bidden to it. "I'm not sure that he's not wasting his money, or that his plans are on a big enough scale to attract people back to Skye, but if it fails, none of it's going to be my fault," and she wished at once, catching the look on Blaine's face, that she had said 'our' fault, though what indeed would there be for him to do there?

He had told her that he was willing to work with the builders, as a navvy, as anything at all, but she had vetoed the suggestion.

"Your hands, Blaine," she said. "It would ruin them."

"Well, what have I got to preserve them for?" he asked with that bitterness of spirit which, for all his superficial acceptance of his position, she knew nothing could entirely eradicate.

She encouraged him to go on with his book, though it now meant that he must write in long hand for her to transcribe on her typewriter in the evenings. His books had been packed up and stored in preparation for his leaving his London flat, and he had these sent to him by a firm of removers, writing to Miss Dove to ask her to see to it for him rather than let Virginia know where he was, and the name he was using.

With Anna's consent, he told Miss Dove of his present circumstances, and that he was living with Anna as her husband. He foresaw that someone might have to know, and that he must keep some contact with his former way of life because he had had to leave a good many loose ends, and he knew that Miss Dove was entirely to be trusted.

He showed Anna her letter, in which she made it clear that she attached no blame to him, did not censure him in any way, and was glad that he had found a way of life in which he could hope for some personal happiness.

"She always liked you, Anna," he said.

"I liked her very much, too, and I'm glad we can think of her as being on our side," said Anna.

Miss Dove spoke of Virginia. She had moved into a flat of her own, and the production in which she had a part, though not the principal one, had gone into rehearsal.

"Please heaven she makes a success of it," commented Blaine. "That's our only hope of her changing her mind about me. She

174

might not then want to fall back into being Lady Belding again."

"She might even find another man," said Anna in a matter-of-fact tone.

"Not much hope of that! She's such a cold fish, and has no interest in men as such. Not like you, sunshine!"

Anna gave a contented little laugh. Their love had fulfilled and completed her being, and had it not been for that undefeatable enemy of Blaine's bitter sense of loss and frustration, and his knowledge of the injustice of the thing that had come upon him, she would have been completely happy.

A knock at the door sent her to open it.

Mr. Gracing stood there, and when Anna had invited him into their one living-room, into which the door opened directly, he looked round with some surprise.

"You've done quite a lot about this place, haven't you?" he asked approvingly, for they had transformed it from the bare, comfortless place it had been into something resembling comfort and even beauty.

Blaine had driven them into Portree, and they had been allowed to turn over the entire stock at the weaving shop and brought away with them lengths of hand-woven material long since stored away and forgotten, and Anna had made curtains of it to shut out the biting winds of Skye, and upholstered the hard old sofa and wooden chairs and given them bright cushions, and she had even persuaded Miss McLay to let them buy some of the old, hand-woven rugs on the shop floor itself, saying that surely the old weaver could make some more to take their place.

In their search for materials, they had discovered the major parts of an old loom which they had bought for a song, and which Anna was proposing to have completed as soon as she could persuade one of the carpenters to do it, after which she hoped to weave materials for herself on the instructions of the weaver.

"We could do a lot more if you'd let us have some men occasionally," laughed Anna.

Mr. Gracing grunted non-committally. It was only with the greatest difficulty they had been able to persuade him to let them

have a man for long enough to turn the out-house into a bathroom, and they were still waiting for the bath, which had been
sent from the mainland with the heating stove, to be fixed. At
present they had to heat the water in big pans over the kitchen
grate, which was old and difficult, and drain the water away
through a loose pipe into what they hoped might some day be a
garden.

"Well, what I've come for is some help," said Mr. Gracing.
"Old Angus's best cow has fallen into the ditch, and we need
an extra hand to help pull her out, so I thought you'd come, Mr.
Banford," looking rather uncertainly from under his beetling
brows at Blaine, who was an unknown quantity to him so far
but who he understood to be a writer of some sort.

"Of course," said Blaine at once, and they both went with
him to the muddy ditch, steep and rock-sided, where the poor
creature was plunging about, trying to get a footing without
success, the ropes round her horns and her neck being insufficient
to help her.

It was a long and difficult job, but they succeeded at last, and
the cow, exhausted, lay in an awkward heap on the rough, uneven
ground and seemed unable to struggle to her feet, though she
was making efforts and sinking back with a groan.

"One minute," said Blaine, waving back the men who were
trying to encourage her. "I think she's got a broken leg," and he
ran his hands knowledgeably over her and found that the leg
was broken in two places, and that she had suffered other
damage more superficially.

"Anna, could you get my case?" he asked, and soothed the
frightened, suffering animal while she sped back to their cottage
and returned, more than a little amused, with the leather case she
knew so well and which Miss Dove had sent with his books.

She watched him set and bind the leg with all the skill he
would have brought to a human patient, and she wondered what
any of the watching men would have thought if they had known
that Flora, the cow, was being attended to by the famous Sir
Blaine Belding!

"I'll give her something to quiet her down now," he said,

"but it won't do her much good to walk on that. Is there a truck or something we could get her into?"

A farm wagon was brought, but Blaine had to give the animal an actual anaesthetic before she could be heaved up into it, and out again into a tumble-down shed where she was to be left until he said she might be allowed out again.

"I'll look in in the morning to see how she is," he said, and Anna hurried on in front so that she could give way to the laughter she could no longer control.

"Oh, Blaine!" she said chokingly when he rejoined her in the cottage. "If only you could have seen and heard yourself! It was so exactly the way you would have behaved if Flora had been Lady Watsname in her London mansion!"

He joined in her laughter.

"I got a lot more satisfaction in having Flora for a patient," he said. "Wonder if I can be hauled up before the Medical Council for that?"

After that, he found himself called upon to attend all sorts of animals for all sorts of ills, dogs and cats as well as cattle, sheep, a goat, and even chickens. "Unofficial veterinary surgeon to Skye," he termed himself to Anna, with sarcasm and yet, she knew, with a certain secret satisfaction in being able to do anything which even remotely resembled the work he loved, and from which he had been torn away.

"You know, Anna," he said, "a vet has to know a lot more than a doctor of mere humans. I've certainly got a new respect for their profession. There's a devil of a lot I don't know," and he wrote for books and apparatus and drugs from Edinburgh, and would sit in the evenings poring over them, absorbed and making occasional comments to her whilst she sat with some sewing or worked at the old loom which she had been able to persuade someone to repair and complete for her, finding weaving an attractive recreation, though she felt it would be a long time before she could weave anything of which she might be justifiably proud.

She had learned to spin as well, starting from the raw fleece, her instructress being an old woman, the wife of one of the crofters, whose speech was so broad as to be almost unintelligible to London-bred Anna.

But they were great friends, and when Blaine went down to the old woman's cottage to meet Anna, as he usually did, he would smile at the laughter which came from the dark little hole of a kitchen where, amidst the peat smoke and the lingering scents of the years of living in it, Anna sat at the old wheel.

She threatened to make him a suit from the first completed skein of wool, a thick rough thread full of lumps which had taken unevenly the dye made from weed which grew in abundance near the cottage and which had been used for dyeing for longer than anyone remembered. The one Anna had proudly produced from it was a particularly hideous yellow made from a weed which had some of the properties of the tropical fustic, but of a brighter and more crude colour.

"If you do, I'll leave you," said Blaine, surveying the result of her efforts, and they both laughed, for they knew there was very little on earth that could separate them now.

Blaine, given an interest in life by his unpaid professional job with the animals, had taken up the work on his book again, and the publishers with whom he had first discussed its production wrote (Miss Dove again the intermediary) to say that they saw no reason why it should not still be published, and asked him to let them have the early chapters as soon as they were available.

"There!" cried Anna in triumph when the letter came. "What did I tell you?"

"How like a woman to say 'I told you so'," said Blaine, and when she pulled a face at him, he chased her through the cottage and out into the place that was gradually beginning to look like a garden, and caught her and, with the laughter suddenly stilled when she was in his arms, carried her into the house and up the broken staircase and into the little room under its sloping ceiling where they had found so much of heaven.

CHAPTER XI

THOUGH they seemed to have found their oasis in the desert in the little cottage in Skye, both of them felt in their hearts that it could not always endure, that it was only an oasis and not a place where they could live for ever, or even for very long, though neither of them wanted to face whatever might come next.

The first sign of the break came when the old earl died suddenly, after only a few days' illness, leaving his work unfinished and not enough money, when death duties had been paid, for it even to go on to any useful stage.

"I doubt if it would ever have been any good," said Mr. Gracing, who, with Anna and Blaine and all the crofters, felt keenly the loss of the kindly old man who had been the friend of all of them. "Perhaps it's a good thing he passed on without knowing. It would have broken his heart."

The work was abandoned, the half-finished buildings left to fall into ruins, the castle itself left empty and desolate except for the one or two old servants who hoped to be able to scratch some sort of living for themselves if they were allowed to remain there. No one was likely to turn them out unless some grasping taxgatherer discovered they were there and made it his duty to see that they did not remain there.

Anna and Blaine sat down to consider what they were to do next.

"It isn't as bad as it might be, dearest," he said. "I've still got something left, and if I can finish the book in a couple of months or so, that should see us through for some time," so that now it was he who was the cheering and confident partner and Anna the one who was depressed by foreboding.

But the real and unexpected solution came when he was informed, in suitably pompous language, that there had been a further meeting of the Medical Council at which it had been decided, in view of Sir Blaine Belding's great contribution to modern surgery of the brain, that he should be reinstated on the rolls.

Blaine sat with the letter in front of him, the look in his eyes making her feel ashamed of the thought that had sprung unbidden to her mind, the thought that this would change their lives utterly, might even separate them though they had believed nothing could do that.

Instead she went to him and kissed him and said, "I'm so glad for you, Blaine darling, so glad."

He held her hand in both his own.

"This need not make—too much difference to us, sweetheart," he said. "It will mean, at least, that I haven't got to worry about the future, or how I am going to take care of you. You won't have to work any more, Anna. At least it means that, and we should have had to leave here in any case."

"Not work?" she asked, forcing a little laugh. "But I'm the working sort. I've always worked, and I shouldn't know what to do with myself if I didn't."

"Well, we'll talk about that," he said easily, and she realized he was not thinking about her at all, or even about them, but about the return to the work he loved and for which he had always hungered when it was denied him.

He was like a boy when the time came, as it very quickly did, for their packing up and preparations for leaving. She wanted to take her loom with her. It would, she felt, always be a concrete reminder of their happiness here, in the little cottage, which had never achieved its fitted bath, and where they were still heating and carrying the pans of water.

He laughed and helped her take it laboriously to pieces, marking each part so that it would not be too difficult to put it together again, though she wondered if she would ever use it again. She did not even know how and where she was to live, since obviously he must live in London, and there would be no place for her in his intimate life as there was here.

He spoke of that on their last evening in Skye, an evening of fog and cold drizzle, with no wind to blow away the fog and the plaintive cries of the sheep and cattle adding to the sense of desolation and loss.

"We'll find somewhere just outside London for you, Anna," he said, taking her on his lap and trying not to feel that these evenings would not come again as they were now. "Not too far, so that I can reach you easily, and—perhaps quite soon—we shall be able to marry, darling. I shall try to make it possible. It means a lot more to me now even than it did before. You're part of me now. Part of my life. I can't let you go out of it. Virginia's got to do something for us."

She did not tell him, but she felt sure that he knew without that, that if Virginia would not divorce him when he had lost the power of his name and the means to maintain her in the luxury she loved, she was not likely to do it now that he had regained both of them.

Instead she said quietly, "Blaine, dear, you'll have to look at this sensibly and carefully. It wouldn't do at all for you to be involved in anything fresh, anything of that sort, just when you've been reinstated and are starting again, with everybody willing to forget the past and give you a clean sheet."

"But you, Anna——"

"I can wait, Blaine. We both can. We must. I'll do as you want and live somewhere not too far away from you. I couldn't bear to be where I could never see you! But we must be careful. Terribly careful."

"I hate that sort of thing between us," he said, but she could see that he knew she was right, and when they reached the outskirts of London, they parted, as they had arranged, he to go on to the hotel where he had engaged a room in his own name, and Anna to take the little car to an hotel in Richmond where she, too, had booked a room in her own name.

She had learned to drive whilst she was at Kenborne, and Blaine persuaded her to accept the Morris for her own use.

"Let me do at least that much for you, Anna," he had said when she protested that she would not need it, and she could not fling back in his face the generosity he had for so long been forced to curb.

It was strange, hurtful, to be Miss Mere again, but she faced it and hid away the wedding ring Blaine had put on her finger and felt that with it she was putting away all the happiness she would ever have. She was determined that she would not stand in his way, that nothing should keep him from becoming what she felt he could and would become, the finest brain surgeon in the world, honoured and untrammelled by any fetters which his association with her, a furtive, secret association now, might lay on him.

He had been hurt and angry when she insisted that she must find herself a job, but in the end he had not been able to break down her determination and had had to agree to it, though he added a proviso that she should allow him to open an account for her so that he could be sure she was never in any money difficulties.

"I don't want you to feel you've ever *got* to work," he said.

In spite of the, to her, substantial sum with which he had opened the account for her, a sum which had seemed to Blaine humiliatingly small but all that he could at the moment afford, she moved out of the Richmond hotel into something more modest whilst she decided on her next step. She was not anxious to become just a typist again, regretting that, with all the things she had learnt to do, she still had not applied herself to the short-hand which would have given her the chance of a better and more interesting job. She did not actually want to go into an office again if she could find an alternative, and at the back of her mind there was the suspicion, which soon became a certainty, that she was to have Blaine's child.

She had meant to tell him before they left Skye, but events had crowded upon them and she still had not told him of her suspicions when he had the news of his reinstatement, and she saw what a complication such a thing would make and had kept silent about it.

Within a few weeks of leaving the island, however, her suspicions were confirmed and she must make her plans accordingly.

Inevitably there was disturbance in her mind about the new

situation, but there was also a deep happiness. Whatever happened now, she would have this indissoluble link with Blaine, something that was his, a legacy of their love-life which could not be taken from her. Not for a moment did it occur to her to try to end her pregnancy. It would have been like murdering love itself, and there had always been something deeply maternal in her being, even before she had known and loved Blaine.

And then, by chance, she saw an advertisement in the paper which might provide her with the answer to her problem.

It was for a partner with a small capital in a handcraft business in an East Coast village. It detailed such things as pottery and leather-work, and added that the introduction of other 'primitive crafts' was under consideration.

Other crafts? Weaving and spinning?

She decided to write for an interview, and a few days later went to Embury in the little Morris to keep the appointment.

She found the Lang Craft Shop, after some difficulty, in two wooden sheds, converted army huts, the trestle tables which were almost their only furniture filled to overflowing with such a miscellaneous assortment of hand-made objects of every sort that Anna wondered how the two Miss Langs, Violet and Rosa, ever found anything at all or managed to sell anything.

They were women in their fifties, Violet tall and thin, Rosa short and plump, grey-haired, cheerful, very enthusiastic about their 'shop' and quite unperturbed about the muddle it was in.

One end of the larger hut was their workshop, with Miss Violet's old, foot-powered potting-wheel and tubs of clay cheek by jowl with Miss Rosa's leather-work and the dolls and puppets, the knitted garments and pin-cushions and lamp-shades which they explained were the joint concern of both of them.

After some thought, Anna had decided that for the child's sake she must pose as a married woman, but she had a strange reluctance to be known again as Mrs. Banford, the name she had shared with Blaine. She felt that every time she heard it on someone's lips, it would stab her with remembrance, and when she had written to the Miss Langs in answer to the advertisement, she had taken a name at random from a book and called herself

Mrs. Bridger. She had felt that until her life settled into some sort of pattern again, she must lose her identity, though it was with some difficulty that she recognized herself under her new name.

The two women were delighted with the contact they had made with her, having decided with so much foreboding that they must invite a third partner to bring some much-needed capital to their rescue and not daring to hope for anyone like 'Mrs. Bridger'. She told them, colouring a little, that she was very recently a widow, and since she would not be anything but quite fair with them, that she was expecting a child.

She saw to her relief that it made very little impression on them, except for a twitter of excitement which was soon lost, to them, in the greater excitement of the possible development of their business.

Anna had told them about the weaving and spinning, that she had her own loom and was prepared to buy a spinning-wheel; also, rather tentatively, that she could bring three hundred pounds into the business.

That completed their determination to get her. They had hoped for one hundred, had toyed with the hope of a possible hundred and fifty, but here was someone, young and obviously much more businesslike than they were, someone they felt they could get on with—and she could bring with her the stupendous sum of three hundred pounds!

Not without some misgiving, Anna had decided that she would risk almost the whole of what Blaine had put into the bank for her, refusing to take into her calculations anything which he might pay in subsequently. She did not want him to do this. Her independent spirit made the thought of being supported by Blaine when they were not living together quite unacceptable, and she was determined to stand on her own feet, whatever the future might bring.

But, since she was to bear his child, she felt she could use his money to establish herself in a position where she could maintain it, and this queer jumble of the Lang Craft Shop seemed to hold such possibilities.

It would never, she realized, bring her a fortune, but she did not desire one. She would be doing work she liked, with women whom she felt she might like very much, and it was obvious that if she went in with them, they would be only too willing for her to put her own ideas to work to make it a better-paying concern.

She went into their haphazard accounts, decided to get some knowledge of scales of profits, and left them with a promise to think the proposition over and write to them.

"I do hope you will decide to come in with us, Mrs. Bridger," said Miss Violet rather wistfully. "You see, my sister and I are not really good business people, and we do feel that we have made a good many mistakes and that there ought to be more money in our little business. No one comes to Embury in the winter, but that is when we do most of our work, and in the summer there are always plenty of visitors. The bathing and the fishing are good, with a very safe beach for children, and there is a summer camp about a mile away, along the shore, and people come here to do their shopping, and they always want to take things back with them, little souvenirs and so on. We do quite a lot of business in the summer, but we do feel that if we were *organized*, we could do so much better."

Anna was fully in agreement there, having been both amused and appalled by the heterogeneous assortment of articles, some good, many just rubbish, on the trestle tables and in the boxes and bundles which cluttered up the shelves.

By the time she reached her temporary home again, she had made up her mind that she would go in for this venture.

She had asked the Miss Langs about living accommodation, and they had looked at each other for a moment, exchanged a nod, and then Miss Violet, usually the spokesman, had made the proposition which had obviously depended on the sort of impression their would-be partner might make on them.

"Well," said Miss Violet, "you *could* live with us. We have room in our little house for another, but we thought, my sister and I, that you might like to have a little place of your own, only a very *tiny* place, but we have a little cottage, a bungalow, that we let in the summer. It's empty just now, of course. We could let you have that. Not, of course, at the rent we get in the summer, as you would be having it all the year round, but we could perhaps agree on a figure, if you would like to have it?"

However small it might be, it would be a home of her own, and this made an even stronger appeal to Anna than the prospect of congenial work and the happy association which she felt she could form with the two maiden ladies. It was a wet, gloomy December day, and she wanted to get back before the fog descended again over London, so she did not go to see the place, but she felt that, after the tumbledown cottage in Skye, nothing could daunt her.

What was she to do now about Blaine?

Though it was like physical pain, sharp and almost intolerable, she knew that it meant parting from him, since she had made up her mind, as soon as she became certain about the child, that that must be hidden from him. She knew that he ardently desired a child, a son, and that that had been one of the factors contributing to the trouble between him and Virginia.

But he would not want a child he could not acknowledge and help to bring up, and if he knew that Anna was to have one, he might go to any lengths to get free to marry her, and that was what she felt in her deep love for him and her understanding of his position, he must not do. He could not be subjected, for any reason at all, to any new scandal. He had felt unclean, utterly in the mire, when he had been dragged through the divorce court by the Freys, and if he now could succeed in getting Virginia to divorce him, all that would be brought up again and he would lose so much of what she knew he was so thankful to have regained. He would not again come under the censure of the B.M.A., since his most heinous offence had been, in their view and according to the rules of the association, that his partner in the scandal had been a patient.

But that was not all. Gradually people's memories would fade, must be fading now. He had come back to find himself urgently needed in his profession, and his letters had shown her how good it felt to him to be back in it, to be re-establishing himself amongst his colleagues, to find doors open to him again and people prepared to bury the past.

She did not believe that Virginia would ever set him free, but even if she could be prevailed upon to do so, Blaine could not escape the calumny a second divorce case would bring with it.

Nor did she feel, in her always humble estimation of herself, that she would be the right wife for him. She derided the thought of herself as Lady Belding. She—Anna Mere! People, his friends and proper associates, would never accept her, and in any case, since the child would be born in six months' time, it could never be made legitimate. Blaine could not go through all the business of getting his freedom by then, even if Virginia could be made to agree, and their subsequent marriage would not legitimate the child since he would have been a married man at the time of its birth.

No, there was no other way, for Blaine.

She wrote two letters when she got back to her room, one to the Miss Langs saying she would come to them under the proposed terms of partnership in a week's time, the other to Blaine, though she did not post that until the week had passed and she was on her way to Embury.

The writing of that letter was the hardest thing she had ever had to do.

She set herself grimly and with fainting heart to the task.

She told him that, having now had time to think things over, she had come to the conclusion that there was nothing for them but to part.

I haven't come to this conclusion lightly, Blaine, but I know that I am right, she wrote. *We have our separate and personal lives to lead, I as well as you, and we must both realize that there is no future we can share. I must be free to plan my life and get the best I can out of it, just as you must be free. I shall remember always that you wanted me to be your wife. It will make me glad and honoured all my days, but I think I have known all the time that it could never be. It would not have been the right thing for either of us. I should have been out of my element. Your sort of life could never be mine. I was not brought up to it nor would I want it. So, Blaine, I am taking this irrevocable step and leaving you. Don't try to find me, or even to feel that you must try. I have found a job in which I think I shall be happy, and it is a long way from London. I am taking the little car, and I am also using the money you left for me in establishing myself in my new life. I know you would like me to do both those things, and will be glad I have done so. I am leaving Richmond. By the time you get this, I shall have gone. I have drawn all the money from the account and closed it, and have not left any address at the bank. I am going out of your life, Blaine.*

I have had very great happiness with you, and I know you have with me. I shall never forget it, or try to. The memory of you will be with me to the end of my life. Thank you, Blaine dear, for it. I shall watch for the mention of your name and shall think with pride of what we once were to each other, with pride and with joy and no regrets. I won't say "Forget me" because I don't think you will, not yet, not for a long time. But I know I am doing the right thing for us both, and I am doing it in this way to spare us both the pain of the actual parting.

Good-bye, Blaine, my darling. I shall love you all my life. Anna.

She dropped the letter into a letter-box and drove on.

The little thud it made as she let it fall from her hand was like the blow of a hammer on her heart, leaving her numb with pain.

It was over. All the love and the happiness, the joy and the anxieties, the laughter and the pain of all they had shared.

She felt empty, lost, desolate. She was alone again.

Then she thought of the child which soon would be stirring beneath her heart, of the new life and work awaiting her, of the friendly women who had sent her an affectionate welcome to the new home where she would live with her child and Blaine's, and thanks and gratitude welled up in her because she had so much left.

The two Miss Langs were in a twitter of excitement about her coming.

They had scarcely dared to hope, after her visit to them, that she would really come. She seemed too direct and generous an answer to their prayers.

"Do you—do you think she really is a widow, Violet?"

asked Miss Rosa a little nervously, not quite sure what her sister's reactions and views might have been.

"I don't know," said Miss Violet. "I should think probably not, and that she's not *Mrs.* Bridger at all, but need that concern us? She must have a sad story, whatever it is, and who are we to judge others? As far as we are concerned, she is what she says, a widow."

Miss Rosa gave a sigh of relief and satisfaction at this robust agreement with her own thoughts.

"I'm glad you think that way, Violet," she said, "and—won't it be rather nice to have a child about the place, a—a baby? It won't be in the way at all. We could have a little cot in here. There's that basket thing we used to have. The one I made when we were doing cane work. Do you remember? I think we used it for logs, but we could clean it and paint it—blue, do you think? Or perhaps cream so that it would do for either a boy or a girl, though I rather hope it will be a girl, a dear little girl we can make things for," and she rambled on happily until the more practical Miss Violet reminded her that before they could make any other arrangements or plans, they must get enough space cleared for Mrs. Bridger's loom and also the spinning-wheel she was going to buy.

"We'll put her near the window in the big room," she said. "For one thing I expect she will want more light than we are accustomed to work by, and for another, it will be such an attraction to have someone actually weaving and spinning where people can see her as they go by. We are really so fortunate, Rosa, and you will remember that it was *my* idea to put in that advertisement, though it did cost us nearly five pounds."

They pushed and dragged things about to make room for the loom. Then they went to the cottage, which was joined to their own, and cleaned and polished, washed and re-hung the curtains, carried cushions to it from the shop, and a brightly coloured rag rug which Miss Rosa had made in a moment of enthusiasm but which had not turned out as she had hoped and had not found a buyer.

"You know, Rosa," said Miss Violet, when they had spread

it on the floor, "you ought not to have put in those bits of your old combs. They don't do with the rest of it at all."

"No, I don't think it's that, dear," said Miss Rosa, her head on one side like a bright, plump little bird. "It was that old coat Mrs. Higgins gave me, but she would have been so hurt if I hadn't used it. Oh look, Violet, there's a bit of that green dress you had. Do you remember it? You always said it was unlucky."

"Well, so it was, for the rug," said Miss Violet, sharing her sister's pleasant contemplation of an article so full of reminders. "I rather like that bit of blue in there. Now, what was that?"

"That, dear? I don't think I—oh yes, of course! It was that petticoat I had, only I dyed it and it didn't come out very well. Such a nice piece of stuff, too. I dyed this bit of pink as well. It was Mary Bright's best blouse. The one she always used to wear at the whist drives until Johnny Gain spilt coffee all down it.

Anna was charmed with the cottage, which she felt had everything she would ever want, two tiny bedrooms, a small sitting-room and a good-size kitchen in which a bath had been fitted, with taps and a proper run-away. It had once formed part of a house of which the Miss Langs had the larger portion, and the garden had been divided so that each cottage had its own private part of it, though they shared the little front garden which, tended by Violet and Rosa, looked much as their 'shop' did, with no particular plan or system, and Anna could imagine that when it was in full bloom, everything ran riot and did as it liked.

"We hope you will like gardening, Mrs. Bridger," said Miss Rosa. "I'm afraid we're not very good at it, but of course we don't have much time, what with the work for the shop, and then there's Maisie and Bruce. Maisie is our cat, a dear thing but she's always having kittens and really I don't think there's anybody left in Embury who has not had one of them, so I don't know what we shall do with the next lot because, of course, we couldn't drown them."

Anna did not have to ask who Bruce was, because at that moment he came bounding up and nearly knocked her over, a large dog of no recognizable breed but possessing, she discovered, the best qualities of most of them. He began as a spaniel, with eyes filled with devoted love for all mankind, but ended, after several digressions, in a long, thin tail which had the secret of perpetual motion. He ran loose about the village, was known in everybody's kitchen, and survived the cars in the road by a miracle of high speed. One ear stood upright and one lay flat, giving him an endearing look of surprise and speculation, and Anna, an inveterate animal lover, loved him on sight.

"Then there are the chickens," said Miss Rosa, when Bruce had thoroughly washed Anna's face, "but you can't really make friends of them, can you? Though of course we've had them such a long time now that they do seem part of the family."

"But if they're so old, do they still lay?" asked Anna, who had become knowledgeable about chickens when she lived with Miss Balchin.

"Well, not often, I'm afraid," admitted Miss Rosa regretfully, "but we haven't really room for any more, and of course we couldn't have them killed. You see, we *know* them."

Bruce had already made his way into the kitchen and was investigating its possibilities, though Anna felt that she already knew enough about the Miss Langs to be sure he would not be hungry.

"I do hope you don't mind him," said Miss Rosa, pushing him out though he returned immediately. "The back door doesn't shut very well, so he just walks in, but we could have something done about it."

"I shall welcome him," said Anna. "I love dogs."

"I hope you won't be lonely, dear, but if you are, you've only to knock on the wall, and one of us will come in—or if you want anything, of course."

Anna soon found that only the slightest tap would be necessary if she did indeed want company or help, for the wall between the two cottages was so thin that she could hear the whole pleasant conduct of the sisters' lives through it and knew that they were as sweet and sound in their private lives as in the more public one of their business.

She bought her spinning-wheel, a rather cumbersome

second-hand one and a good deal more clearance had to be made to accommodate both that and her loom, but since the two sisters were only too glad to have their stock overhauled and put into some sort of order, they gave her a free hand, being as busy as bees themselves with catalogues and price lists which had become of such thrilling interest to them now that Anna's money was available to replenish their meagre stock of materials of all sorts.

Tactfully, for she would have hated to hurt their feelings, Anna suggested the discontinuance of some of the lines which to her mind were unsaleable rubbish, and shelves were filled with things which were to go at bargain prices in a sale they were excitedly planning when 'the season' opened, which would be in about five months' time, though they talked about it as if it were tomorrow.

"So much to do! So many things to think about and prepare for!" twittered Miss Rosa happily.

In five months' time, her baby would be nearly due to be born, thought Anna, a deep peace in her heart at the thought. It was a pity it was to be at the beginning of their busy time, but she felt strong and confident that it would not be very long after that before she could take her full share of the work again, and she was looking forward to the new experience of being a saleswoman.

She was amazed at the vitality and energy of her two partners, especially when it was tactfully directed by her into the most profitable channels. Miss Violet's pottery was acknowledged to be their best-selling line, but since they had no kiln of their own, they had been up against the great difficulty of taking the unfinished work, in a fragile state, to and from the School of Art in the nearest town, some ten miles away, where it was fired. Here Anna's car proved a great convenience and solved the problem for them so that Miss Violet went ahead with great energy, turning out rows and rows of the little pots and bowls and jugs, beakers, ash-trays and a dozen other articles, some of them quite useless to Anna's more practical mind but all of them made with loving care and skill. Before the final firing, Miss Rosa took them in hand and painted little designs on them, or highly moral sentiments, or inhospitable instructions such as 'go canny with the jam', or 'waste not, want not'.

Anna sat at her loom and produced lengths of tweed, of gaily striped curtaining and, in larger quantities, the little head-scarves and mufflers more likely to find a market amongst the sort of people who would come to the holiday camp with a very limited amount to spend. Until she could produce spun wool of a more useful quality than that which had aroused so much mirth in Skye, she proposed to use the spinning-wheel rather as an attraction for sightseers and to lure customers inside than as a producer of profits.

She had not believed she could be so quietly happy and contented so soon after the parting from Blaine, of whom she tried not to think too much, and by night-time, when she had cooked a meal for herself (usually shared by Bruce and often, somewhat disdainfully, by the obviously pregnant Maisie) and set her little home in perfect order again, she was too tired for anything but sleep. Her day began early, since her two partners were usually up and doing before six, and it would in any case have been impossible to go on sleeping with all the cheerful bustle and banging about next door, and she began to like these early morning hours, especially when the days started to lengthen and six o'clock no longer seemed the middle of the night.

They were at the 'shop' by eight, and seldom left it again before the clock had gone right round, having a sandwich lunch with tea made on a Primus stove, though they were debating the possibility of replacing both that and the oil lamps by the electricity which had recently made its appearance in the village, this being another of the things which Anna's partnership made feasible.

The sisters made no attempt to disguise from her their satis-faction over the three hundred pounds, and, very soon, over her presence there.

"You are a real godsend to us, Mrs. Bridger," said Miss Violet. "You have such good ideas, such taste, and like us, you are a worker! We had an offer from a man to go into this partner-ship with us, but for one thing neither Rosa nor myself have had anything to do with men and don't know their ways, and for another, if you want work done, go to a woman for it any time! Women are the real workers in this country, though you would not think it from all the fuss and bother men make about what they do, all these strikes and things. And nobody must tell them what to do, not even the people who pay them!"

Anna listened and chuckled inwardly, for it was clear that Miss Violet and Miss Rosa, if they were not actually man-haters, had a strong predilection for their own sex.

She often thought, with a longing which she crushed at once, how much she would like to write about it all to Blaine, who would appreciate to the full her descriptions of her two partners and the little shop, though there would have been no malice in any of it. She had become too fond of them, admired too much their courage and energy and optimism, to have anything but respect for them, and if she sometimes laughed inwardly at them, it was with a very sincere affection.

By May, the first of the year's visitors began to arrive, part of the holiday camp having been opened for them, and the vagaries of the weather did the shop a good turn, bringing them into Embury rather than tempting them to remain on the beach, and the three partners did quite a bit of business as a result.

Miss Violet's pottery, and the smaller leather articles Miss Rosa made sold the most readily, but Anna found customers for her scarves and even, to her delight, a length of her best-quality tweed, and she took an order for twelve yards of curtain material which would keep her busy for some time, especially as by now she was finding it difficult to sit at the loom for too long at a time.

At first the Miss Langs had been very delicate and reticent about it, but now their interest was too keen for reticence and since Anna showed that she did not mind, they talked about the baby constantly, making all sorts of plans and arrangements for its reception, and it touched her very much when Miss Rosa shyly presented her with some really exquisite baby woollies which she had knitted in secret in her very small amount of spare time.

"How really sweet of you, Miss Rosa," said Anna gratefully.

"Well, dear, you see, never having had any children of our own, Violet and I like to feel that we are going to have a share in yours—especially as it will have no father," flushing a little as she said that and feeling that she had been indelicate.

But all that Anna said was a quiet "No."

"Violet," said Miss Rosa a little later, when they were preparing for bed. They had shared a room as long as they could remember. "Violet, I can't help *wondering* about dear Anna's baby. I really would love to *know*."

"That's just vulgar curiosity, Rosa," said her sister briskly, pulling over her head the sort of nightgown, made of the best-quality cambric, which she had worn all her life, up to the neck and down to the wrists and feet.

She herself would 'love to know', but she would never have admitted it, even to Rosa.

Rosa, donning a similar modest garment, cast her mind back down the years, now nearly thirty of them, back to the time when she herself might have taken such a turning as she felt sure Anna had taken. It was, in the end, only because she could not bear to leave Violet that she had kept on the straight, narrow, and oh, so dull, hard-working path! Only because one could not take one's elder sister to share a life of sin with one, for it had been a life of sin to which she had been invited by a man who was too much married to offer her any other kind. Of course she had been quite right not to go, quite apart from leaving Violet—and yet—Miss Rosa remembered how sweet, how exciting, how tumultuous life had been for those few short weeks when she had given all her heart to her first, and as it turned out, her only love.

What if she *had* gone, if she had been left, as perhaps dear Anna had been left, with a—*baby*!

Miss Rosa's eyes, mercifully hidden by the sudden blowing out of the oil lamp by Violet, were dewy soft, and she quite overlooked the fact that that baby, had there been one, would by now be a grown man, probably with a moustache and a wife of his own by now. To Rosa, the child she had never conceived was always a baby, though her body was still virgin.

"We must be very kind to Anna," she said, though she had not spoken for a long time.

"Of course," said Violet. "Go to sleep, Rosa."

Anna's son was born on a morning in early June, born in the little bedroom from which the Miss Langs could hear, and agonize over, every sound and did the unprecedented thing of turning to kiss each other when his first protest against being thrust into a world of fear and hatred came through the thin wall.

But there was neither fear nor hatred in his small personal world.

Anna could have gone into a hospital, but she wanted her baby to be born where she herself had found happiness, amidst the familiar things, and with love around him instead of the impersonal routine of a hospital ward. There was a good midwife in Embury, and it was to her that Anna turned when, towards the end, she needed help. Until that moment came, she was calm and in complete control of the situation, far less agitated about it than were Miss Violet and Miss Rosa, the latter having been dispatched on her bicycle for Mrs. Grey when Anna decided she had better come.

So the first things that small Colin opened his eyes to were the little rooms of the cottage, to kind Mrs. Grey, to the two enchanted spinsters, and to Anna herself.

Anna had longed for her baby to look like his father, but he seemed to bear no resemblance to either of his parents, fair and chubby, a stockily built little person whose eyes, when they lost their indeterminate baby blueness, were a soft grey-blue which could flash with stormy temper, be sunny with smiles or drowned in tears all in a moment.

Miss Grey pointed out the width of his forehead and the noble proportions of his head.

"He'll do big things, this young man," she said. "He's going to be clever."

Blaine's son, thought Anna lovingly.

"I don't mind about the big things so long as he is kind and good," she said, holding him to her in a passion of love different from anything she had known before.

He was hers, her own, all her own, and if now and then the thought of Blaine, and what she was denying him struck at her heart, and she knew that many times in this young life she would yearn for him to share the responsibility and the happiness, she knew that she had done the best thing—for Blaine.

Probably the thing she would have to fight more strenuously than anything would be the spoiling of Miss Violet and Miss Rosa, to whom nothing as wonderful had ever happened.

The basket cot which Miss Rosa had made, ill-shaped but commodious, was carried to and fro between the cottage and the shop, and Colin throve in the atmosphere of clay and leather and glue, and the noise of the potting wheel and the loom and the coming and going of customers. Anna, throwing aside the many books which she and the Miss Langs had studied before his birth, looked after him as other animals look after their young. She kept him clean and comfortable, fed him when he was hungry at his natural source, and had a contented, happy baby.

So soon the baby days must pass!

It seemed no time at all before he was sitting up, before he had teeth to chew hard crusts, before he was staggering about on uncertain feet with his hands deep in Miss Violet's clay, or investigating the contents of Miss Rosa's boxes and baskets, or unwinding into inextricable confusion his mother's skeins and bobbins.

Anna was sometimes afraid when she saw how quickly his groping young mind fastened on an idea and grasped it. Miss Rosa made him a set of gaily coloured letters in cardboard, and long before he was of school age, he could arrange them on the floor in his own corner to make words which later he could pick out of his picture books, discovering them with shouts of delight.

It looked as though Mrs. Grey had been right in her estimate of his capabilities. Would it be possible for her to give him the sort of chance he should have, both by right of his quick mind and as Blaine Belding's son? She could not look beyond the village school, for the fees of paying schools were out of the question. However hard she worked, and however good the season might be, she could not hope to get out of the little business more than enough to maintain herself and Colin in her present simple style. Was it right for her to deny Blaine's son such things as his father could do for him? What he certainly would do if he knew of the child's existence?

Yet, watching for any mention of Blaine's name in the newspapers, knowing that he had more than re-established himself in his profession, she shrank from making the contact which might damage his reputation again. She knew that he was capable of some action which might do this.

So, though she feared for the possible loss to Colin, and longed with all her heart to see, or hear from, Blaine again, she must let the years bring what they might.

CHAPTER XII

It was not easy for Blaine Belding to make the return to his professional and his private life after the bitter abandonment of both. The hurt to his pride had been deep and lasting, and his attitude, at his return, one of defence.

Though the best of his friends approached him warily, there were others who made it clear that they regarded his return as no more than the exigency of his profession and not a passport to any personal association. As a result, he rejected them proudly and shut himself within his own life, becoming morose and difficult to deal with. He knew that the opinion of the many was that he should have freed himself from his wife whom, after all, he had left to her own devices and profession, in order to marry the woman in the case, Louise Frey.

He took a small, furnished flat in an unfashionable neighbourhood, and a consulting room in Harley Street and took up his work at St. Agatha's, which had been the principal reason for his reinstatement, and moved in that small orbit with little or no outside contacts.

Miss Dove had returned to him, as his receptionist and secretary and almost his only personal friend. She had appeared in his consulting room as soon as he took it.

"Why—Emma!" he said in glad, if uncomfortable, surprise.

"How are you, Blaine?" she asked in her matter-of-fact way. "I've come for a job."

"You? Why? I thought you were staying on with Melcome."

Melcome was the man who had bought the nursing home.

"I was. I have been. Now I want to come back to you."

"But I haven't a job for you."

"Yes you have. You want someone to look after you—oh,

I mean professionally, of course. You know what you are with your engagement book and correspondence and so on. You'll be in a hopeless muddle in no time. Also, since I knew they would want you back and that their Victorian morals would not stand up against the need, I have taken a refresher course and am prepared to act as your personal theatre nurse. You are in a position to have me as such."

"But—Emma——"

He was nonplussed, grateful but inclined to reject any offer of help or friendship.

"No buts," she said briskly. "Do I get the job?"

"You can't touch pitch without getting defiled," he said bitterly.

"Rubbish. Don't start being sorry for yourself, Blaine. I can't stand self-pity. Neither could you at one time. I am ready to start now."

"It's—generous of you, Emma."

"Generous my foot! I want to do it. I've always wanted to get back to my real job, and we understand each other."

He could not refuse her, nor did he want to do so. She would take off his shoulders the burdensome part of his work, and he knew that he could trust her utterly.

So Miss Dove became an integral part of his life again, and her robust good sense, her tact and her refusal to let him go on indulging in self-pity, did much towards the reconstruction of his life.

But she did not intrude into his private life; he lived alone with a man-servant, in the small flat where, when his work was finished, he shut himself in with his books.

He had been back some six weeks and had already established the routine of his life, when he returned to his flat late one afternoon in February to find Collier, his man, in an unusual state of perturbation.

"There's a lady to see you, sir," he said, taking his hat and coat. "She hasn't an appointment and I told her I didn't think it would be convenient, but she said she would come in and wait," apologetically and with a healthy respect for his employer's probable reaction to such a breach of his instructions.

Blaine's heart lifted as a wave of joy swept over him.

Anna!

He reproached himself for not having been out to Richmond to see her, though he had written to her. His days had been very full. Also it had been impossible for him to decide what to do about her, hating the thought of a furtive association with her, with all its sordid little secrets, asking her to live the sort of life which would be so foreign to her. She could and did do things in a big way, such as going with him to Skye and taking, as she had done, all its deprivations and difficulties, but the hidden life, the snatched secret meetings, all the nasty little details of such a life, would be quite wrong for her, as for him.

But she had come to him!

He hurried into the one room which did duty as living-room, sitting-room and study, his face alight.

Then he drew back.

It was not Anna who sat there, a cigarette between her lips, her elegantly shod feet stretched out towards the fire.

"Virginia!" he said and did not dissimulate both his surprise and his disapproval.

She rose, threw the cigarette into the fire, and smiled at him, completely mistress of herself and the situation.

"Hullo, Blaine," she said. "Surprised to see me?"

"Of course," he said shortly. "Why are you here?"

"That's quite a story," she said. "May we have some tea? Your man, by the way, was most reluctant to let me in, so I take it you're living a very secluded life here—unless, of course, your lady friend is with you? And I don't mean Louise Frey! That little cat!"

"I'm alone," he said shortly, and rang the bell and asked Collier to bring them tea.

"Perhaps you'll tell me why you've come," he said when they were alone again.

"I've come back to you," she said calmly.

"Why?" he demanded with curling lip.

"Several reasons. One, though you probably don't believe it or care about it, is that I'm rather fond of you."

He gave a short laugh.

"We can miss that one out," he said.

"I knew, of course, that you would take that attitude. The next one is that I'm rather tired of being on my own."

"Meaning that you're not having much success?" he asked in the same contemptuous tone.

"A little of that too, though I've got enough work ahead for some time and could go on with it. I'm making a film, here in England, and I can go on tour with the play I'm in if I want to. I've done fairly well, Blaine. I can keep myself decently. That should answer your question."

"I've nothing for you, Virginia," he said shortly.

"No? I'm the best judge of that. I know you don't think much of me, Blaine, and I can't really blame you. Whilst we've been apart (and I'm prepared to draw a veil over what has been happening to you in that time), I've done quite a lot of thinking, and I made up my mind that if you came back, as I was sure you would, we could have a go at doing things rather better than we did before. I'm sorry for what happened to you. I don't know if I ever told you that, but you didn't give me much chance, did you? I know you've got a lot against me and I'm not trying to justify myself, but I rather lost my head when you married me. That was nearly four years ago, Blaine, and I've found myself a bit in that time. I'm different now."

"I notice that you did not decide that you were different and wanted to resume your life as my wife when I was down and in disgrace and not likely to be able to provide for you," he said with a grim, set face.

She gave a shrug and a smile.

"No. I didn't know where to find you, for one thing, but I'm not going to pretend anything. It wouldn't be any use, would it? I shouldn't have been any good to you when you were like that. I like good living. I'm no Florence Nightingale with a lamp. You see that at least I'm honest! Well, you're back, and alone. I'm still your wife, Blaine, though if I had thought you really wanted to marry that Frey woman, I might have considered divorcing you."

"You wouldn't do so when I really did want to marry someone else," he reminded her curtly.

"No. That was rather different. I wasn't going to let some other woman take my place and strut around in my name as things were, and if I'd done what people expected me to and divorced you after the Frey case, I should have forced you into marrying her, which I was sure you didn't want at any price."

"At least you're honest," he said.

He felt strangely confused about Virginia who, with all her faults, had, he realized, always been honest with him, even to revealing herself in a bad light. What was he to make of her now?

"Yes," she agreed with a wry smile. "Well, what about it now, Blaine?"

"I still want to marry the other woman," he said.

"I thought you might, but you can't afford another divorce case, unless it is to marry Louise Frey. I know nobody can touch you for these very important operations which probably no other surgeon in the world, certainly in Britain, would take on, but I don't imagine you can live on those rare cases and you'll want the lesser ones as well and when people have a choice in private cases, even in these days a good many would choose someone else if you got yourself wrapped up in a second case—unless, of course, you did it to marry the Frey woman, and I can't imagine you would do that!"

"I wouldn't," he said grimly, "and whilst we are on the subject, will you allow me to say that I—appreciated, and still do, your belief in me over that?"

"Pff! As if *you* would get into a state over a woman like that! Nobody who knew you would credit it. So you see where you are, Blaine. If I divorced you, citing Louise Frey or anybody else, it would cause a stink that you can't afford. And you wouldn't marry the Frey, though she's still waiting for you to do it. She's even been to see me to ask me to divorce you! So, you see Blaine, where we are. I'm not going to divorce you, for your own sake. If you married the Frey, you'd be miserable and it wouldn't last. If you married somebody else, it would look too bad and you'd lose a lot of patients. So what about it?"

He could see the force of her arguments. He had already faced them, but had been prepared to risk whatever might happen if he could marry Anna. But if Virginia were determined, as she seemed to be, not to set him free, where were they?

After a few moments' silence, he spoke deliberately.

"I'm sorry, Virginia," he said, "but I am not disposed in any circumstances to live with you again."

"Why not? Am I so repulsive to you?"

"You're not repulsive at all. As you know, I was very much in love with you when I married you, and I still like you. I like you very much, Virginia. As you say, you've always been honest with me, even when you married me, because I think you really did believe you were in love with me. It was just that you didn't understand the meaning of love, nor that married life, as such, would be so repugnant to you. You're just not made that way, Virginia. There are people like that, men as well as women, and they ought not to marry at all. Why do you want to take up life with me again?"

"I've given you two reasons—one that I'm tired of being on my own and fighting my own way, and the other that I'm fond of you. I really am, Blaine. There is no other man for me and never has been and never will be. I'm nearly twenty-five now. I'm not a child any more, as I realize I was when we were married. I honestly want to make a life for myself with you again and I'll try to make you happy and—as I know you want children, that too."

He walked away from her and stood staring at nothing.

If it were not for Anna, he knew he might be inclined to do as Virginia wanted, to take this thing at its face value and do his best to make it go deeper. He too was lonely. He too wanted a private life of his own.

But not with Virginia. Not without Anna.

When he turned back to her, she knew she had failed.

"I'm sorry, Virginia. I'm honestly sorry. You make it sound

possible, and even attractive. But I'm heart and soul in love with another woman. I've been living with her since I went away. She's waiting for me if—if I can make a proper place for her in my life, and that proper place is that of my wife."

She rose and picked up her coat, the mink he had given her during those early days when he would have given her the earth.

He saw the marks of the years on her face, still young, still lovely, but no longer the face of a child.

"I'm sorry too, Blaine," she said, "but one thing I must make quite clear, and that is that I've no intention at all of getting a divorce. We need not discuss that. I've got a hard streak in me. You know that, and it's right here, where this other woman is concerned. I don't even want to know now who she is. It doesn't matter to me since she will never be your wife, never, whilst I am alive. I'll go now. It doesn't matter about the tea, though your man doesn't seem to be very efficient, does he? This is where I'm living," putting a piece of paper from her bag on the table. "If you get too lonely, or change your mind or anything, you'll be able to find me. Good-bye, Blaine. Or shall we say *au revoir*? Because this is not the end between us. I'll let myself out," and she passed the rather astonished Collier on the way with his laden tea tray and he heard the door close.

He waved the man aside.

"Never mind about that now," he said. "Bring me the whisky and then you can go. I'll get some dinner out if I want any."

The contact with Virginia, the oblique references to Anna, had set him longing to see her again, reproaching himself anew that in all the business of re-settling himself into his new life, he had not done so.

He rang up the hotel, to be told that she had left there and that they did not know her present address. That gave him a shock, for she had not told him of her intention and he had a sense of desolation and loss because he did not know how or where to find her.

And then he had her letter of renunciation.

He read it many times, trying to find in it some hope that she did not mean exactly what she said, that she was going out of his life and would not enter it again. But he knew too well the stability of her mind and the purposeful way in which, having set her course, she steered unflinchingly along it.

He realized how little chance he would have of finding her. She was too capable and efficient to have left a trail for him to follow. All that remained for him was to have the small satisfaction of knowing that she was not entirely without money, and had not been too proud to accept it. He wished he had been able to give her more, but when he had had to leave his profession, in bitterness of spirit he had sold many of his most valuable instruments and books, and had had to replace them, and until he could establish himself with private patients again, he had no large sums coming in.

He did not like to think of Anna being thrown back on her own resources, with only herself to depend upon, though he knew that would represent no hardship to her, independent as she was and used to working for her living.

He went out to Richmond in case, by a miscalculation, she had left even the smallest trace which he could follow, but there was none. She had disappeared as completely as if the earth had opened to swallow her up.

For weeks he nursed his soreness and sense of loss in silence. Then, driven to communication with some human being, he spoke of it to Miss Dove.

"I'm all in," he said one day in his consulting room, when he had seen a number of people by appointment which should not have distressed his mind at all.

"Lost your flair for work?" she asked him with a smile, putting on the electric kettle for their tea, as he had another appointment later which would prevent him from leaving.

"Perhaps. Other things too. Have I been particularly difficult lately, Emma?"

"Like a bear with a sore head. I wonder that anybody but myself stands you. Anything wrong?"

"Yes. Emma, you knew that I was living with Anna Mere in Skye?"

"Yes, you told me," she said. "From the tone of your letters, you sounded happy in spite of everything."

"I was, very happy. In one way, I was almost sorry this thing happened. You see, it's meant parting from her. She's— part of me, Emma. We were very much in love. We are still. At least, I am."

"You don't mean she isn't? You know what I thought about her. I liked and respected her very much, and I was sorry you didn't meet her first."

"Not shocked, Emma?"

She laughed.

"Me? No. I wouldn't have thought of her going in that direction, but if she made you happy, I can only be glad she did. What's happened, Blaine?" since she could see that he was wanting to tell her.

"She's left me. No trouble or quarrel or anything like that. There was nothing but happiness between us. But she thinks she's doing me harm by staying in my life, within my reach, even if I could marry her, which I can't."

"Virginia?"

He nodded and stared moodily into the fire.

"She wants us to live together again," he said.

She considered this in silence, bringing the cups, opening the bottle of milk, calm and methodical.

"Would it be such a bad idea, Blaine?" she asked at last.

"*You* think that, Emma?"

"What is the alternative, if she won't divorce you? And you don't want any more of that. You know that as well as I do, and if she did, what about Mrs. Frey? You need a normal, settled life now, with a proper background. What is Lady Belding's idea? Semi-detached as before?"

"No, though we didn't go into that in detail. I gather that she's ready to give up the stage, and, to be fair with her, it doesn't appear to be the other way round, the stage giving her up. She's making a film at present, and she has one or two other things lined up."

"But she prefers to be Lady Belding?"

"Presumably. Also—she seems prepared to do the thing properly now and have children."

"How do you feel about that?"

"I'd like it. It's what I've always wanted, a completion to one's life, a stake in the future world, if it isn't blown to bits by then. But—I want Anna's."

"We don't often get what we want, all we want, do we? She's right, you know, Blaine. Anna, I mean. And perhaps Virginia's right too. She did stick by you, didn't she? Whatever her purpose, she did that, in the face of the world, and it must have cost her a bit to do it. It would have been easy for her to throw you off then, and give you little option but to marry that dreadful little Mrs. Frey. She saved you from that, and since it meant your disgrace, she must have had something in the back of her mind. She may care for you a lot more than you think."

"Virginia's not capable of caring for anybody but hereslf," he said shortly.

"Well, you're in a better position than I am to decide that," said Miss Dove quietly. "Here's your tea, and I bought some of those biscuits you like. Shall I pour it out?"

"Yes, and stay and have it with me. I don't know what I should do without you, Emma. I sometimes think you're the one I ought to have married," with a smile.

"Hh! Marry your grandmother? If you take so much sugar, and eat those biscuits, you'll get yourself a tummy."

"Why should I care, so long as I can still bend over the operating table? Give me the file on the Dexter case, will you? I can't make up my mind whether to operate or not," and the more personal element was lost in their discussion of the case.

It was some ten days later that he rang up Virginia.

"How about dinner?" he asked without preamble.

"Very nice," she said. "Where?"

"You choose. I don't know much about West End haunts."

"All right. Want me to book a table?"

"Please. Shall I call for you?"

"No. I'll let you know. Shall we recognize each other or will you wear a cauliflower in your buttonhole? Remember?"

He did remember. It was the suggestion she had made, laughing, the first time he had suggested meeting her. It took him back those four years, when she had been the source of all delight to him.

No one could give him back the years that the locust had eaten, but he could not help feeling a pleasure in taking Virginia out again, on these new lines, with the past pushed into the background even if it could never be forgotten.

They dined at a smart restaurant, the cynosure of a good many pairs of eyes of which he was uncomfortably aware though she gaily ignored them, apart from a smiling response to several greetings, as they made their way to their table.

She looked enchanting, and had taken a good deal of trouble to achieve it. Her arms and shoulders were pearly out of the foam of the billowy white in which he had always liked her best in the old days, and round her neck and in her ears were the pearls he had given her as a wedding present. He wondered if she had intentionally given herself the look of a bride, but the orchids she wore gave her a sophistication which she had not worn as a bride.

He looked at them.

"I suppose I should have sent you those," he said. "Who did?"

"Oh—I get them," she said, and he did not pursue the subject.

Actually she had bought them herself, but she preferred him to think they were the gift of some other man.

After that, they met several times, and both knew the direction in which they were going. Virginia would not finish the film she was making for another few weeks, and she had told him that she had decided not to go on tour when her play was taken off in London, so that by the end of May, she would be free.

She had softened a great deal and was anxious to please him, and the hours he spent in her company made his small, not very convenient, flat seem the lonelier and emptier when he went back to it. Everything, he knew, pointed to the common sense of a complete reconciliation with Virginia—everything except his longing for Anna and his knowledge that in Virginia he would find very little of the sort of happiness he had had with her.

Virginia would always be a woman of the world, looking for pleasure, not content unless she were surrounded by friends whose quality was not important so long as they could amuse and entertain her. Virginia could never have shared his life in Skye, with its hardships and discomfort and with only him for companionship and only the crofters, and the gentle old earl, for friends.

Yet what was the alternative to living with her again?

Only his present loneliness, his apology for a home, and no possibility of the son for which he longed.

So, one evening, when they had dined together and could linger over it because she had no longer to go to the theatre, and he had driven out of London and was sitting with her over a final drink in a quiet country inn, he asked her if she were still of the same mind.

"About taking up the cudgels with you again?" she asked.

He smiled.

"Need they be cudgels again?" he asked. "I'd like to think we could be at peace with each other."

"Me too. What about the other woman, Blaine?"

He hesitated. Then he gave her the complete frankness he felt the occasion merited.

"I still care for her, Virginia. I think I always shall. But it's over. By her choice rather than mine. She's gone out of my life and I don't anticipate ever seeing her again. The thing is, can you live with the memory of that? Knowing that my love belongs to someone else? You see how honest I am being, but that's necessary if we are to understand each other."

"I won't pretend that I shall never think of her, because I shall," said Virginia, "but I don't think it will worry me much. I shall have you, you see," with a smile.

"Yes. To that extent, you will," he agreed, returning her smile but with a tinge of sadness in it.

He was burning his boats. This was the point of no return. After this, it would be Virginia and Virginia only, and there must be no bitterness or regret.

"I'm prepared, if you are," said Virginia.

"All right. Shall we drink to it?"

She made a grimace.

"In beer?" she asked, for that was what they were drinking.

"I'm not going to drive on champagne, if that's what you mean," he said, lifting his glass.

"Well, perhaps you're right. And, after all, what we are arranging isn't really on the champagne level, is it? Where do we go from here? Not your horrid little flat."

"No, I wouldn't ask you to come down to that, but don't forget that I haven't got back yet when you're house-unting."

"You want me to find something for us?"

"I should have neither the time nor the energy," he said.

"Nor the interest, Blaine?"

"I suppose I deserved that."

"Don't make it too one-sided. I still have my rag of pride, and I know I'm pushing you into this. Is it quite against your will, Blaine? Can't you find any satisfaction in it at all?"

"I'm sorry, Virginia. I'm not being very nice to you, am I? But I'll do my best to make a success of this. If I weren't prepared to do so, I wouldn't undertake it."

"All right," she said with a smile. "I'm not expecting my bridegroom back, you know. Too many things have happened to us. Shall we go? Mine host is beginning to look anxiously at the clock."

In the car, in the darkness of the now deserted car park, she laid a hand on his arm before he switched on the engine.

"Will you kiss me, Blaine?"

"I'm sorry the suggestion didn't come from me, but I didn't think you would welcome it," he said, and took her face between his hands and kissed her without passion.

That, he felt, was his final good-bye to Anna—his lips on those of another woman.

Virginia found them a home in a converted mews, one of the places now become fashionable and expensive, and furnished it in her own gay, colourful taste, but kept him a room where he could still be himself and where he could work. Collier, who had conceived for her the passion her servants often felt, went with them, as there was a small room which could be made into a room for him, and though Virginia was at first scornful of his association with her, she soon found that he was to be relied upon, and a man about the place had its advantages.

Blaine found considerably more difficulty in settling to the new order of things than either his staff or his wife seemed to do, and it was not until some weeks after they had moved into the house, and after Virginia had said to him, laughing, "I don't want to be actually a stranger to my husband, you know, darling," that he could bring himself to do as she expected, and wanted, and go into her room.

Though Virginia was his wife, and they had been in the closest possible relationship at one time, he had a feeling of betrayal towards his lost Anna, but if Virginia knew it, she gave no indication of doing so. She was sweetly receptive rather than responsive, and tried to infuse into their relationship a warmth which he knew she was incapable of feeling.

He missed Anna the more, for she had been all woman at such times, warm and loving and eager, bringing into such intimate moments a passion which matched and satisfied his own, with no reserves, no reticences such as Virginia, for all her resolve to be what she called a 'real wife' to him, showed. He knew that she was glad when he left her, and would not have welcomed what had been to him and Anna such a sweet relaxation when, passion spent, they lay in each other's arms and slept in serenity and happiness, to wake and look into each other's eyes and know the ever-fresh renewal of their love in their quiet, passionless kiss.

He felt that there was something almost indecent in this association with Virginia, a delight to neither of them, mere animal satisfaction on his part because she was a lovely, yielding woman, and on hers the knowledge of a duty done.

And within a year, Virginia produced her daughter, Sonia.

Though she had made light of her pregnancy, inviting Blaine's satisfaction at her condition, he knew that she resented what it did to the lovely body which had been one of her main preoccupations, and he decided during that time that, even if the child were not his greatly desired son, there should be no others. Virginia did not carry the child as if her body were a temple, a holy of holies, as Anna would have done, he knew. She hated her appearance and towards the end would not go out anywhere, or even look in the mirror for more than the few minutes required for a sketchy make-up.

But after the child was born, she was radiant again.

She went into an expensive clinic, surrounded by every kind of comfort and luxury, and telegrams, letters, flowers, sweets, magazines, poured in as soon as the announcement appeared in *The Times*.

Virginia did everything she was told to do, exercising her body vigorously in her eagerness to get back its lines of beauty. She refused from the first to nurse the child herself.

"I'm not going to be tied down like that, and it makes you ugly," she said, and when she returned to her home, a highly efficient nurse took the care of the baby off her hands and she took up with eager delight the gay social life she loved.

She had no interest in the child. Had it been pretty, she might have shown a certain pride in it, but it was a singularly ugly baby, with her father's dark hair and long face, strange on so young a child.

"How hideous!" had been Virginia's first shocked comment, and after that, she scarcely even looked at it and never held it in her arms.

Blaine felt a yearning tenderness towards the child, soon getting over his disappointment in her sex. He knew that it was from him she must draw all her love, and surely it was to him that she would give it rather than to the lovely, indifferent mother?

Miss Dove, who seldom came to the house, was brought there by him when Sonia was a month old.

"You can leave her here until I ring," said Blaine to the starched, rustling nurse, and when she had done, he picked the baby carefully out of the carrying basket in which it had been brought down and cradled it in his arms.

"Virginia says she's hideous, poor scrap," he said. "One has to agree that at the moment she's no beauty. Too much like me! Let us hope she will grow out of it, and I'm not sure that I think beauty is the best asset for a woman, or even a very desirable one," and Emma Dove knew that he was thinking of Virginia's beauty which had so wrecked his life.

"Would you like to hold her?" he asked sheepishly, and transferred the silk-and-lace wrapped bundle to her arms.

She held Blaine's daughter with pain which did not show in her face, looking down at the tiny thing held in arms which seemed to curve themselves naturally to hold it.

Blaine looked at her.

"You ought to have had children of your own, Emma," he said. "Why have you never married?"

She smiled at him.

"Nobody axed me, sir, she said!"

"Men are such fools," he said shortly. "Is she going to cry? Because if so, the nurse had better have her back and do something about it. Virginia's got some sort of a party on in the other room, and they mustn't be disturbed by the protests of the next generation," his lips curling as he spoke.

Anna saw the announcement of the birth in the paper, and sat with her hands clenched, her face bleak.

She had known, also from the papers at various times, that Blaine was living with his wife again. They were pictured together.

'Sir Blaine Belding, with his lovely wife, were amongst the guests.'

'Sir Blaine and Lady Belding in the paddock.'

'Lady Belding, in mink, at the luncheon given to celebrate the publishing of Sir Blaine Belding's book on brain surgery.'

She had known it, had even felt it was the best course for Blaine to take, but she had not realized that he had taken up life again as Virginia's husband in more than name.

There was some small, unworthy satisfaction in knowing that the child was a daughter, but when she looked at her own sturdy little son, she felt bitter at the loss to both Colin and Blaine.

There was a bitter flavour, too, in the knowledge that Blaine had taken up married life in so intimate a way after such a short interval, only three months at most since their parting. Such a little while for the burying of love.

Still, she refused to indulge in self-pity, that last and final weakness. Instead, she determinedly counted her blessings and knew that they were many.

She was strong and healthy and had never been better in her life than in the keen winds and salt air of the East Coast. She had work which she enjoyed and which brought her in enough for her modest needs, and she worked with the two women whom she regarded with ever-deepening respect and affection and with whom she had formed a lasting friendship.

And above and beyond everything, she had her son.

Colin, emerging with what is to a mother tragic speed from his babyhood, showed a determined and independent spirit which made her both proud and anxious. His stocky little frame, bursting with health, was matched by a mind so quick and retentive that when, at four, he went to the village school, he was soon outstripping senior age groups, learning to read and write and calculate at lightning speed and with an obvious desire to learn.

From necessity, he spent most of his leisure time in the shop, always busy, never bored, the pride and delight of the two Miss Langs, who adored him and spoilt him shamelessly, in spite of Anna's protests and her resentment at being obliged in consequence to be mentor and disciplinarian.

"I can't let him ride roughshod over me as he does over you two," she said to them when they remonstrated, almost in tears, over some well-deserved punishment. "A boy can so easily be ruined with too many adoring women round him and no man," but she did not at any time, by word or hint, satisfy their curiosity about Colin's father, nor, in spite of the close friendship between the three of them, did either of the two ever dare to ask.

There were definite limits in Anna's reserves beyond which they could not go and they were too gentle, too well bred, to let their curiosity master them.

So, in quiet happiness, with Colin the centre and joy of their lives, the three of them pursued their way into the years.

CHAPTER XIII

BLAINE'S daughter was three years old when Virginia went to America again.

She had been restless for some time, and Blaine realized that with the birth of the child, their relationship had begun to slip back into its old channels, only outwardly running together but each set in its separate path.

He had never overcome the feeling of distaste for their marital relationship, not only because he could not see it as other than a betrayal of Anna and his love for her, but also because he had to close his mind to Virginia's own attitude towards it, that of an unpleasant duty duly performed.

After the birth of Sonia, she did not say to him in so many words, 'I hope you're now satisfied', but he knew that that was in her mind, and she made no further overtures to him when she had completely recovered from what had been an easy uncomplicated confinement, but accepted (with relief, he felt sure) the cessation of his visits to her room.

Relieved of that prostitution of love, he let his mind return with more and more longing to Anna, but with no word or sign from her, she was as lost to him as when she had first disappeared from his life, and he sought relief in ever harder work, was seen very little in the social whirl about Virginia, and spent most of his free time in revising and bringing up to date his book, which had become a world text-book, and in adding appendices to it.

Yet, though he had known how far he and Virginia were drifting apart, it was something of a shock to him when she told him that she proposed to make a film in Hollywood.

"I thought you'd finished with all that," he said.

"For the time, I thought so too. I'd got tired of it, but I suppose it's in my blood. My agent has been asking me for some time what I felt about doing something else, and as I'm getting on now (can you believe I'm twenty-eight?) if I'm going to do anything, I'd better do it now. I'm probably forgotten as it is, but it's *Lady of Leisure* they're going to film, and I've been suggested for my own part in it again—produced *à la* Hollywood, of course!" with a light laugh. "It might be fun, and the pay's quite stupendous. Would you mind very much, Blaine?"

"No," he said. "No, I shouldn't mind. After all, it hasn't been a very conspicuous success, has it?"

"Living together again? I've been quite happy, and I thought you were. Still——"

He nodded.

"Yes. As you say, 'still', " he agreed. "How long will you be gone?"

"Impossible to say. They hang about so even when the film is ready to be shot—but they're going to pay me all the time."

"What about Sonia?" he asked.

"Oh, I should leave her here, of course! I couldn't very well drag a baby and a nurse around with me, and she's better here in any case. You wouldn't want her brought up like an American child, I'm sure."

"I didn't realize you were proposing to stay as long as that," he said, "but I'm glad you don't propose to take her, as I couldn't agree to that, even for a short time."

"You're really quite fond of her, aren't you?" she asked, amused. "I wonder why, when you wanted a boy and she's such an ugly little brat."

Blaine drew his brows together and his lips tightened into a thin line. He did not protest against her description of her child. He was even secretly glad that Virginia neither loved nor wanted her, for his small daughter had become the main interest in his life, apart from his work, and he loved her with a deep constancy of purpose, a determination that she should lack nothing in life that he could give her, her mother's love being one of the things he would have to supply by the measure of his own.

She *was* a plain child, with no promise, at three, of her being anything but a plain woman, but she was sweet-natured and tractable and deeply affectionate, showering her love on anyone who showed any response to it or need of it. Collier was her willing slave, and it was he who contrived to house and care for the collection of creatures which seemed to gravitate towards her small person when they were in trouble or need.

A mongrel dog with only three and a half legs, a cat badly mauled in a fight, a bird with a broken wing, a rabbit which had looked mangy and half starved when exhibited for sale in the street, even for a time a spider which had lost some of its legs and had been rescued from the housemaid's broom but which mercifully did not survive the varied diet with which Collier provided it—all such things lived a life of comfort and comparative mutual toleration in the shed at the back of the mews house over which Collier presided without interference, and in which the small Sonia spent entranced hours.

But her father was her hero and her love. Daddy could do everything, even to providing Chop, the dog, with an addition to his half leg which enabled him to get about with more speed and dignity than when she had discovered him, bleeding and half dead from some unknown accident, during a walk in the park with her nurse. There had been such a scene with the usually docile Sonia, that that capable but rather hard-hearted woman had had to bring the poor creature home in the push-chair, Sonia walking manfully beside it and refusing to take its place, however undignified and absurd the situation might make the redoubtable Nanny look.

It was daddy, too, who had doctored the wounds of Micky, the all-sorts cat, who had provided ointment and a diet sheet for Mr. Gloo, the rabbit; daddy, too, who had been greatly relieved when the death of Spike, the spider, had enabled him to escape the loss of face if he had had to admit his inability to provide it with its full complement of legs.

An outing with Sonia was at once a delight and an embarrassment to her father, since he never knew what he might be required to bring home with them. It was on one of these outings, when he had driven them out into the country one

Sunday, that they found the injured thrush, and though had he been alone he would probably have put the suffering little thing out of its misery, he dare not attempt such a thing under Sonia's tearful eyes. They took it back in their lunch basket, Blaine X-rayed it under his daughter's fascinated eyes and occasional instructions, mended the broken wing with great skill, and kept it in a suitable box in his own study until it could fly again, when, after careful explanations to Sonia about its happiness, they set the box on the window-sill and watched it fly away.

He feared for her tender heart, not too useful a possession in the world of today, and yet rejoiced in its sweet affection. He thought, too, with some misgiving about her lack of physical attractions, hoping that when the time came for her to meet the world of men, and attain a knowledge of her own womanhood, that lack of superficial beauty would not leave her as lonely and unsatisfied as were women like Emma Dove. He knew himself, from his own bitter experience, how great a weapon to achieve their heart's desire a woman's mere beauty could be, and how often they missed all that life might have held for them from lack of it.

A woman's whole happiness might depend on the length of her nose!

He was glad that Virginia was prepared so readily to leave Sonia in England, and he knew that, so long as he had the child, he would not greatly miss his wife. In fact, when he was quite honest with himself, he knew that it would be a relief. Apart from the fact that the house was usually filled with her friends far into the night, she herself was a disturbing element in his life, a constant reminder of the failure of his marriage and the barrier between him and the happiness he could have found with his lost Anna.

Virginia wrote fairly regularly at first, then at increasingly long intervals.

She was undoubtedly gay and happy and if she had not found her *métier* in film work, she gave him the impression that she had done so. Her letters were full of references to well-known people, well known even to Blaine, who was not a frequent cinema-goer. She was staying with this one and that, sent him pictures of herself in various situations and in varied company; this important man and that had shown an interest in her work; *Lady of Leisure* had been followed by a contract which, she told him apologetically, would keep her out there 'perhaps as long as another year' though the year lengthened into eighteen months with no suggestion of her return. She adopted the jargon of the studios, much of it unintelligible to him, but as her letters were only of superficial interest to him, he did not trouble to discover their meaning.

Curiosity took him to see the first of these films to be shown in London and he realized that Hollywood had turned her into something different, harder but more glamorous and with her undoubted charms enhanced and pointed by the clothes she wore, or did not wear.

'My wife,' he thought, watching her, but he could not feel that that was the truth, or that he had ever loved her with that early passion, agonized over her lack of love for him, or that, with only the ghost and shadow of that passion left, she had indeed borne him a child, his idolized Sonia.

He felt no distress, was not even surprised, when, nearly two years after she had gone, she wrote and suggested a divorce.

For one thing I don't feel I shall ever want to come back to England, she wrote, *and for another, I want to marry somebody else, Erskine Malley, the producer of my last picture. It will be good for me, and I'm really quite fond of him, and out here one never thinks of a marriage as having to last long, though Erskine is crazy about me. I have promised him to write to you for a divorce. I don't think you'll mind about it and it can't do you any damage now. You wouldn't feel that now you'd have to marry that Frey woman, not after all this time, and I hope you'll have more sense. What about this other woman? I don't know how's the best way for you to set about the divorce, but Mr. Templar will know, and I hope it won't mean having to wait the full three years so that you can get me for desertion. Let me know about that. Things move quickly here, and Erskine won't want to wait a year!*

She added, as a postscript to the letter: *You can keep Sonia, of course. V.*

Blaine laid down the letter and thought of what it would have meant to him a few years ago, but what did it mean now? Very little, except the undisputed possession of the child.

Virginia's letter had been very much to the point, with no waste of words or high phrases about their marriage. She, as well as he, knew that there was no likelihood of happiness for them together, and now that it suited her own purposes, she would be glad to be free from it. Still, to give her her due, she had kept him out of divorce when it could have damaged him, and also she had saved him from feeling obliged to marry Louise Frey. After so long, he did not now feel any such obligation. In fact, it had been rumoured (Virginia had told him this before she left England) that the Freys would eventually come together again.

'What about this other woman?' Virginia asked him now.

'Well, what about her?' he asked himself bitterly.

Oh Anna, Anna, if only I could find you!

What good was a divorce to him now? Yet he could not, in the circumstances, refuse it to Virginia, though after consultation with Jeffrey Templar, he wrote to tell her that she would have to wait for the statutory three years, as the simplest way, since she was no longer in England, of putting it through.

She was disappointed, with a good many things to say about the British marriage laws and the simplicity of the 'much better system' where she was, but she had to wait the third year, not writing again to Blaine except, when the time was ripe, to remind him of it.

It was a simple procedure, with no complications and very little publicity, so that the news of it did not reach Anna.

She had a very considerable trouble and anxiety of her own at that time.

In the early summer of that year, Colin, who was six, had an accident which at the time did not seem likely to have any far-reaching consequences.

Always a bit of a desperado, getting knocks and bruises, and bits chipped off him so that Anna was wont to say she never had a completely whole child, unadorned by bandages or bits of plaster, he came from school one day with a wrist dangling at an odd angle, his face very white.

Anna, who was desperately trying to finish the weaving of some towels for which she had an order, left her loom at sight of him.

"Darling, what on earth have you done *now*?" she exclaimed.

"It's nothing, Mummy," he said, trying to speak reassuringly. "I only fell off the roof."

"Off the roof!" she cried. "What on earth were you doing up there?"

"It was only a dare," he said. "Jimmy Logan bet me I couldn't, and—I could," and he slipped to the floor, unconscious.

When Miss Rosa had sold a leather wallet for half its proper price, and Miss Violet had dropped and broken one of her best bowls, they closed the shop and hurried to Anna's cottage, where Colin had been taken in the doctor's car and had had a broken wrist set.

"But why should he have fainted?" asked Miss Violet anxiously. "He's such a strong little fellow."

"And so brave," quavered Miss Rosa, in tears.

Dr. Brent knew them well, as did everybody else in the neighbourhood, and knew that for the whole of his six years, young Colin Bridger had been the pride and joy of their lives.

"Well, it was a bit of a shock for him, of course, and perhaps just as well," he said consolingly. "Anyway, he seems all right now, and Mrs. Bridger knows what to do for him, and I'll look in tomorrow."

"Don't think about the shop, Anna dear," said Miss Violet. "Don't worry about anything but Colin."

"There are those towels to finish," said Anna with a frown.

"Never mind about them. We can explain that there's been an accident and they can be sent on by post. Now if there's anything Colin wants, you let us know, and if you want us in the night, just rap on the wall."

Their affection and kindness lapped Anna about. She went back to the shop whenever she could, getting a neighbour to stay with Colin, who was a surprisingly long time recovering from the shock of the accident.

The wrist healed quickly and satisfactorily, and even in a few days there was no apparent reason why he should not return to school, but he lay about lethargically, taking no interest in anything, and Anna was more worried than she cared to admit. He was so unlike himself, for he had loved school and all his pursuits there, proud of his position at top of the class of considerably older boys and in the ordinary way would be desperately anxious to get back.

When a month had gone by, Anna managed to persuade him to go back for the last few weeks of the summer term, but when he did so, he seemed to have lost all interest in his work and quickly descended almost to the bottom of the class.

"I can't think what's the matter with you, Colin," said Anna, badly worried. "You know we've always talked about your being able to win a scholarship when you're older so that you can go to a very nice school, but at this rate, you won't even be able to go up into the next class next term. What *is* the matter, darling? Don't you feel well? Does your wrist really hurt still?" for he was no more anxious to join in the games and the fun than to work at his lessons, though he had always been the ring-leader, his quick brain evolving all sorts of wild schemes for the general edification, one of which had been the cause of the present disaster.

"I'm all right," he said, pushing her hand away roughly and going off to his bedroom alone, both things increasing her anxiety so much that she consulted Dr. Brent again.

"He's been so different since the accident," she said. "He's not the same boy at all. He moons about by himself, doesn't even want to come to the shop any more, and the other day he was really rude to kind Miss Rosa."

The doctor, a busy man, did not at first take very much notice of her complaint, gave the boy a tonic and said that if the weather improved so that he could get down on the beach more, he would no doubt be all right again.

But the summer holidays came and went, and Colin was worse rather than better, his black moods more frequent and prolonged, his formerly sunny temper spoilt. He would fly into wild rages at some small cause, or with no apparent cause at all, and when the school re-opened, he refused point blank to return and when Anna in desperation took him to the door herself and left him there, he ran away and was missing for the whole day. When he returned in the evening, the whole village by now in an uproar because he could not be found, he either could not or would not give any account of how and where he had spent the day.

Dr. Brent began to take it more seriously, and advised Anna to take him to the hospital to get a second and more specialized opinion.

From there Anna started a weary and ever more frightening round of visits, even in the end having to take the child up to London to see a specialist in nervous diseases. There was obviously something quite wrong with Colin, and it dated from the accident which at the time had seemed no more than a broken wrist.

Again and again she had to go through the whole miserable procedure of details, many of which seemed to her irrelevant but which pointed more and more to the secret dread in her mind, which was that Colin must have struck his head in his fall from the school roof in such a way as to leave no outward sign of an injury to the brain.

And the last doctor she saw spoke the name which had been trembling in her own mind for weeks.

"We are inclined to think, Mrs. Bridger," he said with formal kindness, "that the boy ought to be seen by Sir Blaine Belding. You've probably heard of him? The finest brain specialist in England, probably in the world."

"Yes," said Anna faintly. "Yes, I—I've heard of him."

"I think it could be arranged. He is, of course, a very busy man, but he could see the boy at St. Agatha's and it would not, of course, cost you anything. Whatever has to be done could be done under the National Health Scheme."

"Whatever has to be done?" she echoed shrinkingly. "You mean—an operation? There may be an operation?"

"That would be for Sir Blaine Belding to say, but you can rest assured, Mrs. Bridger, that whatever Sir Blaine decides will be absolutely for the best, *absolutely*. Now shall I arrange for him to see your boy?"

"Yes. Yes, of course," murmured Anna. "Would it—must I—should I be obliged to go with him?"

He looked surprised.

"Well, somebody will have to take him, of course. Even if he were older, he is not in a fit state to go anywhere alone," he said.

"Oh no, I wouldn't send him alone," she said quickly. "It's just that—that I don't want to go myself—to see Sir Blaine Belding."

"Well, you will be told what appointment can be made, Mrs. Bridger," he said, and ended the interview.

She could not go to meet Blaine again, to take her son to him, knowing that he would realize at once that Colin was his own son. It would reopen everything, give Blaine all that pain and regret. And it was unthinkable that Blaine might have to operate, if an operation were necessary, on the child he knew to be his own.

At all costs, Blaine must not know, and when the letter came making the appointment, she asked Miss Violet if she would go to London with Colin.

"I've gone through so much, taken him to so many places and people," she said, "I don't feel I can do it again. Would you do this for me, dear Miss Violet?"

"But, my dear, of course I will! I'm proud and honoured that you should ask me, and trust me, and you know the dear child will be completely safe with me. I won't let him out of my sight for an instant," for by this time, it was definitely not safe to leave Colin alone. His actions were unpredictable.

She waited in an agony of apprehension for their return to Embury, but Miss Violet could say little about it.

"Sir Blaine Belding is such a very nice man," she said. "Grave, you know. Rather stern. He didn't say much, didn't even ask a great many questions, but thorough, and really interested. You liked him too, didn't you, Colin?"

"Yes," said the child in the surly, monosyllabic fashion so heart-breakingly different from his former cheerful, incessant chatter.

Anna looked at him, her heart in her eyes.

He knew Blaine now. They had met, had spoken to each other, neither knowing how close was the link between them. For the first time she was thankful that there was no resemblance between them. Blaine could not possibly have had any idea.

"What actually was his opinion?" asked Anna when Colin had gone to bed.

"Well, of course, he didn't tell me. Doctors never do, do they? And Colin was there all the time. I didn't see Sir Blaine alone. All he said was that he would write to you."

It was Miss Dove who wrote the letter.

It gave Anna a jolt to see the familiar signature, though now it was 'E. Dove, Secretary to Sir Blaine Belding'.

So Miss Dove was with him again. She was glad of that. At least he was not alone at such times as Virginia was away, for Anna had read that Virginia was, or had been, in Hollywood making films.

Miss Dove wrote to say that Sir Blaine had gone very carefully into the case, and had decided that, if Mrs. Bridger were willing, he would operate to remove the pressure on the brain.

Sir Blaine wishes me to tell you that such an operation, though serious, is not dangerous and he is confident that you will consent to it. Sir Blaine will perform the operation himself, and a date will be arranged for your son's admission to St. Agatha's Hospital, where he is likely to remain for at least a fortnight.

Anna wrote at once, typing the letter and signing herself 'A. Bridger' in what she hoped did not look like the writing of

227

Anna Mere, and in due course Miss Violet took the child to St. Agatha's and, at Anna's urgent request and at her expense, stayed in an hotel near the hospital until the operation was over.

"Are you sure you won't go yourself, Anna?" she asked. "He will want you as soon as it's over, you know."

Anna gave a sad little smile.

"He hasn't wanted any of us lately," she said, "so if he does want me, we shall know that it's been a success. I'd rather you went if you will, Miss Violet. Will you?"

"I'd do anything for you, Anna. You know that. We're so fond of you, Rosa and I. You and Colin have made all the difference to our dull lives. We do hope you'll never have to leave us."

"I'm not likely to do that. I'm too happy here," said Anna, touched as she always was by a gratuitous expression of kindness and affection.

"You might some day marry again," said Miss Violet gently. "It would be good for Colin to have a father."

"Nothing could ever replace his own," said Anna in a quiet voice.

"You loved him, my dear?"

"More than my life, and always shall. Miss Violet, I know you must at times have felt that I might—tell you about Colin, but it's just one of those things I can never talk about. I've been most grateful to you and Miss Rosa for taking me on trust as you have. I would like to tell you, but—it isn't just my story."

Miss Violet touched her arm for a moment.

"We should never ask it or expect it, Anna dear," she said. "I know that Colin's father must have been a fine man or you would not have loved him. Shall we not talk about it any more? And if you really wish me to take Colin to London, of course I will."

On the day of the operation, Anna had a white, drawn face and stayed very close to the telephone which had recently been installed in the shop, and late in the afternoon, Miss Violet's call came through.

"Well, Anna dear, it's over," she said cheerfully. "I have seen Sir Blaine Belding (what a nice man he is!) and he says he has every confidence that the operation has been a complete success, and that all that remains now is for him to be looked after well and given every chance to recover. There's no need for you to worry at all."

Anna gave the receiver blindly into the waiting hand of Miss Rosa and collapsed, her head on the table, her whole body shaking with the intensity of the relief after the hours of strain in which she had not eaten and had scarcely spoken.

She had known, she had *known*, that Blaine would save Colin, but the suspense had been terrific.

Miss Rosa's bird-like voice finished the conversation for her, and she put up the receiver and gave Anna a convulsive little hug.

"Now you must have something to eat, dear," she said, "and I will tell you a little secret. Violet bought a bottle of port for us before she went! She said she was sure you would need something when this was over. She did not know quite what to buy because, of course, we ourselves are not accustomed to drinking any sort of intoxicant, but we felt that port is a *ladylike* drink. Our dear mother used to take it, just a small glass when she felt the need of a little stimulant," and she bustled about in pleased importance, produced two tumblers, poured a very large amount for Anna and a very small one for herself and set it down on the table with the dainty meal of sandwiches and little cakes.

"You know, I never take anything," she said delightedly, "but I'm really going to have a little sip with you now. I hope it won't go to my head! What a scandal *that* would be for Embury! I think I had better close the shop and pull down the blinds just in case!" doing so.

"Now I think we should make it a little toast," she said. "What shall we say? To little Colin, of course—and I think it would be nice to say Sir Blaine Belding as well, don't you? Because, of course, our present happiness is due to him."

Anna, not quite dry-eyed, nodded and smiled.

"To Colin and—Sir Blaine Belding," she said shakily.

"To Colin and Sir Blaine Belding, bless them both!" said Miss Rosa and took an infinitesimal sip of the port, feeling herself a very gay dog indeed.

In spite of her fear of ever meeting Blaine, Anna could not keep away from Colin for more than the first week. Then Miss Violet returned, and Anna took her place.

It was not difficult to find out at St. Agatha's when Sir Blaine was expected, and she took care to pay her own visits at such times as she could feel safe, though at each opening of the door in the small private room into which the child had been put, her heart was in her mouth.

"Sir Blaine thought he should be alone for the present, as it is so essential for him to be kept quite quiet," the nurse told her, "but he is getting on so well that we may be able to move him into the ward room. He is such a dear little boy, and so good—and simply devoted to Sir Blaine!"

"Sir Blaine has been so very kind," said Anna unsteadily.

"He's very fond of children, you know, and he seems to have taken a great fancy to Colin. I think one reason why he wants to keep him in here instead of in the ward is so that he can spend more time with him than with the others! In fact, I don't ever remember his visiting a patient so often after the operation is really over and the patient on the way to recovery."

The girl smiled as she said it.

"I don't think he has a son of his own, has he?" asked Anna in a low voice.

It was so wonderful to be able to talk about Blaine again, to say and to hear his name.

"No, just a little girl. He was telling Colin about her yesterday and saying that one day he might bring her to see him. Children are not allowed at all here as visitors, but of course Sir Blaine is a law unto himself!"

"What is she like, his little girl?"

"Actually a very plain child. He brought her here to wait for him one day when he was going to take her to the Zoo. Quite a dear little girl, but—with such a beautiful mother as Lady Belding——!"

"Yes. Very beautiful," said Anna, feeling a certain malicious satisfaction in the knowledge that the lovely Virginia had produced a plain little girl whilst she, Anna, had produced Colin!

One day, when Colin had been in the hospital a month and his return to his home could be considered, the sister stopped Anna on her way to the little room where Colin still remained.

"Oh, Mrs. Bridger, Sir Blaine would like to see you the next time he comes," she said. "I will let you know when he will be free."

Anna took fright. She had been anticipating something of the sort, however, and was prepared.

"I'm very sorry, Sister," she said, "but I must go home today—at once, in fact. It will not be possible for me to see Sir Blaine."

The sister looked surprised and displeased.

"Surely one day would not be too difficult for you, Mrs. Bridger?" she asked coldly. "After all, we regard Sir Blaine Belding's wishes as commands here, you know."

"I am sorry," repeated Anna firmly, "but it is not possible. Will you please tell Sir Blaine? Please say that I am very— grateful to him, but—I can't stay."

The sister's eyebrows went up still further.

"That does not sound very grateful, Mrs. Bridger," she said. "I should have thought you would want to see Sir Blaine. He has done a great deal for your little boy and takes a great interest in him."

"I'm sorry," said Anna again, and closed her lips.

The sister gave a little shrug.

"Well, of course, if you feel that your own affairs are more important than seeing Sir Blaine, I suppose there is nothing more to say. I will tell him," and she marched off in high dudgeon.

She could not know the passionate longing Anna felt to have been able to give a different answer. To see him again! To hear his voice, touch his hand!

It did not make it any easier for her to know that Colin was full of enthusiasm for the man he called '*my* doctor', and could not be kept off the subject.

He had been out of bed for some days, wrapped up in the gay little dressing-gown Anna had made from material which she had woven for the purpose, and except that he still looked pale and had lost a lot of weight, he was almost himself again, the old sweet, chattering self, interested in everything.

Today he was sitting on the floor playing with a collection of the little toy motor cars he loved, and when he saw his mother, he gave a shout of joy.

"Mummy, look what my doctor brought me this morning! Two new Dinkies, a petrol lorry and an ambulance. He said I could go home in the ambulance! As if I could! I couldn't even get one toe into it. Aren't they smashing? And he says that when I go home, he'll give me a big garage to keep them all in."

"Sir Blaine spoils you, darling," said Anna, sitting on the floor with him to examine the new toys. "I'm afraid you're going to miss him when you come home."

"Yes, I am," he said frankly, "but, Mummy, he says that if you'll let me, I can go and stay sometimes at his house. He lives in the country, and he's got a little girl called Sonia. She came to see me yesterday with my doctor. I like her very much and she likes to play with the sort of things I like. Of course she's *much* younger than I am. She's only five!" from the superior heights of six and a half. "Mummy, do you think I could go and stay with them? They've got a dog called Chop and a cat called Micky, and a sand pit and a paddling pool and all sorts of things. Could I?"

"You want to very much, don't you, darling?" she asked, a tug at her heart-strings because he was no longer all her own.

Blaine was taking his share of him after all!

"Yes, terribly," said Colin. "He said you could come too if you wanted to."

"I don't think I'd want to," said Anna. "You see, I've got my work to do, and since your illness, I haven't done much, but if you'd really like to go to stay with Sir Blaine, well, when he asks you, I think you could go. You won't forget, though, that they live a very different sort of life from ours, will you, darling? They have a lot more money than we have, and I wouldn't like you to think—well, that your home isn't a very good one after theirs."

He moved across the floor to give her a convulsive hug.

"No, of course not, Mummy," he said. "I should never think that."

But Anna remained unconvinced and apprehensive, knowing how impressionable Colin was, how devoted to Blaine, and how much eager delight he would derive from such things as Blaine would have provided for his own child.

When Blaine was told the next day that Mrs. Bridger had had to go home without seeing him, he gave one of his wry grimaces.

"Oh well," he said, "it's the boy I'm interested in, of course. What sort of woman is the mother, Sister?"

"Oh—quite an ordinary type, quiet, well-spoken. Not well off, I should say. Colin says they have some sort of shop."

"No husband presumably? It was she who signed the papers, I believe."

"Yes. I asked Colin if he had a father, but he said no, he has never had one. Possibly——?"

Blaine nodded.

"Let's be charitable and say she's a widow," he said. "Well, I'll go in and see the child, and I think we could arrange for him to leave in a few days. I take it he has a comfortable home? Would be looked after?"

"Oh yes, I should say so, and she seems quite fond of the him, though you remember we thought it strange that she did not come with him in the first place, but sent someone else, a Miss Lang. And not wanting to stay to see *you*!"

"Oh well, we won't worry about that," he said. "There's nothing the matter with the boy now that time won't cure," and he went off to see Colin.

He did not quite understand his exceptional interest in this particular patient. It had been a tricky but not desperate operation for a surgeon of his experience, and he had not had any serious doubt of its success, and the boy had made normal and satisfactory progress after it. There was no reason why he should regard it as in any way an exceptional case, and yet he had that

233

feeling of being drawn to him, of not wanting to lose touch with him as he did when other patients left the hospital cured, to return to their homes.

After his usual delighted welcome, Colin informed him that his mother had said he might go and stay with Blaine and Sonia if he were asked.

Blaine had almost regretted having made the suggestion, for why, after all, should he want to retain such a contact?

Still, he could not change his mind now, in face of the boy's delighted anticipation, and it would be good for Sonia, who was rather a lonely little soul.

"Well, we'll see about it, old chap," he said. "You're going home first, though. You're glad of that?"

"Oh yes, but I like it here," said Colin, "and I don't want to leave you. Sonia's lucky, isn't she?"

"Well, so are you," said Blaine, but it gave him a thrill of pleasure to hear the real affection in Colin's voice.

If only he had had a son like this! Sonia was the apple of his eye, and he felt he could never have loved any child better, but this Colin Bridger was such a fine little chap, bright and happy now, and undoubtedly possessed of a very good brain, a son one could have been proud of.

Miss Violet went to bring Colin home, since Anna felt she could not risk any further request that she should see Blaine, and during the summer holidays, before the boy's return to school, the invitation came for him to spend a fortnight with the Beldings at their home in Kent.

Blaine himself wrote the letter, and added that if it were convenient to Mrs. Bridger to bring Colin to London, he himself would take him down to The Beacon in his car.

Anna was in a quandary. If she did as he suggested, and took Colin to the Harley Street consulting room, how was she to avoid meeting Blaine? Finally she devised a scheme which was not devoid of risk, but which worked satisfactorily.

She took Colin from the London station in a taxi to Harley Street and left him at the door.

"I don't want to come in, dear," she said. "I have a lot to

do whilst I am in London, so I'll just sit in the taxi whilst you ring the bell, and when I've seen you go in, I shall know you're all right. Good-bye, darling. Have a good time."

"Oh, I shall, Mummy," he said blithely, kissed her and ran across the path with his little case of clothes in his hand, his pockets stuffed with his cars and with a cardboard box tied to the case containing a doll which Anna had bought and dressed for Sonia.

'He's not a bit concerned about leaving me,' she thought with a little stab, and then pulled herself together with an effort. How could she expect him, at six, to be anything but filled with excitement and anticipation at such a visit? She was just 'Mummy', always there, familiar and unexciting, and this was an adventure.

She had provided him with note-paper and stamped, addressed envelopes, and his scrappy letters, laboriously written in his big, unformed writing told her all sorts of things, though nothing she really wanted to know—except that he was happy.

Sonia and me went fishing in the goldfish pond only she cryed when we cort one which was silly becos it was only a net and we put them back. It was good fun.

Sonia and me bilt a big castel in the garden but the gardner didnt mind. He is called Rush and he has a big pimpel on his nose that is called Alik. Rush is very funny.

We went to the sea yesterday and Uncle Blane is going to teach me to swim. Sonia only paddles but then she is only a girl and Uncle Blane says it dosnt matter if a girl cant swim but he says a boy must. I want to swim like him. I want to do everything like him. He is smashing. Do I have to come home yet? Uncle Blane says I can stay as long as you will let me.

'Uncle Blane'!

So he had progressed as far as that? Colin's letters were full of him now. He was obviously the boy's hero, and Anna tried not to harbour the feeling that could only be jealousy. Was it not what she had always wanted, without seeing the least chance

235

of its happening? That Blaine and Colin should know and love each other?

Colin, at his urgent request, stayed until the day before he was due back at school, and returned brown-faced, bright-eyed, fit and sturdy again and bringing with him an assortment of new possessions, including a rabbit in a hutch.

When Blaine wrote that he was driving the boy down to Embury himself, Anna in a panic absented herself, making some excuse so that only the two Miss Langs were there to welcome him.

"Where's Mummy?" he demanded, wide-eyed and disappointed.

"She's very sorry, dear, but she had made an appointment to go and see somebody in Yarmouth, a very important customer who is a cripple and not able to get up and whom Mummy is teaching to weave lying in bed. She had to go today," explained Miss Violet, though it had puzzled her, for surely all days were the same to Mrs. Elder?

"I am very sorry not to meet Mrs. Bridger," said Sir Blaine. "I should like to have told her myself how pleased my little daughter and I have been to have Colin. Will you tell her so? And that I hope she will let him visit us again in his next holidays?"

"Yes. Yes, of course I will, Sir Blaine," said Miss Violet whilst Miss Rosa, excited and flustered by her first meeting with anyone so illustrious, got the tea and dropped things until the small Sonia, grave-eyed and capable, came to her rescue, carrying plates from the little kitchen to the living-room, loving the smallness of everything. Later Miss Rosa took her to see the latest of Maisie's family, and when she and her father returned home, they were accompanied by a small, fluffy kitten.

"May I really have any one I like, Miss Rosa?" asked Sonia, her arms full of the family.

"Yes, dear, whichever you like. Look, isn't this a pretty one?" picking out the fluffiest and fattest and more lively.

"Yes," agreed Sonia, but in the end she put down four of the kittens and kept in her arms the smallest and weakest, a rather poor little thing which was always being bowled over by the others in their rough play and seemed unable to stand up for itself.

"This is the one I'd really like," she said politely, "if you're sure you can spare it."

"But that's such a poor, weak little thing, and not even very pretty," protested Miss Rosa, whilst the others looked on.

"I know, but that's why. You see, perhaps nobody else will want it and it needs more loving than the others because it's so small and isn't so pretty. May I have this one, Daddy? I shall call her Lovely because it may make her feel better."

"Perhaps it isn't a girl kitten," he said, and raised an inquiring eyebrow at Miss Rosa, who was covered with confusion.

"I don't know," she admitted. "We never know, I'm afraid. Do you—do you mind?"

He smiled.

"Not a bit, if it's the one Sonia wants," he said. "Come along now, chicken. It's time for us to go. Say good-bye to everybody."

She said it sweetly, with thanks for 'my nice tea', and a tearful hug for Colin, who himself blinked a little, and then they were gone.

Anna heard all about it when she returned, what a dear little girl Sonia was and how distinguished and important-looking Sir Blaine was—"but so friendly and nice, Anna, that you'd never think he's who he is! Such a pity you couldn't have been here!"

She realized what a profound impression Blaine had made on Colin's mind and wondered many times whether it would not have been better if she had not let him pay the visit. Then she checked herself for selfishness. It was Colin's *right* to know his father and to enjoy the way he lived, and all the things which she herself could not give him.

But it was a deep pain to her to feel that, to some extent, she had been supplanted by Blaine. Nothing could destroy the child's love for her, but it was no longer all her own and when, towards the end of the term, Blaine wrote to her to ask if Colin might spend part of the holidays with them, she had to fight down the impulse to refuse.

We shall have a quiet Christmas, he wrote, *though there will be a few parties now that Sonia goes to a nursery school and has some little friends, but as I feel sure you would not like to spend Christmas without Colin, I shall be pleased if you will come with him and, if you have to return to your work, leave him with us for a little while.*

Well, she couldn't do that, of course.

Sonia had written in big, printing letters to Colin, *PLEASE SPEND XMAS WITH US. X X X X X*, and he was wild to go.

"Do let me, Mummy. Oh please, please let me!" he begged.

"But I can't go myself, darling," she said. "You know we're opening the shop for Christmas," though she knew that such little business as might result could perfectly well be done by the Miss Langs.

"But I could go, Mummy!" he said with the unconscious cruelty of children.

"And leave me? At Christmas?" she could not keep herself from asking.

He hugged her, suddenly contrite.

"But you could come too, Mummy. Really you could. I'll ask Auntie Violet if you can. It's lovely at The Beacon, and you'd have a lovely great big room as big as—oh as big as all our cottage!"

In the end it was arranged that he should spend Christmas Day at Embury, and go to the Beldings the next day, and that they would postpone their celebration of Christmas Day itself to Boxing Day at Blaine's house so that Colin would not miss it.

He went off in wild spirits, put in charge of the guard to London, where Blaine would meet the train, and Anna knew that though she had done everything she could think of to make his Christmas Day a happy and exciting one, it had paled before his anticipations of what he would find at The Beacon.

Uncle Blaine would do this. Uncle Blaine would have that. Uncle Blaine had promised so-and-so, a fancy-dress party, a visit to the circus and to a pantomime, and, if there should be the snow for which Colin passionately wished, a snowman and snow-balling in the garden.

"But the snow would be just the same here, darling, and probably lots more of it, and all the fields for snow-balling and a snowman," Anna pointed out, but none of it would be as good, in Colin's view, as the snow that would fall on The Beacon garden which was 'miles and miles', though probably no more than an acre at most.

Still—there was always work. And Colin was happy. And Blaine would be happy.

And the child was *hers*. Nothing could make any real difference to that.

CHAPTER XIV

SINCE Colin had made no mention of Virginia after his summer visit to The Beacon, Anna had concluded that she was still in Hollywood making the pictures she sometimes saw advertised, but after the Christmas visit, she could no longer restrain herself from asking the question nagging at her mind.

"What about Sonia's Mummy?" she asked casually, when he was giving her further rapturous accounts of their doings.

"Oh, there isn't a Mummy," he said. "They're debossed. What's debossed, Mummy?"

Her heart gave a lurch and then seemed to stand still.

Blaine was free then. If she had waited, not cut herself adrift from him——

But sanity returned. She *had* cut herself adrift, to do the best thing for him. It was still the best, her life and ways so far removed from his. If he ever knew where she was to be found, and especially if he knew about their child, he would feel a compulsion to marry her and who was she, now, to become Lady Belding? Her lip curled in contempt of herself at the thought. No, this was her life, the sort of life to which she really belonged, and after all these years, she would be only a bitter-sweet memory to Blaine.

"What *is* debossed, Mummy?" Colin repeated, tugging at her arm. "Sonia didn't know either."

"Well, you haven't got the word quite right, darling," she said, pulling herself together, "but it doesn't matter. It's not a very nice word or one that you need to know. It only means that when two people are married, and they—they're not very happy together, and—don't want to go on living in the same home together—then they don't—they don't have to."

"Oh well, Uncle Blaine and Sonia don't mind about being debossed," said Colin cheerfully. "Sonia can't remember her very well but I don't think she liked her much. Mummy, were you and my daddy debossed?"

Anna drew a deep, anxious breath. Some day this would have to come. She wondered that it had been so long in coming. What was she to say?

She took refuge in temporization.

"No, darling," she said. "Nothing like that. One day I'll tell you all about it, but not just yet. You are not quite old enough to understand it, but when you are—I'll tell you. Will you just not talk about it till then?"

"O.K.," he agreed at once. "I think it would be nice to have a daddy, but I don't suppose he'd have been like Uncle Blaine, would he? And I've got him, haven't I? Mummy, it's stopped raining. Can I go out and get some sweets? I've still got some of the money Uncle Blaine gave me."

She heaved a sigh of relief. It was over for the time being, even if only put off.

What was she going to tell Colin when the time came? Now that he knew Blaine, it was going to be so much more difficult. She could never tell him the whole truth. She would have to fall back on the thing she had resolved she would not do, and tell lies to Colin about his birth.

Bringing her mingled happiness and sadness, Blaine began to write to her with some regularity, obviously feeling that Colin had constituted a bond between them and seeking to know more about her, and she had to reply to the letters, typing them and signing them 'A. Bridger', and gradually they became less formal, not such a burden to her to write, just as his took on a more friendly tone and seemed to invite her interest in his work and his life.

There was not a great deal that she could tell him in reply. The happenings at Embury were very small, though she infused the telling of them with a sly, unmalicious humour which pleased him, and which reminded him of Anna. In fact, there was a lot about these letters of hers which reminded him of Anna. There was a certain bitter happiness in the reminders, and his letters became more frequent in consequence.

In one of them, he struck a more personal note than he had done so far.

Though we have never met (that is hardly due to me!) I feel that I know you from these letters of yours, but only as 'Mrs. A. Bridger', Colin's mother. When you write again, won't you implement the initial so that I can think of you as someone a little more personal than 'Mrs. Bridger'? he wrote, and the next time she signed her name, she wrote 'Ann Bridger', not daring to put the rather less popular name of 'Anna'.

And when next he wrote, he started: *My dear Ann, you see how quickly I have taken advantage of my new knowledge.*

She tried in her letters not to sound too much like herself, not to use phrases which he might associate with her and having no idea that she herself permeated the whole letter, her likes and dislikes, her particular brand of humour which had been his as well, her wide tolerance of others, her sympathy and understanding.

And then, after Colin had paid yet another visit to them at The Beacon, came a letter which filled her with a mixture of pain, happiness, elation and despair.

My dear Ann, he wrote, as always now,

I have done a lot of thinking lately and I want you to share these thoughts and, I hope and think that they are good ones.

You probably know that Sonia has no mother. She has been cared for by a trained children's nurse from birth, but now that she is going to school, there is no need for me to retain the nurse's services, nor does she wish to stay, and she is leaving very shortly. She has been more or less looking after the housekeeping, though I have servants, of course, and it has occurred to me that the best way for me to fill the vacancy she will leave is by engaging a housekeeper.

You will realize now what I have in mind.

I cannot help knowing something of your circumstances and that you must work for your living and Colin's, and you may not be disposed to give up your present independence, and the shop, for what will, after all, be only a job. I hope, however, that you will consider it, if not for your own sake, then for Colin's. You know that I am very fond of him, and he is undoubtedly very happy to be here with my little daughter—and I think I may add, with me. I need not stress the point to you that he is an extremely intelligent child, much above the average, and both deserves and would profit by a better education than you are able to give him, even if later on he can win scholarships. This better education I can give him, and will do so if you can agree to my proposition.

In different circumstances, I might ask you to let me adopt him, take him as my son and give him my name. But from the little I know of you, I hesitate to do this as it would mean your giving him up entirely. It may be a selfish attitude to take, but I am not prepared to share him to the extent of his having two homes with two completely different environments. It would not be fair to him, and there would be difficulties in the future, when he is, for instance, at a public school, which might cause suffering both to him and to you.

On the other hand, if you came to me as my housekeeper, you and Colin would have your home here, and you, as his mother, would not be put into the normal position as my paid housekeeper. I should see to it that your position in my household would be one not incompatible with the one I should wish Colin to occupy. You would act as my hostess and be received by my friends and treated in every way as an equal.

I will not elaborate this at the moment by speaking of salary and conditions, though naturally I should expect to pay you enough to keep up the position you would occupy.

I am not an easy man to live with, Ann. I have been a lonely man for many years, with its natural consequences, but since the continued presence of Colin in my life would depend on your being able to put up with such of my company as you could not avoid, I should try to make myself not utterly unbearable! Nor would you need to see a great deal of me, as I have rooms in town which I use frequently when my work makes it advisable, and I could spend more time there in the children's school terms if you did find me too unbearable as a companion.

243

I have not disguised from you that my real interest in this matter is Colin. I have never had a son, and I would not change my little Sonia for any child on earth, but I should have felt myself singularly blest had I a son like Colin.

I will leave this with you now. Take what time you need to think it over, and if you feel it would be a workable scheme for both of us, we can at long last meet to discuss it. I confess that I should look forward to that.

Yours very sincerely,
Blaine Belding.

She read the long letter through several times, though its full import had been clear to her at the first reading.

Such a thing had never occurred to her, and her mind was in a state of chaos.

What he suggested was, of course, impossible, though he could not know that.

But where did she herself stand in the matter? Had Blaine forgotten Anna Mere? Was that episode in his life so far in the background that her return would be no more than an embarrassment to him? Did he love that memory still? Would he want to have that love revived if such a thing were possible when they met again?

She realized that, if they did meet so that he became aware of her identity, there were only two alternatives possible. They must either marry or part irrevocably. There was no middle way.

Her heart throbbed painfully at the thought of marrying Blaine, that unimaginable and surely impossible happiness, for how would such a marriage affect him? Would it do so adversely now, after all these years, and with no barrier of Virginia or a divorce between them? Could she hold such a position? What had his life become? His friends?

She looked at his letter again.

If she went to him as a paid housekeeper, she was to be 'received by his friends and treated in every way as an equal'.

She smiled a little at his ignorance of the ways of the world, his world, if he imagined that that could be so, that a woman who was living in his house as a paid employee would ever be regarded as an equal by his friends. In fact, almost certainly, if he tried to put her in such a position, she would be regarded as his mistress!

But the main thing in her mind, as he had so frankly stated was in his, was Colin.

The thought of his education and his future had long been a source of anxiety to her. Whilst he was so young, only just out of babyhood, the village school could supply his needs, but what after that? He *might* win a scholarship when the time came. She certainly hoped that he would, and the school-mistress encouraged her in the belief that he would, but what if he did not? Competition, she knew, was keen, and a boy had to be actually brilliant, not merely above average, to get the coveted award. And meantime he was here in Embury, his friends and associates the cheerful little ruffians whom he was even now beginning to resemble, his speech and manners deteriorating, his ideas not always the ones she had tried to give him.

Blaine could give him everything he needed, and now, from the beginning.

The other alternative, to part from Blaine entirely, was an anguish to her, and she realized how much it had meant to her to have him even at such a distance, and so impersonally, in her life.

For Blaine's sake, if she were convinced that it would be the best thing for him, she could do it again as she had done it once —but what about Colin then? The boy was devoted to his father and would not only bitterly resent being torn away from this association with him, but might also be changed in his very nature by such a ruthless act, resentful and frustrated and unforgiving, no matter what reason she could give him for the break, nor whether she put the blame of it on his father or on her own shoulders.

If she and Blaine parted, could she bear to give Colin up? In his letter, he said he might have suggested adopting him, in which case a condition would be complete surrender of the boy.

Had she the courage, the strength, the utter selflessness, to do that for Colin?

She could not believe herself capable of such a thing. The agony of it could not yet even be contemplated, and her heart knew such bitterness as it had never felt that Blaine, not realizing what he was doing, should be in a position to ask this sacrifice of her. Had she not suffered enough already through him? Was yet another punishment to he laid on her for taking that short happiness when it was put into her hands?

In the end, torn by her indecision, she spoke on the telephone to Emma Dove. Surely that sane and well-balanced mind could help her to see the right path, and to take it whatever it cost?

"Is it you, Miss Dove?" she asked.

"Yes? Sir Blaine Belding's secretary," said the brisk, remembered voice.

"Miss Dove, I want so much to see you," said Anna, feeling awkward and embarrassed now that the moment had come. "Do you remember my voice at all?"

"No. Should I?"

"Are you alone in the room?"

"Yes."

"It's—Anna. Anna Mere."

She heard the gasp of surprise.

"Good gracious! After all these years? Where are you?"

"I'm some distance away, in Suffolk, but I could come up to London if you can let me talk to you for a little while. Will you?"

"Yes, certainly. When? Not today," Anna heard the turning of pages. "Tomorrow some time? Not till the evening, I'm afraid. Do you mind that?"

"No. I can be anywhere you like, and at any time."

"Then make it tomorrow evening. Six o'clock? I'll go to my club. Will you take down the address?"

Anna did so, and then said rather breathlessly, "You won't tell Sir Blaine, will you? Not that I have rung up or anything?"

"Not if you don't want me to," said Miss Dove in her rather

246

brusque fashion. "Tomorrow then. I'll try not to be late, but if I am, wait in the lounge and order yourself a drink."

Anna laughed a little, though rather shakily.

"I'm not likely to do that, but of course I'll wait," she said and rang off.

The die was cast. She was resolved to do whatever Emma Dove thought she should do, even the unthinkable thing of giving up Colin.

She had to wait only a few minutes before Miss Dove, a friendly hand outstretched, came across the club lounge to her.

"Anna!" she said. "You don't look a day older."

Anna smiled unbelievingly, though Miss Dove was no flatterer.

"I often feel a hundred," she said. "It's so nice of you to see me."

"Nonsense. It's a pleasure. We can't talk here. Let's go into one of the little writing-rooms, and presently we can have dinner. You can stay for that?"

"Thank you. I'd like to," said Anna, who had arranged for Colin to sleep in the Langs' cottage, as he sometimes did.

"Now what's it all about?" asked Miss Dove when they had found an empty room with a good fire.

"I don't know quite where to begin," said Anna awkwardly, "but—does the name Bridger mean anything to you?"

"Bridger? Why, of course. Isn't that the name of the little boy Sir Blaine operated on and has befriended? Had him down at his house?"

Anna nodded and looked away. She did not know quite how much Emma Dove had known about Skye, but now she had to know.

"Yes. Colin. Colin—Bridger. He—I—I'm his mother, Miss Dove."

"Really? And Sir Blaine doesn't know?" asked Miss Dove, plainly surprised.

"No. We've not met."

"You're married then, Anna?"

Anna faced her steadily. her head held up. She was not going to tell this as a shame-faced, sordid thing.

"No. I've never married," she said. "I call myself Mrs. Bridger for Colin's sake."

Something in her look, her tone, gave Miss Dove the first glimmering of an astounding idea.

"How old is the boy?" she asked.

"Seven," said Anna.

Seven. Miss Dove thought rapidly. Seven years ago, just over seven years ago, Blaine was in Skye.

"Anna, why have you come to me?" she asked directly. "It's about the boy, isn't it?"

"Yes."

"And about—Blaine? Is he—Blaine's son, Anna?"

"Yes," said Anna simply, and there was a long silence between them whilst Emma digested this information and all that it implied.

"Does Blaine know?" she asked at last.

"No."

"I see. Difficult, isn't it? He's very fond of the boy. Unreasonably so, I've thought. But now——" and she paused.

"I never meant them to meet at all," said Anna. "It was just the coincidence, the—the rather frightening coincidence of the operation Colin had to have, though I never thought at the time that anything like this could possibly come out of it."

"Why have you told me this, Anna?"

"Things have become—so terribly confused and difficult. Blaine and I have been corresponding for some time, though he hasn't known, doesn't know, who I am. Then, the other day, he sent me this letter. I'd like you to read it," taking it from her bag.

Miss Dove read it through slowly and then folded it and handed it back. Her face was very serious and thoughtful.

"Yes, I see," she said. "I see how difficult it is. What did you feel about it when you had it?"

"All sorts of things. Confusion and chaos mostly. I don't

feel very differently now. You see, it would be quite impossible for me to do what he suggests."

"Yes, I see that, of course," said Miss Dove slowly. "May I ask you something?"

"Yes. Anything."

"Then—this wasn't just an isolated thing? Not just a passing affair? Anna, I knew that you and Blaine were living together in Skye."

"Yes, we were. For about eight months. We were—happy, in spite of everything."

"Yes. Looking back, I know that. He *was* happy, in spite of everything, as you say. What happened then?"

"I went away. I left him. He didn't want me to, but I could see it would be wrong for him, do him harm, especially just then, when he had come back and had all that to face. I couldn't do anything for him, except go away from him."

"Did you know about the child? Did he know?"

"No. I was fairly sure, but he had no idea. If he had had, he —might have made it too difficult for me to go," she said painfully.

"You're a brave woman, Anna."

"It wasn't easy. It hasn't been easy since, especially now that he and Colin have met. You see how it is, don't you? He could not know I was Colin's mother without also knowing that he is his own son."

"Yes. Quite," said Miss Dove and paused again.

"You know about Virginia?" she asked then.

Anna nodded.

"Yes," she said, with a shadowy ghost of a smile. "Colin told me that according to Sonia, they were 'debossed'."

Miss Dove laughed.

"A grand word for what happened! Of all fantastic things, Virginia did somehow manage to be the boss. At any rate, she seemed to be the one able to dictate all the time. He got a divorce for desertion. She wanted it and I shouldn't think he minded at all. Good riddance to bad rubbish, to my mind. She's married to somebody else now, living in America."

"But Blaine? There's—not been anybody else?"

"No. No interest in women. At least—what am I to think about that now?" with a quizzical smile.

"He may not even remember me," said Anna in a low voice.

"Blaine's a faithful person, and I should not say he has ever had much to do with women, probably none at all but you and Virginia. He's very unlikely to have forgotten you. Why not give yourself the chance to find out, Anna, my dear?"

"But, don't you see, if he ever finds out who Colin is, he might feel *bound* to ask me to marry him," said Anna, distressed.

"Why *bound*? He wouldn't have married the Frey woman even if Virginia had made it possible."

"I think he might have done," said Anna.

"Well, Virginia saved him from that, anyway. Give the devil his due, though she'd never be likely to give up anything she had unless she'd got something as good, or better, to take its place. But leaving aside whether he'd feel *obliged* to ask you to marry him, what would be the matter with your doing so if he did?"

"I—I'm not right for him, Miss Dove. I'm not his equal in any way."

"Not his mental equal perhaps. Who is? But as for anything else, rubbish, my dear, rubbish. Blaine has had his basinful of beautiful bodies and social climbers. What he wants now is a *wife*, a woman to come home to, somebody who cares for him for himself, and a mother for Sonia and perhaps for other children."

"At my age?" asked Anna with a wintry smile. "I'm forty, nearly."

"Well, what of it? Especially these days? I think you should give Blaine the chance, anyway."

The look on Anna's face, the sudden light in her eyes, told their own tale. She had wanted so desperately to be told to do just this thing, but had not dared even to hope that she would be.

"You think I—should marry him if he asks me to, Miss Dove?"

"Of course you should. I told him years ago that you were the one for him, and I know he thought so too."

"Only if he really wants me, for myself," said Anna shakily. "Not just because he feels he has to, nor even for Colin. Only, if I see him, let him know about Colin——"

"You will have burnt your boats?" Miss Dove finished for her when she paused. "Well, burn 'em! Have a big bonfire of them, a glorious conflagration, and I'll help you push them into the fire if you need any help. I think he would be happy with you. I know he would. I've been with him for many years now, and his happiness means a lot to me. Don't try to look as though you don't know what I mean. I'm a silly old woman. Always have been where Blaine is concerned, though thank God he's never known it. I hated it when he married Virginia. Not for myself, because of course that was always impossible, but for him. I knew she'd never be able to make him happy, and of course she didn't. But you can, Anna, and now at last I'm able to do something towards his happiness. That's why I say—let him know. Go to him. Write to him. Do it anyway you like, but tell him. Let him at least have some sort of choice. Now let's go and have dinner, and you can chew on what I've said as well as the tough steak they give you here. Ready?" rising from her chair.

"You've been wonderfully kind to me, Miss Dove," faltered Anna.

"Rubbish. Don't let's say any more about it. It's up to you now, and don't be an idiot any longer."

The next evening, when Colin had gone to bed and the little cottage was quiet except for the cheerful sounds from the adjoining house, Anna sat down to write to Blaine.

She could not tell him the truth in a letter. She felt she must be with him, able to see him when he discovered it. Only in that way, without giving him time for thought, could she be sure of his feelings, of what he had brought through the years of that memory they had shared.

Dear Sir Blaine, she wrote, *I am deeply interested in your letter and the proposition you make. Before we can go any further with it, however, I think we should meet to discuss it and I could come to London or, if convenient to you, see you here. Will you let me know about this, and suggest a day and time? Yours sincerely, Ann.*

For the first time, she left out any surname, and he noticed it with a little feeling of discomfort.

Though he had taken to addressing her like that, her own use of it brought into his mind the vague feeling which he had tried not to harbour, namely that she might be thinking of his proposition in quite different terms from the ones he meant to convey. What if she meant to work her way into his life, not as his house-keeper but eventually as his wife?

Would he mind that so much? He was lonely, and Sonia was motherless, and he could so easily come to regard Colin as his own son. What if he did eventually feel he could marry her? Since Anna was lost irrevocably to him, there would be no other woman for him, and these letters he had exchanged with Colin's mother had given him, he felt, a certain knowledge of her which had seemed all good and pleasing.

Well, he would let it ride. At any rate, he would see her.

He would see her in her own home, he decided. Later she must come to The Beacon, but at their first interview, she would feel more comfortable and relaxed in the familiar atmosphere of her own home.

He wrote to her accordingly, and when the time came, Anna was in a fever of apprehension, altering her mind several times about what she should wear out of her scanty wardrobe, but in the end deciding on the things in which she would be most at ease, most herself, the tweed suit she wore in the shop and a freshly laundered blouse. She would not give herself frills. She was a working woman, able to look after herself and remain independent if——

But she would not let her mind go further than that 'if'.

Colin was out playing, and she had told him he might stay to tea with his boon companions if he were asked, as he usually was.

The March day was beginning to close in by the time she heard the car draw up outside, and she felt suddenly that she could not meet him there at the door, and she left it ajar and went into the kitchen and stood, her heart beating wildly, leaning against the sink and wondering how she could bear to face him now that the moment she had longed for and dreaded had come.

Now, at any moment, she would *know*.

She heard him knock at the half-open door which led straight into the living-room. He waited for a moment, knocked again and then she heard the creaking of the door as it opened wider, and he walked into the room. From where she stood, in the dimly lit kitchen, she could see him through the open doorway.

He looked round the empty room.

"Mrs. Bridger?" he said uncertainly.

"I'm here. Here in the kitchen," she said in a voice that was little more than a whisper, her throat thick.

She had spent so long making the living-room bright and sweet for him, with newly washed curtains, with everything shining and flowers on the table—and yet when he came to her, it was in the kitchen, with the tentative preparations for a meal all round her, and herself leaning against the sink!

He pushed the door wider, and then stood quite still, looking at her.

The next moment he had crossed the space between them in a couple of strides and she was in his arms.

"Anna—oh, Anna!"

And she knew.

Beyond all doubt, beyond the power of thought, beyond anything but the consciousness of his nearness, of his arms about her, she knew.

"You?" he asked incredulously. "Has it been you all the time? Are *you* Ann Bridger?"

She nodded. She could not speak. She could not even look at him because of the glory that was in her eyes, because of the glory too deep to bear that was in her heart.

253

He still held her, not attempting to kiss her, but looking down into her face with that bewildered look on his own.

"And—alone, Anna?"

"Yes," she whispered.

"Have you always been alone?"

"Yes," she said again.

"Nobody else called Bridger?"

She shook her head.

"No. I—I got it out of a book," she said—in the foolish, meaningless way one speaks when the heart is too full of meaning.

"And—Colin? *Colin*, Anna?"

Then she looked at him, with love, with a pleading, beseeching look in her eyes.

"Yes," she said. "Yes, Blaine."

He gathered her closer, held her against his heart, looked out over her head with eyes which saw nothing but looked down the vista of the years, looked at things he had never dreamed had been.

"Oh, Anna," he said again. "Anna, my darling."